EAST DUNBARTONSHIRE LIBRARIES

3 8060 07006 050 4

ED LEISURE · CULTURE
Libraries

BEARSDEN	777 3021		
BISHOPBRIGGS	777 3155		
CRAIGHEAD	01360 311925	WESTERTON	943 0780
LENNOXTOWN	777 3151	WILLIAM PATRICK	777 3141

MILNGAVIE LIBRARY

1 8 JAN 2024

2 0 FEB 2020

- 9 MAR 2020   8 JAN 2024

- 4 APR 2020

2 7 OCT 2021

2 4 MAR 2022

- 7 OCT 2022

Please return this book on or before the last stamped date.
It may be renewed if not in demand.

EAST DUNBARTONSHIRE LEISURE & CULTURE TRUST	
3 8060 07006 050 4	
Askews & Holts	22-Jan-2020
AF	£7.99
MIG	

PROLOGUE

Eddie looked around at the crime scene. As usual, it looked nothing like those on the cop shows he'd seen on TV. No photographer, no blue and white police tape or flashing blue lights; just him and his little black case. A small crowd of onlookers surrounded him and to be fair, they gave him a little room to work, but that may have been because of the smell.

This was the third of three similar cases that Eddie had worked in the space of two years, and he briefly wondered if they could be connected. Flies buzzed around his face and he flapped his hand at them ineffectively. The victim had been dead for a couple of days, and there was a sticky pool of blood and faeces on the ground below the body. A length of wood extended from the anus, and another from the mouth; from the position of the body, Eddie surmised that it was the same piece of wood, because it was supporting the corpse in mid-air across two rusty steel barrels, as if it were a spit roast about to be barbecued. Eddie hoped that death had come before the skewering.

He was concentrating hard, so it gave him a bit of a start when a voice interrupted his thoughts.

"Hey mister, who the fuck wid dae that tae a fucken cat?"

CHAPTER 1 Eddie

Ever since he could remember, Eddie had wanted to be a vet. As one of the few vets in Scotland who specialised in animal abuse and poisoning, he was often called out by the SSPCA when an animal was suspected of having been poisoned or tortured, which is why he found himself in the middle of a patch of waste ground on the outskirts of Glasgow.

He had started out as a fairly ordinary vet, qualifying with a veterinary degree from Glasgow University including distinctions in medicine, pathology, physiology and biochemistry. This was all the more remarkable when you knew his background; one of four children from a one-parent family brought up on one of Glasgow's toughest housing estates, Castlemilk. University had been a struggle at times, both financially and emotionally, although he had coped better with the academic side of the veterinary degree, being, according to his friend Brian, "a clever cunt".

Despite his upbringing he had almost fitted in, but he couldn't quite manage the don't-give-a-fuck attitude that some of the better-off students had and, although he joined in with many of the social activities normally associated with students, most of his fellow classmates considered him to be somewhat stand-offish, perhaps with a bit of a chip on his shoulder. Eddie himself would have told anybody who asked that he enjoyed his time at university, but that he'd had to grow up a lot quicker than his fellow students, helping to bring up his three younger siblings and working from an early age to earn enough to help with the housekeeping and have a little money for himself.

He took some photographs of the unlucky animal in situ, measured the length of the wood impaling it, and then, using the small hacksaw from his case, he cut the wood close to where it emerged from both ends of the cat, which allowed him to place the animal into the thick polythene bag that he'd brought for that purpose. As he did this, he thought of his first few years in practice, when he had soon become bored with much of the daily routine work that he needed to get through. He wasn't really a people person, so it was often an effort to be "nice" to the clients, although he generally got on a little better with his patients. None of the pet-owners in any of the practices where he'd worked particularly disliked him, but he'd never developed a loyal following of clients like some of the other vets he'd worked with.

He'd also struggled at times to fit in with the other practice staff until, about five years earlier, he'd moved to a small-animal practice in Paisley, just to the South West of Glasgow. The senior partner and the other vets in the practice realised before long that in Eddie, they had a very useful addition to the team. His strong interest in medicine and pathology made him indispensable in handling the kind of lengthy and complex cases that they struggled with, and his solid knowledge of lab work combined with his scientific and ordered approach meant that his work in the background let the other vets get on with keeping the customers happy and doing most of the day-to-day stuff that he found tedious. As a result he was offered a partnership in the practice, which he had accepted two years after joining them.

Encouraged by his position as the practice "expert" in biochemistry and post-mortem work, and his interest in the occasional poisoning case that the practice dealt with, he decided to take the unusual step of studying for a certificate in veterinary forensic pathology. It meant that he had to attend seminars and lectures periodically at Cambridge University, which was a bit of a bitch, but the practice paid for it, and he soon found himself involved in intriguing, though sometimes horrific, animal welfare cases.

Strangely, Eddie had fitted in at Cambridge. The other post-grads he studied with at the veterinary faculty were similar to him in many respects. Their backgrounds varied enormously, but they all had the same drive to learn, and a benign disdain for anyone who didn't strive to further their knowledge. He even had a brief fling with one of his fellow students, Anna, but bizarrely, their post-coital chat was usually about forensic pathology rather than any plans they might have to carry on the romance away from the university's rarefied environment.

The crowd had dispersed with the disappearance of the sorry corpse, and Eddie laid it gently in the large plastic box that he kept in his car for the purpose. Putting his case in the car as well, he took one last look around then pulled off the blue overalls that he usually wore for such jobs, more to keep himself clean than for any forensic reasons. He checked the cat for a microchip which, if present, would enable Eddie to identify its owner.

Eddie groaned when the reader pinged and the number appeared on the screen. It meant a particularly unpleasant phone call he'd have to make later, breaking the news to a distraught owner, getting their permission to do a post-mortem examination and send appropriate samples off to the lab. He headed back to the surgery, anxious to get on with it; it would mean a very late finish, as he also wanted to write up his interim findings and send his preliminary report to Mike George at the SSPCA before going home.

-o-

Eddie arrived at work sharp the next morning, hoping to get all the loose ends from the skewered cat investigation tidied up, but one of the younger vets was also an early starter, and wanted his input on a case that was troubling her.

"I've done full bloods, X-rays and ultrasound on this dog, but I can't find anything abnormal," Lesley complained, frustrated at her inability to find the cause of the young Labrador's vomiting and diarrhoea.

Eddie tried not to show his annoyance at the interruption to his plans; despite his awkwardness with the public, he was generally very good with the younger members of the staff. They in turn found that he was often the best person to approach for clinical advice, not only because of his patience with them, but also due to his excellent technical knowledge.

"Give me the full story," he said, taking out a pad to make a few notes.

"Well, Opus is a male, nine-month-old Lab. He's entire and weighs 24.8Kg. He presented three weeks ago with what appeared to be a mild acute gastroenteritis, and he seemed to respond initially to anti-emetics and antibiotics. He was non-pyrexic; his temp was 37.8 degrees, and his pulse, colour and respiratory parameters were normal. As usual, I advised the owners to withdraw food for twenty-four hours."

She paused and looked at Eddie for a response. He just nodded for her to continue.

"He's been back in three times since for the same problem; mostly vomiting, so we did some bloods. Everything looks normal. Urea, creatinine, ALT, AST and bile acids all were within normal ranges, so the liver and kidneys look good. All the haematology was normal, too.

"What about electrolytes?" Eddie asked.

"I didn't run them, the dog wasn't dehydrated."

"What was he like when you palpated his abdomen?"

"No real discomfort and I couldn't feel anything unusual, either."

"OK, what did you do next?"

"We did an abdominal ultrasound; well, Jenny did it with me. It was normal." Jenny was better than everybody else in the practice at getting the most out of the ultrasound scanner.

"Good. Now, you said you took some X-rays?"

"Yes, we anaesthetised Opus yesterday and did a couple of plates of his abdomen, then we passed a stomach tube and did a barium study as well. The plain films were normal and the barium passed through with no problem. He is a bit of a chewer and I had wondered if he might have had a gastric foreign body; a piece of plastic toy, or a sock or something, but there was nothing there and the stomach emptied without leaving a barium outline of anything abnormal."

"Was a note of his heart rate made at any point?"

"Hold on a sec, I'll go and check. As far as I remember it was OK."

She disappeared, and Eddie got on with filling out the submission forms for the samples he'd taken from the cat the previous evening. The post-mortem had been as bad as he had expected – there was widespread haemorrhage in the abdominal and thoracic cavities, and in the pharynx, which meant that the poor cat had been alive when the piece of wood had been inserted into its anus, pushed all the way through, and out of its mouth at the other end.

It had caused extensive lacerations to the anus and had penetrated the rectum before rupturing some of the mesenteric blood vessels supplying the intestines. Continuing its journey through the abdomen, it had passed through the stomach and liver, prior to rupturing the diaphragm, a sheet of muscle that separates the abdomen from the thorax. It had then travelled along through the mediastinum between the lungs, miraculously sliding over the heart base and through the thoracic opening into the neck, just nicking the pulmonary vein on the way through. After it had passed along the neck, beside the trachea and oesophagus, it penetrated the pharynx and exited the mouth, taking half the tongue with it. Eddie felt sick, and as angry as he had ever been, thinking of the pain the cat must have gone through at every single thrust that the sick bastard must have used to push the oversized skewer through the whole length of the body. He estimated that the cat could have taken up to an hour to die, as none of the ruptured blood vessels were large enough to cause the animal to bleed to death quickly. Either the culprit knew what he was doing and avoided the major arteries and veins, which he found hard to believe, or he had just achieved it by luck alone.

At each stage of the post-mortem Eddie photographed the body from all angles, and he collected the usual samples – such as blood and urine – as he went along. He had also measured the cat and weighed it before starting, and would subtract the weight of the piece of wood at the end to calculate the cat's true weight.

Even taking into account the major trauma that was evident in the abdomen, Eddie noticed that the kidneys looked a bit strange. They hadn't been affected by the passage of the wood, but he was sufficiently intrigued by their appearance to remove one of them, divide it in two and fix one half in formol saline for histological examination to determine if the kidneys were damaged. The other half, the unfixed piece of kidney, he placed in a container with a sample of liver, to allow the lab to run toxicology assays, vital in cases where poisoning was suspected.

All these samples needed accompanying paperwork. He had just finished it, and had bagged everything up to send to the lab, when Lesley returned.

"Opus's heart rate was in the low sixties on both occasions that it was noted," she told Eddie.

Eddie wrote this down on his notepad.

"Is there any history of Opus collapsing, or having any ataxia?" he asked, referring to any blackouts or balance problems the dog might have.

"The owner didn't report any, and I think they're the kind of owners who would have told us if they'd seen something."

"OK, Lesley, I think that you should run electrolytes and do an ECG on Opus." He paused again. "Why do you think they would be useful in this case?"

Lesley realised now what Eddie was hinting at.

"Shit, do you think it might have Addison's disease? I didn't think of that because there was no sign of an Addisonian crisis."

She was alluding to the dangerous collapsed state that dogs with Addison's disease sometimes died from, where the blood levels of the crucial hormones, cortisol and aldosterone, fell dangerously low. In Opus's case, Eddie suspected that he hadn't quite reached that level, but that the dog might be suffering from Addison's all the same, his adrenal glands unable to produce enough of those critical chemicals that control the levels of sodium and potassium in the body, as well as the blood glucose level. These fluctuations could affect the heart and other organs, and would explain the moderately low heart rate, and the intermittent vomiting.

"It certainly needs checking, and I wouldn't be surprised if that's what it turns out to be."

"Thanks Eddie, I'll get that all checked, and get him dripped and started on medication right away if it is. I should have bloody thought of that myself."

Eddie smiled. "Don't beat yourself up, it's hard to diagnose when it's that mild." He knew that she wouldn't miss it again; she was thorough and would learn from every case she dealt with.

-o-

The results from the lab came back quicker than Eddie expected, and he wasn't surprised when he read that there was extensive damage to the tissue of the kidneys; they'd looked abnormal on gross examination. What slightly surprised him was that the report stated that there were extensive deposits of oxalate crystals in the tubules of the kidney, but he realised that this unexpected finding could explain how it had been possible for the person responsible for this sick act of cruelty to achieve it. Making the assumption that it would have been very difficult, if not impossible, to restrain a cat thoroughly enough to impale it so effectively, he had presumed that the cat must have been at least semi-conscious. In the absence of any trauma to the head, he had come to the conclusion that some form of sedative or anaesthetic had been used, but he had wondered where the person who had done this had managed to get hold of an appropriate drug, and use it correctly.

He contacted the lab and asked them to check for ethylene glycol toxicity on the samples that he had already sent to them. An hour later, he had the results he expected.

He phoned Mike George, knowing that the SSPCA would

be keen to know the results as soon as possible, especially as this was a new departure, in Eddie's experience, from the familiar string of cruelty cases that happened on a weekly, or sometimes daily, basis.

"Mike," he said, when the SSPCA regional superintendent answered the phone, "I've got an interesting one for you today."

"Eddie, how's tricks? Is this about the cat we sent you to investigate?"

"Aye, it certainly is. We have a nutcase with a new twist on killing cats. This poor little moggy was poisoned with antifreeze first, probably to immobilise it, then impaled on a stick while it was still alive."

"What a sick bastard. It makes you wonder how far people will go when it comes to torturing animals." Mike knew that death by antifreeze poisoning was horrible, but to suffer the impaling in addition was almost unimaginable. "Do you think those other two cases last year were the same?" he asked.

"I was just coming on to that. Because they were so autolysed, I couldn't tell if there were any kidney changes, and there was no point in doing histopathology on either of them." Both cats had been dead for at least a week before they were found, and were partly decomposed when Eddie post-mortemed them, but there was no mistaking the fact that both had died from having different, but equally lethal, penetrating objects inserted through their anuses. "I retained tissue from both cases, so I'm sending off liver and kidney samples for ethylene glycol toxicology. I suspect that antifreeze was used to immobilise these cats to allow the subsequent mutilation to take place."

"That's a new one for us. I can't recall a case like this before, and I've been involved with this side of things at the SSPCA for the last twenty years."

"I've got something else. I know it's a long shot, but when I examined this cat's claws, there was some tissue under four of them. I looked at a smear under the microscope of this tissue, and although I'm no expert, I think it might be human."

Mike laughed, then apologised. "I know I shouldn't have laughed, but I was just thinking what the police would say if we asked them to use their DNA database to find our cat killer. They'd tell us to take a hike."

"I know," Eddie replied, slightly annoyed, "but if we do find someone for this, there's no reason why we couldn't use DNA matching to confirm that he had been in close contact with the cat."

Mike sounded doubtful. "I'm not sure of the legal implications or the financial costs, but we've certainly never used it before."

"OK, so at least we have it as an option. I've frozen the whole cadaver, so that we have the DNA evidence in the bag, so to speak, if we should ever need it." He paused. "Can you send an Inspector over to Nitshill to ask around and see if anyone knows anything? I asked the bystanders a few questions at the time, but drew a blank. The cat was found near a boarded up block of flats due for demolition, so it would have been fairly secluded. We might not get much."

Mike agreed to send one of his officers over the next day and asked Eddie if there was anything else he could do.

"No, I'm going to ask around the local practices, to see if any of the vets in the area have come across similar cases. Let's see what we get from that, and from the toxicology in the other two cases we have tissue for."

"Good. I'll trawl through our records and get a list of cases we've dealt with that could fit in with these ones. Our IT guys should be able to come up with something for us." He continued. "I'll speak to you as soon as I've done that. In the meantime, can you keep me up to date with any progress?" There was a pause while he wrote down a few notes. "We should really arrange a meeting once we have a bit more to go on, and get Sally from the press side in on it. She might come up with ways to push the investigation through the media."

They agreed to keep in touch, and Eddie hung up. He finished writing up his final report and popped it in with the practice mail for posting the next day.

He phoned the cat's owner to tell her the results, not as difficult a task as his first phone call to her, informing her of her pet's demise, had been. This time she was marginally less distressed, but he still felt genuinely sorry for her, an old age pensioner, living alone, losing her only companion in such a horrible way.

-o-

Eddie worked his butt off for the rest of the week. The practice was extremely busy with a parvovirus outbreak in the local dog population, not helped by the fact that a large percentage of dogs in the area were unvaccinated. There was also a rash of heatstroke cases caused by the exceptionally warm weather that had hit central Scotland during early June. If dogs weren't on an IV drip for the severe dehydration caused by the profuse diarrhoea and vomiting associated with parvo, they were on a regime of cold water showering *and* an IV drip passed through ice-water to counteract the overheating resulting from them being left in parked cars, even those with their windows left open a crack. The more severe cases needed a tepid rectal lavage in addition to the drip, which didn't please the nurses.

It was only during his rushed lunch hours that he managed to find time to contact the other practices in and around Glasgow. It took over a week, and he suffered a bit with indigestion due to wolfing down lunches, or missing them altogether, but he had such a good response initially that he widened his research to the whole of Scotland.

When the results arrived from the samples Eddie had sent in from the two cases he'd investigated previously, they confirmed that the two animals had been poisoned with ethylene glycol. Armed with this, he composed letters, and posted them to *The Veterinary Record* and a couple of other veterinary publications, asking for information about any poisoning or cruelty cases in Scotland within the previous five years.

Finally, he wrote to the local and national veterinary associations, and all the Scottish veterinary diagnostic laboratories, requesting any information of relevance to his investigation.

It came flooding in. Even Eddie was surprised just how many animals were involved. From Scotland as a whole, a spreadsheet supplied by the SSPCA listed about 3,650 cases of animals, mostly cats, that had been poisoned with antifreeze in the last five years. When he added case reports that he'd gathered from his other research that didn't already appear on the list, this grew to 4,821. Many of these could have been accidental, as cats were prone to sit under parked cars and leaked antifreeze had a sweet taste that seemed to appeal to them. Only twenty-three were reported as having survived, and of these, just eight had confirmation by blood analysis of ethylene glycol toxicity. Of the four thousand and odd total cases, only a handful involved some form of mutilation in addition to the fact that they'd been poisoned, and they were all cats.

In addition, there were another 2,359 cases of deliberate mutilation, from the SSPCA and external sources, without any evidence of poisoning.

Eddie was no IT geek, but he had enough computer skills to do some basic analysis of the data. He sorted the list by date and location, and flagged whether or not there was any mutilation or poisoning involved. Sharon, the practice manager, helped him to set up a map of Scotland on Photoshop, with fifteen overlying layers. For each of the five years, there were three categories: The poisoning cases, which were marked with a small round dot; mutilation cases, which were given a triangular mark; and cases which had been poisoned and mutilated, which were denoted by a square. Each year was represented by a different colour.

Eddie laboriously plotted all the cases in their appropriate layers, according to the year they were reported and their category, but with them all visible there were too many marks on the screen, and the pattern was seemingly random, as if someone had fired a shotgun at the map from a distance.

However, when he started playing about with the layers there was a bit more of a pattern to it. The most telling were the layers showing the cats that had been poisoned *and* mutilated. There were two clusters. He had expected the one in and around the Paisley area, where there were five cases, but he was surprised to see that the only other three reported cases were all within ten miles of each other, in or near to the city of Dundee.

His first thought was that there were two individuals that had the same perverted way of jacking off. All the Dundee cases were all on the SSPCA list, so he phoned the SSPCA centre in Dundee, and asked to speak to one of the Inspectors. A woman came to the phone and introduced herself as Inspector Julie Elliot.

He explained that he was making enquiries about a series

of cases in Glasgow, and asked her if she could fill in the details of the three instances of poisoning and mutilation in the Dundee area that were on the list, in case they were related in any way to the one in Glasgow.

"We only dealt with two of these cases, but we got nowhere with them. If the other one was south of the river, it may have been the Dunfermline branch that dealt with it. You could try them."

"What about the two cases that you did deal with?"

"I remember thinking at the time that we had a fair chance of getting a prosecution, because they were so blatant; somebody must have known about it or have seen something, but there was nothing. One cat was nailed to a wooden door, but would have been almost dead from antifreeze poisoning by the time that happened, according to the pathologist at the University of Edinburgh Vet School. We found it in a derelict factory after a phone call from a member of the public. The second cat had been hung by a noose around its neck, but the pathologist's report stated that the noose had been knotted, and it wouldn't have tightened enough to strangle the cat immediately. The cord had abraded the skin right through to the flesh in places, as the cat struggled for what must have been a considerable amount of time. This cat was also shown to have severe renal failure due to ethylene glycol poisoning, and may have been pretty far gone by the time it was strung up. It was reported by a family out walking, who found it hanging from a tree in Magdalen Park, down by the Tay Railway Bridge."

"Can you send me the reports, if that's possible? They seem to be similar to the case I'm dealing with already. There probably isn't a link, but I'm not ruling it out."

After making a few notes about their conversation, he phoned the Fife office, based in Dunfermline, and discovered that Julie Elliot had been right. The third case had been found on the beach at Tayport, on the south bank of the Tay Estuary, just as it flows into the North Sea.

The inspector wasn't in, but the woman in the office promised to get him to ring back. When he did, it turned out that he knew Eddie from his time as an inspector in Glasgow, a few years previously.

"Eddie, it's nice to talk to you again. It must have been four years now, eh?"

"Graham," replied Eddie, recognising his voice after a few seconds, "I'd forgotten you'd moved up to Fife. How are you enjoying it up there?"

They spent a few minutes catching up, but Eddie was keen to get down to business, and steered the conversation round to the case of "the cat on the raft". It hadn't been in such an advanced stage of antifreeze toxicity, so it would have been conscious when it was nailed to a kitchen cupboard door with an industrial nail gun, and floated down the Tay. By the time it beached at Tayport it was dead, but it would have taken a long time to die. Although it had taken some water into its lungs, it had probably died of hypothermia and shock. A couple walking along the beach had found it washed up on the shore, and had taken it to the SSPCA facility in their home town of Dunfermline, demanding that whoever had done this should be locked up. The staff had explained that while they would do what they could, it might be difficult to find out who had been responsible.

After talking to Graham, Eddie was curious about the two clusters and started playing around with the layers that divided these cases into groups according to the year that they had occurred in. The Dundee cases had all taken place in one year, and only one Glasgow case had taken place that same year. He went back to the original spreadsheet and sorted the eight cases into date order. They had all taken place over the last three years, two before the Dundee cluster and three after, including the three cases he'd investigated himself.

It made it more likely that one person had been responsible for all the cases, and that he or she had lived in Dundee for a period of just under a year.

-o-

"Eddie, it's unlikely that the police are going to look at an investigation with so little information, and the PF will only consider a prosecution if we have a definite suspect and a very strong case," said Mike George.

He'd called in to the practice after Eddie contacted him about his concerns and suggested that the police should be brought in, or that the case should be reported to the PF, or Procurator Fiscal. The SSPCA is almost unique among animal welfare charities. In most parts of the world, animal charities have the same rights as ordinary citizens to bring private prosecutions of individuals who have broken animal welfare laws. Because there are ineffective provisions for private prosecutions in Scottish law, the SSPCA has been granted the status of a specialist reporting agency to the Crown Office and Procurator Fiscal Service, allowing it to lay reports for prosecutions directly to the Fiscal. Their inspectors have powers of entry, seizure, and issue of binding notices like "care notices", that force people to care for their animals or have them removed by the SSPCA.

Mike George was being realistic and pragmatic, but it seemed to Eddie that he was also being too cautious.

"Mike, this is not just your wee mindless thug that thinks it's funny to see an animal suffering or someone playing the big man to his mates; this is a guy who is serious about torturing animals and he *is* going to continue."

"I know that, Eddie. Don't forget that I've been doing this for a long time. In my experience, it's better to wait until we are further down the line before we go to the police or the PF, but I fully understand your frustration."

"So we just wait for the next one, and hope that Joe Public sees him and reports it to us?"

"No, of course not. We'll put a couple of inspectors on it for a while to see if we can come up with something more substantial. After all, somebody somewhere must have seen something. And don't get me wrong, what you've done already is fantastic, especially with that map on the computer; it gives our guys much more of a chance to make progress."

Eddie was still annoyed, but part of him could see Mike's point. Even so, he didn't feel like backing down completely.

"OK, I'll give it two weeks. But if you've got nothing by then, or there's another case in the meantime, I think we should go to the police."

Mike could see that Eddie was adamant. As a veterinary consultant Eddie was a useful asset to the SSPCA and Mike didn't want to curb the younger man's enthusiasm and determination, so he came up with a compromise.

"Tell you what," he said, "let's make it a month and if there's still nothing, I'll ring Paisley CID myself."

It wasn't ideal, but it was something. "Okay," said Eddie, reluctantly, "we'll give it a month."

-o-

As Eddie had suspected, despite the efforts of the SSPCA

Inspectors assigned to the case, no more information came to light during the month. In fairness to Mike, Eddie didn't have to push him; he kept to his word, and phoned Eddie to tell him that he had contacted Paisley CID. Eddie knew he was referring to the Criminal Investigation Department of the Strathclyde Police force; he'd worked with them on a couple of occasions before.

"The police are going to be phoning you at some point in the next few days," said Mike. "I thought it better that they talked to you first, as you have more in-depth knowledge about the case and I'm up to my ears with this pet shop chain that has been importing dodgy exotics and keeping them in totally unsuitable conditions."

"Mike, that's fine, I don't mind dealing with it. Good luck with the pet shops. What species are you talking about?"

"Mainly lizards and snakes, but there are some terrapins and turtles too. We've had to euthanase half of them, due to the state they were in."

"They should stop exotics being kept as pets altogether, in my opinion, or at least allow it only under licence by trained owners, but I don't suppose that will ever happen!"

"Sadly, I think you're right. Are you OK time wise for dealing with CID? We can't pay you for all of this, but I'll see if we can do something with expenses to help out."

"Don't worry about it, I don't mind doing it. Call it pro bono, if you want."

"Thanks, Eddie, much appreciated. The name of the officer you'll be working with is DC Catherine Douglas. I gave her your mobile number; she'll contact you."

Eddie was about to put the phone down, when he heard Mike say something else.

"What was that, Mike?"

"Sorry, Eddie, I meant to say, I'll also have to organise some identification as a temporary SSPCA Inspector for you. That will put you on a better footing legally, and make it easier for the police to work with you. Can you send me a current passport style photo of yourself?"

"Aye, no bother. I'll take one just now and email it to you."

CHAPTER 2 Stevie

Stevie Reilly never really had much of a chance in life, but what little hope he had of ever succeeding at any level was snuffed out by his drug habit. His switch from a combination of alcohol and marijuana to heroin was the point at which everyone who knew him, and was willing to help him, gave up.

His friends, with whom he would share a bottle of Buckie and a few spliffs, became acquaintances who would sell his kidneys for a score of smack, if they had the opportunity.

His favoured haunt was an abandoned and boarded up service station at the entrance to the derelict industrial estate on the edge of town. Once a busy fuelling spot for workers driving to and from work, it now lay deserted amidst the abandoned factories of post-Thatcherite Scotland. It seemed that nobody else ever went there, so he always had the place to himself and, more importantly, he didn't have to share his stash.

It was at least a twenty minute walk from the centre of town and he hated the dismal dampness as he forced a fast pace on himself in his desperation to load up. The Tesco bag holding his gear, and a couple of cans of Special Brew as an extra treat, occasionally banged against his leg as he walked, causing him to curse quietly. As he approached the edge of town, passing the thought-provoking "Haste ye back" and "Thank you for driving carefully" signs, the houses dwindled, and the long section of manicured grass which fronted the industrial estate, still cut by the council to keep up appearances, faced a muddy field with some sorry looking animals in it; some type of cattle, which he

barely even noticed.

When he came close to his bolthole he looked round quickly, as he usually did, just to check that there were no scrounging bastards following him, looking for some of his score. He cursed again, suddenly noticing a figure maybe a couple of hundred yards back on the other side of the road, walking out from the centre of town like he had. He slowed down, then sat on the low metal barrier separating the pavement from the grass, pulled out one of his cans and cracked the ring-pull open. He took a large slug of the "super-lager", feeling it burn his throat, waiting for the kick that he always got from Special Brew while he watched for the stupid cunt opposite to pass by.

Stupit bastard, walkin' for the sake ae it, just get the fuck oot the way, man, he thought to himself.

The stranger looked over at him and nodded as he walked by. It wasn't some healthy bastard looking for fresh air and exercise, although he wore a hoodie and an Adidas top, with matching trainers and jogging bottoms. This was one of his own kind, which made Stevie much more nervous, wondering if the cunt was on the make. He relaxed a bit as his fellow jakey kept on walking past him, striding out to fuck-knows-where.

He gave it a few minutes until the man was out of sight then, where a corner of the corrugated tin sheet and the underlying plywood had been prised off enough to allow it to flex out a foot or two, he squeezed through into what had previously been the forecourt shop. It had been stripped of everything but the hardened glass booth where the attendant could sit safely at night, securely locked in, taking payments for fuel and handing out occasional goods from the steel shuttered and closed shop, in the sure knowledge that he wouldn't be robbed at knifepoint.

Stevie, or Stevo, as he was known to his fellow junkies, sat in the corner on a stained and ripped mattress rescued from a skip, his kit beside him. There was just enough light from the solitary skylight in the ceiling, against which large drops of rain were beginning to batter loudly. He prepared to shoot up, the smack bought with the cash he'd got from the sale of a laptop he'd removed from a car parked outside the mini-mart in the row of shops that served as a shopping centre for the whole estate. *Served the stupid bastard right, leavin' the fucken thing in the boot in the first place.* It had been a ten second job to prise open the lock and grab the computer, having seen the silly cunt put it in there for safety. Now his world was right again and for a while, as the needle punctured his skin and delivered its beautiful load into his worn out vein, the pain and torment that was his normal state faded into fucken greatness.

He must have fallen asleep at some point, because he woke with a start to a scraping sound behind him. Turning slowly, still floating, he saw the board at the entrance to his sanctuary being pulled open and a foot, then a leg, followed by the rest of the cunt he had seen earlier, appearing through the gap, looking around in the gloom as he did so. He watched warily as the guy shook himself, shedding rainwater in a cloud of droplets like a dog.

"Hey," the stranger said, "ye aw right, man?"

"Aye. Whit dae ye want, man?"

"Nuthin', man, just gettin in oot o' that fucken rain. Saw you comin' in here earlier and thought I'd gie it a go."

Stevo wasn't happy, but what could he say? He resigned himself to sharing his "squat" with a fellow ned.

"Ma name's Jacko, by the way, man." The newcomer offered his hand in the strangely formal way that jakeys sometimes do.

Stevo shook his hand and pointed to the mattress. "Ah'm Stevo, park yer arse therr, if ye want."

Jacko pulled a bottle out of his bag, opened it, put it to his lips and threw his head back, slugging as he did so. He handed the bottle to Stevo.

"Here, huv some ae this, man."

Stevo took the bottle and looked at it strangely. It was a plastic lemonade bottle, filled with a blue coloured liquid. "Whit the fuck is it?" he asked, grimacing.

"Hame made Blue Wicked, man, cheap as fuck, an' just as guid. Cheap voddy, some lemonade, an' ye knaw that crap the weans drink? Thon blue dilutin' juice stuff, cannae mind its name just aff the tap o' ma heid, but ye just get a boattle o' that an' add as much voddy as ye feel like."

Stevo took a drink. It was a bit rough, but sweet, and he'd tasted worse. Much worse. He took another long slug, and passed it back to his new pal, who put it on the floor between his legs. Jacko took out a ten packet of Pall Mall king size, offered one to Stevo and took one himself.

"Man, that stuff's aw right, ye knaw," Stevo said between puffs, eyeing up the almost empty bottle.

"Here, huv some mair, there's plenty o' it, man."

Stevo took the plastic bottle from him again, and downed most of the remainder. He could feel the familiar warm glow in his belly, spreading out through his body. It would help when he started to come down off the junk.

"You're no' drinkin' much yersel, Jacko."

"Ye kiddin', man. That'll be ma sixth boattle; ah tanned quite a few awready oan ma way up here."

"Where wur ye goin' earlier when ah saw ye?"

"Ah knaw a place oot the road a bit. It's an auld farm or sumfin', and it's got a bit in it ye can doss down in. Therr's a few boys go up therr; ye get peace, an' sometimes a bit o' fanny goes up an' aw, an' ye get the chance o' a ride, man." He grinned, pumping his arms in the universal shag-mime. "There wis naebody therr the day, so I came back doon tae wherr ah'd seen you."

"Ah thought ye hadnae seen me comin' in here. I like tae keep this for masel', but yer welcome tae use it if ye want. Just don't tell any other cunt."

"Hey, ye don't huv tae worry about that man, ye'll no' be bothered wi' onywan 'cos ae me." He looked at Stevie and grinned, but there was something in his face that made Stevie look away, suddenly uncomfortable.

Stevie shivered. Trust him to get hooked up with some psycho. The guy had seemed all right at first.

But it passed, and Stevie took another drink, then another bottle when Jacko offered again. Within an hour, he'd downed two or three bottles of the stuff. He could feel the alcohol hitting home, on top of the heroin he'd taken earlier. He took out his packet of Golden Virginia and his Rizlas and rolled a fag, offering Jacko the chance to roll one as well, but he shook his head and took one of his own. "Ah'll stick tae these. Ah'm no a big fan o' roll-ups apart fae an odd spliff."

Stevie lay back on the mattress smoking with one hand behind his head, almost drifting off. When he finally did go to sleep, Jacko took the still lit fag from him and stubbed it out on the floor, so the mattress didn't catch fire.

He sat on the edge of the mattress watching Stevie as he fell into a deeper sleep, the drink kicking in. Fifteen minutes later Jacko lit another cigarette, took a long puff and pressed the glowing end against Stevie's arm. Stevie groaned slightly, but didn't wake up. Jacko looked round at the glass cubicle in the corner and checked that the door was open, then grabbed Stevie's legs. There was a thump as his head hit the floor when he pulled him off the mattress and a smear of blood marked the track of Stevie's head across the vinyl tiles as he dragged him into the booth.

Jacko propped him up against the back corner, so that he could shut the door. He couldn't resist cupping Stevie's chin in his hand, squeezing it roughly and saying, "Ye silly, trustin' bastard, ye've made a big mistake, ya cunt, bumpin' intae me. Just your luck, Stevo boy."

With that he left the booth, closing the door behind him. He looked around and saw what he was looking for in a small pile of discarded shop fittings in the corner. He chose a suitable metal fitting, previously used to hang packets or jump leads or furry seat covers, and jammed it through the large, curved, brushed steel handle on the outside of the class cubicle. Just to make sure, he ripped a piece of wire from one of the vandalised light fittings and wrapped it round both the handle and the metal bar, to hold it all in place.

After he'd done all this, he double-checked that everything was to his satisfaction, and lay down on the mattress for a kip.

He awoke to the sound of Stevie groaning and thumping at the glass. *Here we go*, he thought to himself, feeling the familiar rush of adrenalin and accompanying sexual arousal that he knew would heighten during the next few hours, or even days.

Jacko knew almost exactly what to expect, but there were a few differences from his previous subjects that he hoped might show up, and the fact that this one was human ramped up the excitement and fear ten-fold. Although he didn't know the precise mechanisms for each phase of Stevie's chemical torture, he had a very good idea of how Stevie would die, because of the cats.

He wondered if he had time to go for a quick wank, but he forced himself to put it off, knowing that it would be so much fucken better if he waited.

As Jacko approached the booth, Stevie raised his head slowly and stared at him, doubled over in agony, a look of fear, confusion, pain and incomprehension in his eyes. Saliva dripped down his chin, and his fingers were already bleeding from his attempts to escape from the booth. The glass was smeared with blood around the door edges, and there were also palm prints and spots of blood on the glass at the front of the booth.

"Help me, man," Stevie rasped, his speech almost unintelligible as spittle dribbled from his chin on to the counter.

"Didn't quite catch that, Stevo," replied Jacko, smiling and leaning towards him, cupping his ear as if to help Stevie make himself understood.

Stevie screamed and smashed his forehead off the counter. He clutched at his midriff with his hands as shards of pain shot up his back. Looking up through the glass, he could see a blurred shape, vaguely human. There were gaps in his vision; he couldn't see anything on his left hand side and there was a red blotch in the middle, which half blotted out the face of the person in front of him. Pulsing waves of pain shot from the front to the back of his head, and he could hear a roaring sound in his ears.

"Ah must have had some bad junk, man. Gie's a fucken hand here, fur christ's sake."

There was no response. He tried again, grimacing with

pain.

"Help me, fur fuck's sake, man, ah'm fucken dyin' here."

This time Jacko replied, grinning.

"Ah knaw, ya junkie cunt, that's the general fucken idea. Ah'd be disappointed if ye goat better."

Stevie screamed again, collapsing on the floor, writhing around in the small space, his head banging off the walls as he did. His bladder suddenly let go, soaking the front of his trackie bottoms and saturating the floor with urine.

Jacko moved round to the door to watch his victim's attempts to get up, but Stevie's balance was badly affected and he couldn't straighten up easily. The intense pain started in his pelvis and crept up to his neck, almost meeting the agonising stabs of pain travelling through his head like glass shards. The wet floor didn't help, and Stevie failed two or three times, falling heavily on to his knees and hips as he did so, lucky not to break a leg. He got himself into a kneeling position and, just when he thought it couldn't get any worse, he felt a wave of nausea, the like of which he'd never felt before, sweep over him, and he retched violently, adding to the level of slime on the now swimming floor, and a stench of urine and vomit that only made his nausea worse.

He made another heroic attempt to get up, and managed to drag his chest up as far as the counter. His eyes were bloodshot and staring wildly, and he could see less than before. The headaches were so bad that when the pain was at its worst, all he could see was an incredibly bright light. When they subsided a little, he became aware of blurred shapes in front of him. It looked like two Jackos standing outside the booth, but he knew there was only one.

Again he screamed as the pain became unbearable, and it seemed to take an eternity to pass.

"Whit the fuck's happened tae me?" he whimpered to both the Jackos.

"Well, ye see, ye drank some antifreeze, ya stupit bas, ye; that's why yer kidneys are fucked up an' yer goin' tae die."

Stevo struggled to think, but he vaguely remembered drinking with Jacko yesterday. Was it yesterday? He didn't know.

"Was that the stuff we wis drinkin' yester...?" he asked, the question unfinished as another stab of pain tore at his body.

"Naw, that wis the stuff you were drinking. Ah didnae drink any o' it."

"But ah seen ye."

"Ah didnae swallow it, ya dopey bam, ye, ah just put it up tae ma mooth, so that ye'd think ah wis drinkin' it." Jacko grinned again but it was wasted, because at that moment Stevie let out another scream and fell over, sliding sideways on the counter before hitting the side of the kiosk with his head on the way down; blood spilled out from where a piece of his scalp had been torn off.

As he lay on the floor, half-conscious, he realised that there was a new pain appearing, this time in his guts, and that he had a sudden urge to empty his bowels. Even in the state he was in, he tried to haul himself up the wall, pulling down his jogging trousers at the same time, but he ended up falling over again. He attempted to hold it in, but the pain and pressure overcame him and as he lay on his side, he could feel a mixture of gas and fluid explode from his rectum, the warmth spreading all down his body and on to the hand and arm that were stuck underneath him.

As the smell reached his nostrils, he started to gag again. He believed Jacko when he had told him he was going to die, and wished that it would happen soon, as he couldn't bear any more of the suffering that he was being subjected to. He started crying, when he wasn't screaming, all the time aware of being watched from outside the glass.

It took Stevie another twenty-seven hours to die. He was conscious for about half that time, alternately pleading for water to quench his raging thirst and begging for alcohol or drugs to numb the pain. He would scream and repeatedly hit his head off the glass, trying to render himself unconscious, or lie in the pool of his own urine, vomit and faeces, whimpering and occasionally taking convulsions, especially towards the end. Jacko hardly said a word, but spent most of the time watching.

In the last brief lucid spell before he slipped into a terminal comatose stupor, Stevie asked only one question.

"Why, ya cunt? Why? Why? Why?"

Jacko's voice sounded different and distant, as if he was getting further away, or he was someone else entirely.

"Well, Stevo, in more ways than one, ye were just a bit fucken unlucky. It wisnae necessarily needin' tae be you, but somewan like ye; some wee junkie that nae one would gie a fuck aboot. Ye see, some o' us get a right buzz frae bein' right proper cruel bastards, an' you were a wee experiment tae see if it was mair fun tae kill a human wi' antifreeze as it wis fir tae kill a cat. If it's any consolation tae ye, it's been much better in a lot ae ways; ye don't get the chat frae a cat that there's been frae you, so all in all it's been worth it." He paused, and then carried on, taunting his victim. "An' when yer deid, ah'll take the bar oot o' the door; an' when they find you, they'll just think it's another stupid jakey whit drank the wrang stuff comin' doon frae a score. An' they'll all say, (yer maw as well), what a daft wee cunt ye wur, what a waste. But you an' me, we'll knaw better, Stevo, eh."

Two weeks passed before Stevie Reilly's body was found. A springer spaniel, ironically with the name of Jack, managed to slip through the small gap that had been Stevie's secret entrance into the filling station, and when he refused to come out, his owner had squeezed his way in to retrieve him, to be confronted by the smell and the sight of Stevie's decomposing remains, a cloud of flies and a mass of maggots writhing in the dark pool of fluid that had emanated from his body before and after his death.

The police investigated his death but, as far as could be determined and taking into consideration the level of decomposition, acute kidney failure was given as the cause of death. There was moderate trauma to various parts of the body, but all of it could be reasonably attributed to falls and self-inflicted damage. A comment was made about a cigarette burn on the right arm, but again, the police assumed that this had happened when he had become unconscious while smoking. Dried blood and tissue were found on the floor and edges within the booth that supported this, and some empty bottles that had contained alcohol were present in the building. Lab work done on the liquid after the results of the post-mortem confirmed that it contained high levels of ethylene glycol.

There was a bit of puzzlement as to why Stevie had got stuck in the booth, but it was suggested that the combination of drugs and ethylene glycol may have caused blindness, and the subsequent panic rendered him unable to find his way out.

The Procurator Fiscal gave *accidental ingestion of ethylene glycol leading to acute kidney failure* as the cause of death.

At Stevie's funeral, his mum wept for her lost son. The remainder of the small group of mourners in the main looked embarrassed for her, and didn't want to be there. There had been no intimation notice in the paper; she didn't want Stevie's druggie friends turning up for the free food and drink, and a chance to wallow in their drug-fuelled pseudo-grief, giving insincere monologues about what a good friend Stevie had been to them.

CHAPTER 3 DC Douglas

Detective Constable Catherine Douglas turned out to be a pretty but rather serious-looking policewoman. She contacted Eddie the day after he'd spoken to Mike and arranged to come to the practice to have a chat with him.

When Mike had said that she was a DC, Eddie didn't want to appear ill-informed, so he went online to find out what sort of policewoman she was.

It turned out that the "D" stood for detective, and the following letter, or letters denoted the rank. She was a DC, a Constable, which was the lowest ranked officer. The next up was a DS, a Sergeant, followed by an DI, an Inspector, then a DCI, a Detective Chief Inspector and finally the Detective Superintendent. He was the highest ranked CID officer, and would answer to a Deputy Chief Constable, and the Chief Constable in overall charge of Strathclyde police force.

The women at the reception desk were all curious when DC Douglas came in and asked for Dr Henderson. She was told that vets weren't called doctor this or that, but if she took a seat Mr Henderson would see her shortly.

She was dressed in a two-piece business suit, dark grey, with an almost black three-quarter length coat. Her hair was tied in a tight bun at the back, and she wore very little make-up, and sensible shoes, but when Eddie came out to guide her through reception he got all flustered, and he could hear the stifled giggles from his admin staff as he retreated with the policewoman to the partners' office, up the stairs behind the dispensary. He ushered her into the sizable room, took her coat and showed her to a seat. One of the other partners, Gavin Usher, was at a desk on the far side of the room. He looked up, said a quick hello, and then got back to what he had been doing when they entered; something to do with practice duty rotas.

Eddie asked her if she wanted a cup of something and when she said yes he buzzed one of the receptionists to bring up a couple of coffees for them, adding one for Gavin when he indicated he'd like one, too. He didn't normally get his staff to run after him, but he thought he would teach them a lesson for taking the piss earlier. While waiting for the coffee to arrive they made awkward small talk, but once the still-grinning secretary delivered their drinks, they got down to discussing the horrific torture cases that were the object of their meeting.

Gavin initially tried to look as if he wasn't listening, but he gave up pretending as the story unfolded. It became obvious that DC Douglas had a fondness for animals, which pleased Eddie greatly because he felt that she would have empathy with the victims and be more inclined to treat the investigation with the seriousness it deserved. Eddie explained that cruelty against animals generally fitted into one of three categories. The first was *neglect*, often starvation or inadequate provision of veterinary care. The second was *casual cruelty* or *malicious killing*, like drowning unwanted kittens. The last category was *deliberate cruelty*. The crimes they were investigating fell into this last category.

He detailed the individual cases that he'd found and she took brief notes the whole way through. She also taped the interview, with Eddie's consent, and when they finished, Eddie promised to copy all the documentation associated with the case and have it sent over to her within the next few days. He showed her the work he'd done on his laptop, mapping all the locations and dates, which he assured her he would email to her. Finally, they discussed the way forward, and considered what resources they would need to make progress.

"What we need is a list of what we know, what we suspect, and what we don't know," she told him, taking an A4 pad out of her shoulder bag, "and also a course of possible actions that we should think about taking."

At this point Gavin interrupted.

"Listen, I have to go. I've got a clinic starting soon. Let me know if there's anything I can help you with. It was nice meeting you, Miss Douglas." He got up, shook her hand and left the room.

"Gavin's all right, but I doubt he'll be of too much help unless the hours are billable." Eddie didn't say this nastily, just in the matter of fact way he did with most things.

"Listen, Mr Henderson, I think we'll find that this investigation will be down to you and I. There's no chance of us getting any more help from my end, and I'll only be able to do this part of the time, and for a very limited period."

"Please call me Eddie, everyone else does, Detective Constable. I'm OK to put a little bit of official work in on this, but it will mostly have to be in my spare time; my partners will get annoyed if I do too much during working hours without getting paid for it, and to be fair, they're right to feel that way."

"It's Catherine. We may as well be on first name terms, but if you contact the station, or there are other officers about, I'd appreciate it if you'd address me as DC Douglas. I get a bit of flak at work because I'm a woman and because I won't play their games, so I try to keep everything as workmanlike as I can."

Eddie was a little taken aback, but didn't pursue it any further, sensing that this was a raw spot with her. Instead he made a few suggestions for her list, a sort of "case summary", which soon started to take shape. After an hour it was more or less complete, which wasn't saying that much.

The things that they already knew were that a series of animal mutilation cases had taken place over the last three years, all of the victims were cats, and they'd all been poisoned first. The first two had taken place on the south side of Glasgow between May and July, 2010, then there were three further cases in the Dundee area from October to December of the same year. Finally, there were the last three cases in Paisley and the south of Glasgow.

They suspected that all the crimes had been committed by the same person, who lived in the Paisley area or a neighbouring part of Glasgow, and that statistically, the culprit would most likely be male. He may have lived in Dundee for a period in 2010.

They didn't have a description for the suspect, or any idea of his age or background, or a motive for the killings.

Both Eddie and Catherine decided that they needed to collect more historical data for the relevant areas, to try to narrow the search down by further analysis of the updated data, and that a search of police files for any reports of similar cases not on Eddie's list could be helpful.

Eddie suggested that a look at crime reports from Glasgow and Dundee for any instances of stolen nail guns would be worthwhile, and Catherine agreed that this would be relatively straightforward, but she was less optimistic that his idea to collect employment records from companies with branches in both cities would be as manageable.

"There's just too many, and we don't have the resources for such a long shot."

They decided to divide the proposed actions between

them. Eddie would look at the information again to see if there was anything more he could get from it, and he would get the SSPCA to give him records going back another fifteen to twenty years. He would also look into the drifting pattern for the Tayport cat. If wind and tide data was available, he might be able to work out where the cat was dumped into the water.

Catherine would search back through the Strathclyde and Dundee police files for additional cases, and for any records of a stolen nail gun. She would also go up to Dundee and meet with a colleague in CID that she knew from her college days, to see if she could get a little help at that end, especially with things like trying to trace antifreeze sales. She would leave Eddie to contact or visit garages and auto spares outlets in the Paisley area.

"There's a problem here, Eddie," she said, tidying her pad and pens into her bag ready to head back to the station, "you don't have any official standing in this investigation, so there's a lot of things you can't do. Just be careful that you don't overstep the mark at any point, or you could jeopardise any future prosecutions."

"Oh, right, the SSPCA is already dealing with that. They are making me a temporary inspector so that I have an official role. Up until now I've just freelanced for them on the pathology side."

"That might help, but with or without that just be careful, and keep me updated at all times so that I can keep everything on the right track. Here's my work mobile and my personal mobile number." She gave him a business card with her name, her rank, the station phone number and her personal and police mobile numbers printed on it. As an afterthought, she took the card back, and wrote another number on it. "That's my home number as well. Neither of my mobiles work anywhere about the house. For God's sake, don't lose it or hand my number out to anyone else."

"Of course not." Eddie stood up and they shook hands before leaving the way they'd come in. The reception staff tried and failed to get a look at her without being obvious, and she gave them a frosty look for their efforts. She knew from experience that would unnerve them a little; with the exception of criminals, even people who've done nothing remotely unlawful feel slightly nervous when there's a police officer about.

-o-

When Eddie passed back through reception, one of the receptionists waved the phone and, making a grimace, told him that Brian Gardner was on the line for him.

Eddie told her that he'd take the call up in the office. She rolled her eyes at him, and pressed the button to put Brian on hold.

None of the staff liked Brian Gardner, but he was the nearest thing Eddie had to a friend, although they sometimes didn't have any contact for months at a time. Brian was a bit of a waster, but Eddie had a soft spot for him, having known each other since they'd been infants playing in the muddy back yard shared by four blocks of flats in the council estate where they were brought up.

Even before he picked up the phone, Eddie knew that Brian was in trouble again.

"What's happened now?" he asked.

The voice on the line sounded hollow and echoing.

"Ah'm in the polis station. Ah've been detained. The duty sarge let me phone ye."

"Shit. What have you done this time?" asked Eddie,

sighing.

"Nuffin, man, honest. Ah did nuffin."

"You must have done something for them to arrest you."

"Honest, man, ah've been set up. Ah've kept masel' oot o' trouble fir months.'

Strangely, Eddie believed him. Brian would usually admit to his crimes, at least to Eddie. Over the years there had been numerous phone calls in a similar vein, and Brian had spent various lengths of time incarcerated in penal establishments from young offenders' institutions through to Low Moss low security prison and HMP Greenock, all for repetitive petty crimes of a non-violent nature.

"OK, Brian; I believe you. You have been doing pretty well, recently. What do you want me to do?"

"Well, ah wid normally jist use the duty solicitor, 'cos usually ah've done it, but ah wis thinkin' that ah might need somewan wi' a bit mair swagger, wi' me bein' set up by the cunts an' that. Ye aye spoke aboot yon friend ye hud that wis a lawyer. Ah jist wunnered if he wid be interested. Ah get legal aid."

"Terry Gallagher. He was at university the same time as me. He hung about with a couple of the guys in my year."

"Can ye ask him fir me?"

"He *is* a defence lawyer, but I've not spoken to him for years. I don't mind phoning him, though."

"Ah'll leave it with ye, then."

He hung up. The last time Brian had been locked up, it was for resetting stolen goods, when he wisely kept his mouth shut about the source of the thirty £200 phones he was caught punting for forty quid each at the Barras, Glasgow's East End market. That was over a year ago, and Eddie had done his best to push Brian into legitimate but menial employment.

He looked up the phone number for the law firm where Terry was a partner, McCluskey & Gallagher solicitors, and rang them immediately. He was lucky enough to catch him in the office.

Terry was delighted to hear from him, although they'd never been close friends.

"How's it going, Eddie? Still shoving your hand up cows' arses?"

Eddie laughed dutifully. "I do that very rarely now; mostly fingers up dogs' rectums these days, I'm afraid," he replied, as always amazed by people's fascination with the orifices it was part of his job to occasionally explore.

"Is this a social call, or have you been arrested for murdering someone?"

"No, I'm calling on behalf of a friend of mine who asked me to contact you because he'd heard that I knew you. He's been arrested, and maintains that he's been set up."

"He must have heard my reputation. Best young defence lawyer in town."

Eddie laughed. "I'm not sure on either count. It depends on what you call young and what town it is."

They both laughed this time, but Eddie was anxious to help his friend and, hoping that he'd been sociable enough, he went on to give Terry Brian's resume.

"Brian, a friend of mine, is a bit of a habitual petty thief and has done some time here and there. I've been trying to get him straightened out and I thought that I was succeeding, until today. He's been arrested for something he says he didn't do, and I don't want to see him lose his job and get locked up for it."

"This might sound cynical, but do you believe him?"

"I do, although that might seem naive to you. He's always been up front with me in the past when he's been guilty."

"What's the story with you and Brian?"

"Well, as you probably remember, I was brought up in Castlemilk, which was rough at times, and Brian lived next door, so I've known him all my life. We went through school together, and through his association with the more delinquent elements in both primary and secondary schools, I was protected from the worst of the bullying that most kids like me suffered."

He hesitated.

"I don't mind paying. We've always just got on, despite our differences. It's as simple as that."

"OK. I'll take it on. He'll get legal aid, so that shouldn't be a problem, but I'll keep your offer in mind. Give me his details and I'll get down there. It is the main Paisley police station he's being held in?"

"Shit, I didn't ask. Sorry."

"It's OK. I'll phone first, in case it's Ferguslie Park."

-o-

A few hours later, Eddie left to pick Brian up from the front door of the police station, hoping that he didn't bump into DC Douglas. He spoke briefly to Terry Gallagher, and thanked him.

"It was no bother. They were just trying it on, rounding up a few previous offenders who were possible suspects."

Eddie felt that he couldn't refuse Terry's offer of a quick pint, so the three of them headed across the street to the Kelbourne. When Eddie was up at the bar getting the drinks in, Brian explained his and Eddie's relationship.

"He's a kinda cross between a big brother an' a social worker. He's always on ma back aboot sumfin, but a will say, he's no' that bad for a posh cunt."

"He said you'd watched his back all through school, though."

"Ah suppose. He was aye a clevir bastard, an' he stuck oot like a plook oan a tart's coupon. He wid have goat mair do-ins if he hadnae knawn me, that's fir sure." He laughed. "He wis aye tryin tae get me tae learn stuff, an ah sometimes wished ah'd listened tae him, but ..."

Eddie returned with the drinks, and asked them what was so funny.

"Nuthin, man. Ah was jist tellin' Terry here that yer aye oan ma case."

Eddie grinned. "Not that it does any good, most of the time," he said.

Brian tried to look hurt, but quickly cheered up when Eddie slid his pint over to him.

"This feels magic, after spendin' aw that time in thon cell."

Eddie couldn't help laughing again.

As they finished their drinks, Brian continued. "Terry showed thae bastards where they could put their fucken detention, onyhow."

Terry handed Brian his card, saying "You did the right thing; 'No comment' always works, then phone me, if there's a next time."

Eddie and Brian had another pint after Terry left. Even though Brian had been in the police station where Catherine Douglas worked, Eddie didn't mention her or his involvement with CID, although he did tell Brian about his work with the SSPCA, investigating the mutilated cats, on the off-chance that Brian might have heard something at street level about who might be involved. Perhaps he thought that telling Brian about his involvement with the police might have made him nervous, scathing or both.

CHAPTER 4 Craig

Craig Ferguson stood for a few moments in the open doorway, savouring the damp air and his first taste of freedom in a year.

"Fuck this, man, I need a score."

Craig had just completed twelve months of a two year sentence for a burglary that had gone wrong, during which he'd allegedly assaulted the homeowner, who'd appeared unexpectedly and at the wrong moment to discover Craig and another jakey trashing his house in the search for saleable items. The cunt was supposed to have been at work, but had come back early and let himself in the front door to be confronted by Craig, holding a top of the range home cinema sound unit in his arms and making for the back door, where the lock had been forced earlier. They had both panicked in their own way, the homeowner shouting and screaming at Craig, who responded by launching the substantial black, sharp-edged box in the general direction of the unfortunate man. Despite an arm thrown out to save himself, the corner of the box had connected with the side of the homeowner's head, causing a large gash, which bled profusely, and a loud thud as he collapsed on to the floor, breaking a glass display cabinet on the way down. Craig watched in horror as the man lay at a strange angle, unmoving, blood pouring from his head. His accomplice, entering the hall at that point, made things worse by telling Craig that he'd "fucken topped the bastard".

In Craig's defence, he then did two things which ultimately saved him from a long prison stretch, but almost guaranteed that he would get caught. He checked the man's neck for a pulse but, because he couldn't feel it, he took off his right glove. Finally feeling a pulse but realising that the man needed help, he picked up the phone, dialled 999, and told the operator that there was a badly injured man at the address he was phoning from. It then dawned on him that he was holding the phone without a glove on, so he transferred it over to his gloved hand, wiped the handset with his sleeve, dropped it, and ran out the back door in the footsteps of his pal, who'd split as soon as he'd pointed out that the man had been "topped".

Unfortunately for Craig, despite his efforts at cleaning them off, he'd left one print and a couple of partials on the phone. As he'd done time previously and his prints were on file, he was picked up the next day, high on heroin, and charged with theft by housebreaking, with assault. At the trial, the defence had argued that he hadn't meant to seriously hurt the homeowner, merely to facilitate his escape. The prosecutor conceded that checking the man's pulse and phoning for an ambulance weren't the acts of a ruthless killer, besides which the injured man had recovered consciousness before the emergency services had arrived and had asked, in a letter sent to the court, that Craig be shown some leniency because of his actions in summoning help. The judge was not completely unsympathetic, and gave him a shorter sentence than he could have, but made drug rehabilitation compulsory as a condition of his tolerance.

While in prison Craig did well initially, but access to drugs inside was too easy and he eventually slipped back into the familiar routine of either being under the influence of drugs or desperately trying to get some.

Now he was out on licence. As he stood on the pavement outside Barlinnie prison, with next to no money in his pocket, he wondered what his best plan of action was. At his mum's he would be looked after, but she was careful about leaving money about when he was there and she would try and keep him in the house and straighten him out, which he couldn't cope with.

As part of his supervised release order, he had to attend a drug rehabilitation centre and his criminal justice social worker had given him an address for one in Paisley, but that would be just as bad. *"Turnarounds" for fuck's sake. Fucken do-gooders.* Still, he needed an address for the Social, to get money.

The fine drizzle that had been falling was beginning to soak through his thin Adidas top, so he decided to start walking in the general direction of the city centre. He would make up his mind later; *get a score first*. He had enough cash for that. Maybe even do a bit of begging if he could find a pitch that wasn't already nabbed by an Albanian or Kurd, but that would be risky; he'd chance getting picked up and put back inside for breaking his parole conditions.

He'd not gone far when a car pulled up at the kerb beside him. The window rolled down as it stopped.

"Want a lift, man?"

Craig looked suspiciously at the car, a dark grey BMW, and the driver.

"Well, dae ye want a lift or no?"

Craig vaguely recognised the guy, he'd seen him around the estate from time to time. A Ferguslie Park boy. He'd never seen him with a car, though.

"Is it yer ain car, or is it knocked off?"

"It's ma ain. Why? Are ye gettin' in or no?"

"Aye, ah will. Ah wis just askin', man. Ah cannae afford tae get caught in a hot motor. Ah'm just oot ae the jail, man."

"Get in, man, it's fucken wet oot there. Ah stopped 'cos ah thought ah recognised ye."

Craig knew he would be happier on the south side of the city, away from this dump.

"Thanks man, ah wis just headin' intae town tae see a mate, get some gear."

"Ye got any cash oan ye?"

"Enough. Ah'll go up tae ma ma's and lend a few quid aff her later oan."

The driver reached under his dashboard, up behind the steering column, and produced a couple of plastic bags. Craig's eyes widened, but he tried to keep his face from giving away his hunger to grab them out of the guy's hand.

"How much?" he asked, not sure if the crumpled notes and the few coins he had in his pocket would cover it.

"Ah'll tell ye whit, ye can have this for whatever ye have oan ye, seein' as yer just oot the jail, man. Just mind and get yer stuff frae me in the future."

Craig knew he was going to owe this guy; at some point a favour would need to be returned, probably with interest, but he couldn't say no with the gear so close. He turned out his pocket on to the plastic dashboard tray, taking a risk and leaving a screwed up note in his pocket.

If the driver knew that Craig was holding out on him, he never let on. He gave Craig the bags and fished out a new syringe and a kit in a brown bag to cook up with.

"Here, ye'll need that. Where are ye stayin'?"

"Ah think ah'll stay at ma ma's. She's a pain, always oan

at me, but ah need an address for ma fucken social worker. But ah'll need tae fin' somewhere tae shoot up first."

"Where does yer ma stay? Ah've seen ye up at the Tannahill Road end, huven't ah?

"Aye, we stay in Tannahill Terrace. Ah've seen you about an' aw."

"Yer right, doon at the bottom end, but ah keep where ah live tae masel', just in case."

"Right, man, ah can appreciate that, what wi' you dealin' an' that."

The driver turned to Craig, who wondered if he'd gone too far, but his benefactor didn't seem to react.

"Ah knaw a guid squat that's empty, if ye want. It's no' that far frae yer ma's, an' ye can get peace frae her, but be close enough for yer social shirker."

Craig grinned at that, but looked at him suspiciously, wondering again what this guy would expect in return for all these favours.

"Whit dae ye want frae me? Ah mean, ye've got tae want me to dae somethin', huvn't ye?"

"Listen mate, ah've been in your shoes before; done some time, an' that. Some cunts huv helped me oot in the past, so ah'm just doin' the same. An' ah'm aye on the lookout fur punters as well. Think o' it as an introductory package, like ye get wi' Sky TV."

That seemed to settle Craig's anxiety, which was replaced with an impatience to get the gear inside him. If he could have got away with it, he'd have cooked up in the car. The two men didn't speak as the car crossed Glasgow, heading over the Kingston Bridge along the busy M8 to Paisley, and turned into the car park of a block of flats, currently unoccupied, awaiting conversion into accommodation for asylum seekers. The original contractors for the job had gone into liquidation, and a new but shortened tender process had only just started. The driver had a set of keys for the block, and for the fifth floor flat that they climbed up to.

"Nae lifts man; nae electricity at aw. But there's a couple o' wee solar gairden lights. Ye've goat tae remember tae leave them oot on the veranda durin' the day tae charge up. They don't gie ye much light, but enough fir whit yehs wid need, man."

Craig looked around. It wasn't a bad gaff. In one room there were even two beds that had been left by the last tenants before the building was emptied, and that hadn't quite reached one of the two skips sitting directly below. They were already filling up with all the shite from miles around, an open invitation for opportunists wanting to dump anything from discarded bikes to a dead cat. The previous occupants must have been healthy cunts, as there was an old exercise bike which was past its best, with a cracked saddle and one pedal, and a weightlifter's bench oozing stuffing from the torn, black, padded PVC cushion. There were a few weights lying about, and two of the lighter ones were on the ends of the long, rusting metal lifting bar that lay across the bench's side supports.

"Don't be doin' too much weights, man," joked the driver, "it's no guid fur ye." He laughed, and Craig joined in.

"This is the berries man, the dug's baws. Thanks, man."

"Nae probs, mate, they'll probably no' start workin' on this place fur anither month, onyway." He moved towards the door, turning and throwing a set of keys towards Craig before leaving. Craig immediately set about getting ready to cook up. The lighter, the spoon, the syringe and needle were sitting on top of the bed alongside one of the two packets the driver had given him. Before he started, he rushed over to the window, swung it half open and looked down, to see the driver crossing the tarmacked pavement to the parking space the BMW sat in.

He shouted down, "Hey man, whit's yer name, mister?"

The driver opened his door then turned and looked up at Craig, whose head was sticking out the window.

"Just call me Jacko."

-o-

Eddie and Catherine's third meeting took place in Eddie's flat. She arrived exactly on time, a point noted by Eddie in her favour, dressed in her normal efficient manner, porting her shoulder bag and a file storage box full of the case files.

"Here, let me take those. Come in and sit down." He showed her into his living room, a large south-facing room with a panoramic bay window facing Brodie Park. The room retained most of the original features affirming its Victorian origins, and it had been restored in an understated fashion, combining modern furniture with painted floorboards and an ornate fireplace. Catherine glanced approvingly around, sat down and accepted the offer of a cup of coffee, which Eddie went to make in the large kitchen across the hall.

Their previous meeting had been in the CID office in the police station in the centre of Paisley, where she had a small cubicle and desk, but there were too many distractions and she was getting comments from some of the more obnoxious male officers about taking up with a vet because honest hardworking policemen apparently weren't good enough for her. Most of them at some point had tried it on with her, since the messy break-up with her long-time boyfriend, latterly fiancé, now a two-timing sergeant in C division.

Eddie, on the other hand, was all business, although pleasant enough with it. In their phone conversations and meetings, he would be impatient to get past the small talk, and down to discussing any new developments in the case.

On his side, he had come up with some interesting new leads that would be worth following up. The extra data he'd received from the SSPCA contained a few details that excited Eddie. There was a cluster of cases near Paisley, where several cats and one dog, had been poisoned with antifreeze over the previous seven years. There had been a series of animal mutilations in the same locality over an even longer period. The levels were above what might have been expected as the typical background rate of sporadic accidental poisonings, deliberate killing of cats by disgruntled cat haters, and random acts of violence and torture of all species of animals that seems to be endemic in human culture. Eddie thought that this could mean that it *was* the same person who was responsible for these cases and the ones he had already investigated, and if it was, this would tie the culprit to the Paisley area for a much longer time. It could be that there was more chance that a witness would be found who could identify him. It meant going through all the data in detail to see if any of the cases fitted in with the way their suspect worked.

Catherine's search through police archives hadn't been as productive, but there was one possible case that could be added. The SSPCA hadn't been involved because it had come to light during a police investigation that didn't initially involve any animals.

About four years previously, a routine call out to the aftermath of a warehouse fire, which was flagged up as a possible arson, led to the discovery of two bricked up cats. In a corner of the warehouse, which had been used for the long-term storage of MOD surplus items and had, to all intents and purposes, been forgotten about, a dummy wall had been built. Part of the warehouse wall behind this had collapsed due to the heat from the burning cladding, and in the exposed recess the police found two dead cats. One was a dismembered skeleton, but the other was desiccated, remaining reasonably well preserved. There was a capping slab on the recess, which was about eight feet tall, and eighteen inches square, almost like a short chimney. The police concluded that, as there was no access in and out of the recess, the cats had been incarcerated deliberately, or had become trapped by accident while the structure was being built. The latter was unlikely, as the structure was fairly compact, and two cats would have been observed entering into it and, in addition, the structure seemed to have no other function other than to contain the unfortunate animals. The bricks and the mortar used in the construction appeared to be much more modern than those in the original warehouse, so it was thought that somebody had got access to the warehouse, had built the brick enclosure and then dropped two cats in it. Whether or not the person had kept checking the cats over the days from the open top, or whether they had simply put the capping slab on and left them to die unobserved, the police could only guess.

It must have been winter when the cats died; only in cold weather would a cat's body not have decomposed before it dried out.

The police never found the arsonist and they certainly weren't likely to find the person who had killed the cats, as there were no records of any further investigation of the case. Eddie surmised that one of the cats had either died or been killed by the other cat, and the surviving animal had eaten the dead one – the body had been totally dismembered and some of the bones had been gnawed. It would have only delayed the second cat's demise by one or two weeks, and it died in quite an emaciated state, according to the notes, even accounting for the water loss that occurred during the desiccation process. Whatever happened, both cats suffered horribly, and Eddie could easily believe that it could have been the same sad individual involved in all of the cases.

There were no post-mortem results and the cats had long been disposed of, so it was impossible to know if there was any use of antifreeze, but the longest surviving cat couldn't have been fatally poisoned as it wouldn't then have survived long enough for the effects of starvation to be so marked.

Eddie renewed his appeal that employment records should be checked and emphasised that this time it could be much more focused, as there was a distinct possibility that the killer worked in the building trade and may have had some easy way of gaining access to the warehouse legitimately, but it fell on deaf ears.

Catherine's initial visit to Dundee had been unproductive in providing new evidence, but she had made good contacts in the Dundee force that she felt might prove useful at a later stage.

Eddie had trawled through an online business directory and had made a list on his computer of all the service stations, branches of Halfords and independent auto stores in Paisley and the surrounding area, and he repeated the process for Dundee. He sent a form letter to every one of them outlining his concern about a serial poisoner and requested any information about unusual buying patterns or out of season purchases. He got little response, despite following most of the letters up with a phone call.

Catherine offered to try, with the clout of a police investigation behind her, but said she would have to run it past her sergeant first as she was racking up more hours than had been originally allotted to her for this investigation.

In the event, when she was called in to see the sergeant and the inspector the next day and asked to report on the progress of the investigation, she was told that it was being pulled. When she asked for the reasons, they said that it was because of a combination of an extremely large caseload for the department, and a poor projected outcome for this particular enquiry.

When she phoned Eddie he was livid, but he kept his anger under control, not wanting to take it out on her. In a way, he'd known this was coming, and he couldn't quite decide what he was most disappointed about: the investigation being closed down or the fact that he wouldn't be working with Catherine Douglas any more.

"I'll keep going," he told her, determined to let her see that he wasn't quitting on it. "I can probably get a bit of help from one of the SSPCA inspectors. I've convinced them that this is all connected, and I think they'd be loath to let it slip away now, without covering every angle."

"Eddie, I can still help you with this, just not officially. I'm just as committed to this as you are; I've had cats of my own, as you know, and I think it's important to get the guy who's doing this to these poor animals."

Eddie was relieved and pleased. He enjoyed working with Catherine. He felt that they made a good team, and he enjoyed her company, thinking of her already as a friend as well as a colleague.

"I'll call you, and we can meet up. It will have to be at the practice or at your flat, as I can't be seen moonlighting on this one. Technically it wouldn't be wrong unless I got caught using police resources, but it would be heavily frowned upon by the brass."

They agreed to meet the following week, when both their

off duties coincided, and left it at that.

-o-

Craig awoke with the mother of all hangovers, and in a very strange position. His head was throbbing, his mouth tasted awful, he felt sick and he had a tight knot in his stomach that was just short of a cramp, but the strangest thing, apart from his slightly blurred vision, was that he was unable to move his arms or legs. He tried, but he seemed to be stuck – he could feel something tight around his ankles and around his arms, which were stretched out to the side and resting uncomfortably on something hard between his elbows and his shoulders. In addition, he was kneeling on the floor, but bent at the waist to lie face down on a soft and padded surface that supported his torso from his pelvis to his neck. He tried to struggle again, but realised that he was securely tied, and as he craned his neck to look under him, he could see that it was probably the weight bench he was strapped to.

"Hoy," he shouted, struggling, trying to look left and right to see where he was and who was there. Every time he moved it hurt more. "What the fuck's goin' on, man?"

There was only silence. He knew now that he was in the squat and tried to remember anything that could explain how he got into the position he was now in. Surely he hadn't got so wasted that he had entered into some sort of sexual game with some cunt? *Aw fuck, ah hope it wisnae a bloke*, he thought, but he still had his jeans on, and there was no anal discomfort to speak of.

Gradually, as his brain became less fuzzled, he started to remember vague moments from the night before. As soon as his benefactor had driven away, Craig had cooked up the gear and shot up, and it was the best of junk, not like some of the shite he'd had to make do with in prison.

At some point, the driver, Jacko, had returned, letting himself in. He must have had spare keys for the block and for the flat. He had a couple of Tesco bags with him, from which he produced a dozen bottles of booze; *one of thae fancy alcopops. Bright fucken blue. Whit wis wrang wi' good ol' Buckie?* Craig would have rather tapped the guy for some more gear but knew better than to push it, so when he was offered a bottle, he accepted it gratefully. The guy pulled out a couple of large bags of Doritos, and chucked one to Craig, along with a bottle opener.

"Listen man, ah'm no a homo, just in case ye think … ye knaw whit a mean, man."

Jacko laughed. "Craig, yer quite safe, ah'm no interested in ye that way, ah'm strictly a fanny man masel', so yer aw right."

Craig had laughed, relieved that he wasn't expected to put out. He'd had to give a guy in prison a hand job on a number of occasions to get drugs, but had gagged at the critical point when he'd been told that he wouldn't be getting any more drugs for anything less than a blow job, and his supplier had relented and contented himself with Craig's hand again.

Craig sipped from his bottle, relishing the taste after being so long without a decent drink. Alcohol was available in prison, but it was too easy for the screws to smell it on your breath, so he'd done without, sticking instead to whatever drugs he could get hold of.

The first couple of bottles had tasted wonderful, but to be honest, he had gone off the taste after that and had been desperate to ask Jacko for some more gear. His new mentor, if that was the word, had knocked back quite a few bottles as well, and seemed keen to chew the fat with Craig, talking about prison, life outside, women, football and drugs.

- o -

The last thing Craig remembered before waking up strapped to the workout bench was Jacko telling him that he'd take care of him, and laughing as he said it.

Craig was by now really worried. *It must have been that cunt Jacko, or maybe some fud frae one of thae ither flats, tyin' him up fir a laugh.* He shouted again.

"Haw, ya bastards, ye. Let me oot o' here; ye've had yer laughs; it's no funny any mair."

Nothing. Just silence, and a distant lorry grunting up the hill, grinding its way through the gears.

He nearly shit himself when a voice no more than a couple of feet behind him broke the silence.

"Well, Craig, sonny boy. Just what the fuck have ye got yersel' intae?"

Jacko. The cunty bawed bastard! It was him all along.

"Just get me out o' this, Jacko. Please, man, ah'm as sair as fuck here, an' a need a piss, man, an' maybe a shite."

"Now, Craig, ah think that's the least o' yer worries. Why d'ye think yer here?"

"Ah don't fucken know, man, whit huv ah done tae you, fur fucks sake?" A sudden thought struck Craig. "Aw, man, ye found the tenner in ma pocket. Ah didnae mean tae keep it; it must huv got stuck in the corner, man, Ah noticed it later on, an' ah didnae want tae say nuthin' in case ye thought ah'd been lyin' tae ye. Ah'm sorry, man."

"Craig, ah knew ye kept some cash back, aw you wee jakey bastards always do. Anyhow, that's no why yer here." Jacko got up off the chair he'd been sitting on for the last few hours, waiting for Craig to wake up, and walked round to stand in front of him.

Craig stretched his head back painfully to see Jacko, but he could only see as far up as his chest. Jacko reached down, grabbed a handful of hair, and pulled Craig's head back another couple of inches to help them make eye contact. Spittle frothed at Craig's mouth, and he screamed until Jacko let him go. His head fell, and his throat pressed against the front of the bench, momentarily choking him.

"So ye need a piss and a shite, do ye?" Craig sensed Jacko moving behind him again, and felt a sudden pull on his belt. There was a ripping sound, then a sharp pain on one of his arse-cheeks, and coldness as his now halved trousers and boxers were pulled down to his knees. *The cunt must have cut them with a Stanley knife or something.* He could feel the warm drip of blood from his buttock run down the side of his leg.

"Naw. Naw. Naw. Yer goin' tae rape me, ya dirty cunt, ye. Ye said ye wernie a poof, ya fucken arse-bandit, ye."

"Craig, Craig. A bit less o' the abuse, please. Ah think ye've forgot whit position yer in. Ah'd be more polite if ah were you." He moved round in front again, and squatted down, smiling at Craig. "Ah'll tell ye a story, jakey boy. How are ye feelin'?"

"Like shite, ya cunt. Whit dae ye fucken think, man?"

"Do ye knaw why ye feel like shite?"

Craig didn't answer.

"Ye think that ye've got a bit o' a hangover fae the drink, an' yer also feelin' rough 'cos ye need a score, naw?"

Still no answer.

"Sulkin', eh? Well, anyway, see if ah wis tae tell ye that if a let ye go now, ye wid die anyway, whit wid ye say tae that?"

"Yer talkin' shite, man; utter fucken shite."

"Oh, yer speakin' tae me again, ur ye? Well, ah've got bad news fur ye, ah'm no tellin' porkies, yer goin' tae die whitever happens."

Craig had gradually come to the same conclusion, and was now terrified. A trickle of piss came away from him involuntarily, and he could feel the previously mild cramps in his bowels becoming stronger.

"Ah really am goin' tae shite, man; let me up tae go tae the bog or ah cannae promise tae keep it in."

"Go ahead, Craig, it's no matterin' a fuck tae me. Ah don't live here or nuthin', an' anyhow, ah wis tellin' ye why yer as good as deid."

Jacko reached over for one of the bottles from the night before. Craig noticed with horror that he was wearing medical gloves. He put the bottle on the floor inches in front of Craig's face. "See this? Did ye enjoy yer wee swallow last night? Don't answer; I saw ye lappin' it up. It wisnae sae good efter the first couple, wis it? D'ye know why?" he paused to look at Craig's uncomprehending face, then continued. "The rest of the ones ye drank wernae strictly kosher. More of a kinda cocktail, ye might say. Maistly antifreeze, tae be totally frank wi' ye, wi' just enough o' the real stuff tae keep the taste fae bein' too different."

Tears were starting to roll down Craig's face from his bloodshot eyes. He didn't quite understand the full implications of what Jacko was telling him, but it was beginning to sink in.

"Well, that antifreeze stuff, it's great fur motors, keeps ma BMW goin' in winter, man. Doesnae do people much guid, though. Fucks ye up, right royal, an' there's nae cure, even if ye get tae a hospital, they just have tae haud yer haun til ye die."

"Why wid ye want tae … dae that tae me? Whit huv ah … done tae ye?" Craig now spoke through loud sobs, snot bubbling and pouring from his nose.

"That's the funny thing, Craig; ye've done nothing." Jacko paused for emphasis. "Ah'll admit ah don't like wee junkie bams like you, but that's by-the-by. Naw, this is just whit ah dae, an' you invited yersel tae the party, wee man."

Jacko got up and walked over to the window. Craig heard him picking up the bar with the weights on. He came round, and did a few squats in front of Craig.

Craig could hardly watch. Apart from it becoming almost physically impossible to strain his now exhausted neck muscles to keep his head high enough to see Jacko, he was having very bad thoughts about what the bastard was going to do with the weights, and he was feeling sicker and sicker by the minute. *Maybe that cunt was tellin' the truth.*

Jacko finished his squats, laid the bar down on the floor, and started to unscrew the locking wheel at one end. He removed the two weights from that end of the bar, and showed it to Craig, but his head had drooped almost to the floor and his eyes were closed.

He propped the bar against the wall and picked up a bottle of water from the floor. He took a long drink, then poured the rest of the bottle over Craig's head. It had the desired effect. It revived Craig a little and he groaned and cried out. Jacko couldn't make out exactly what he was saying, but Craig, for the first time in his life, was praying. He didn't know who or what he was pleading with for his life, making mumbled promises and offering anything for the big deal. "Just get me fucken out of here, man, an' ah'll get masel' cleaned up an' live wi' ma mither. Ah'll get a job. Ah don't want tae die, fur fuck's sake."

He became slowly aware that Jacko had moved away from where he could see him, and he could hear sounds behind him, then nothing. *Had he gone?*

Then Jacko's voice cut through everything,

"My advice tae you, wee man, is tae relax and take a deep breath, 'cos this might be a wee bit uncomfortable."

Craig screamed. He knew he was going to be raped, and vowed to himself that if he ever got out of this alive, he would search down this cunt, and kill him.

Jacko stood behind him, spat on his hand and smeared the end of the weight bar with his phlegm, then gently slipped the tip between Craig's cheeks until it rested on his anus. Craig screamed again, and tried to struggle, but he was too weak by now, and tied too firmly to the bench to move much.

Jacko put all his weight behind the weights on the other end of the bar and pushed. For a few seconds, Craig made no sound at all other than a desperate gasp, as he fought to get air into his lungs. The pain was intense and at his very core. When he did finally stop breathing in, he let out a scream that would have woken all the residents of the flats in the block, had there been any. Jacko let the bar down, which caused the end that was inside Craig to suddenly angle upwards against the inside of his spine, ramping up the agony to a new level. Even though there was no one to hear, he came forward to stuff a rag in Craig's mouth and wrapped his head with duct tape, to stop it falling out.

"Can't huv any passers by hearin' ye, can we?"

"MMMMNNNNNNNNGGGGGGGGG."

"Sorry, mate, ah cannae really make that out, an' tae be honest, ah don't gie a fuck. Ah wis just bein' rhetorical.'

Craig's body arched in spasm as far as the restraints would let it. A little relief came when Jacko lifted the end of the bar from the floor and held it level, but it was only a prelude to Craig's further torture, as he put his shoulder behind the weight and pushed again. Craig vomited as the pole inside him pushed further up, pressing on his stomach. He was pretty sure that all sort of things inside him were ruptured, but he couldn't even think of a name for any of them.

Jacko seemed to be able to read his mind, because he started to give him a commentary on what was happening to him.

"Ah reckon it's in about a fit noo; that's quite a lot o' metal bar tae be stuck up yer jacksie, ma friend." He paused. "Now, ah'm nae expert, but a reckon yer rectum's mair than likely burst noo, an' yer shit is floatin' aboot inside ye, which isnae that healthy."

Craig struggled desperately, sweating profusely with the effort and the pain, alternately moaning and trying to scream. His bladder, which must have been intact, had emptied and soaked the carpet below. Vomit had come down his nose because of the gag, making it burn, and it was more difficult to breathe.

"Ah'm gonnae shove it in a wee bit more. Ye might feel somethin' a bit like heartburn, only worse, an' there is a possibility, if I'm a bit heavy handed, that ye'll maybe lose a lot o' blood internal like, very quickly, an' pass oot, an' maybe die, but ah'll try and keep ye goin' as long as ah can."

Craig arched his neck and tried to look round, grimacing

with pain and hatred. He felt Jacko pushing again; there was an overwhelming pressure in the middle of his chest then a deep ripping sensation that released some of the pressure, but only added to the pain. His head slumped forward as he lost consciousness, mercifully.

If he had been able to listen, he would have heard the scrape of a chair on lino flooring, and footsteps from the kitchen into the living room, then Jacko's voice.

"Aw Spencey, man, ah'm sorry. Ah think ah've killed the cunt."

A new voice spoke out, one that it was doubtful Craig would ever hear.

"Jacko, yer aw right, man, ye did yer best. It's no' your fault if he's deid." The newcomer, also wearing surgical gloves, reached under Craig's head and pinched his nose hard. A feeble groan came from Craig's mouth. "Anyhow, ah don't think ye've killed him yet." He stood still and watched for a few seconds. "Look, he's breathin'."

Sure enough, Craig's breathing, which had seemed to stop completely for a few minutes, was now starting again, and was increasing in tempo rapidly, and becoming ragged again.

"He's comin' round, Jacko, ah told ye."

"Right, will ah shove this right up now?"

"Naw, gie it a minute, it'll be better if he knaws whit's happenin', the wee cunt. But fair dos, Jacko, ye've done it just like we talked aboot."

Jacko grinned. "Thanks, Spencey, ah don't knaw why you don't want tae dae somethin'; ah get aw the fun, and you just sit an' watch."

"Jacko, that's the bit ah like. Watchin' you enjoyin' yoursel', just the way we planned it. Now, the cunt's nearly awake again; away an' shove that pole in as far as it can go, you knaw whit ah want tae see, don't ye?"

"Aye, ah knaw, but I might need a haun. It's gettin' awfy tight."

"Hit it with thon other weight if it willnae go; ye'll manage right enough."

Craig was slipping in and out of consciousness, but he was sure there were two people talking. Through a blur of pain and weakness, he knew one was Jacko. There was definitely another man speaking; *perhaps somewan has come tae stop all this. Surely if they get me tae hospital, they can fix me up.*

A metallic thud deep within his body put paid to any more thoughts about getting out of this alive. He screamed as a second blow reverberated throughout his whole torso, and he realised that Jacko, or someone else, was hammering the bar into him, like a nail into wood. The pain had started again. It had never gone, but in between times when the bar wasn't being forced through his body, it subsided a bit, although it had now become incredibly painful to breathe in. Or out. With every thump it got worse, and his windpipe seemed to be on fire. He tried to suck air in but the pain was so intense that he had to fight hard to suppress the need to cough and clear his airway. His last thought before he lost consciousness again was that he could feel the pole pushing up through the base of his neck.

-o-

"He's still alive. Get a doc up as quick as you can, and nobody moves anything here."

The distant voice reached Craig, but he didn't believe it.

There had been too many false hopes, and each one that was shattered left him further in the depths of despair. He was in the same position and in the same place as before. He still expected Jacko to appear in front of him, grinning viciously.

But as he drifted in and out of consciousness, he gradually became aware that the people trying to help him were not imaginary. Because of the severity of his injuries, and the fact that he had a metal pole passing through almost the whole length of his body, it took the doctor a long time to get him prepared for transport to hospital, and even longer for the ambulance men and paramedics to get him down to the stairs. They'd had to sedate him before they moved him but just before the doctor had given him the drugs through the IV tube that the paramedics had inserted that would knock him out, they had allowed the police to have a word with him. Unfortunately, Craig's ability to breathe, far less speak, was so heavily compromised that he could do no more than grunt and mouth answers to the few questions they managed to ask before they were told that enough was enough, the patient was becoming too distressed and that they would have to question him after he was out of danger.

That never happened. Craig died, aged twenty-four, two days later. On arrival at hospital, his blood tests had demonstrated severe acute kidney failure, which had required twenty-four hours of dialysis to enable him to be taken to theatre the next day. In a complex operation, lasting over twelve hours and involving four surgeons, they successfully removed the bar but, despite further dialysis, his kidney function deteriorated rapidly and he died less than twelve hours after surgery, from a combination of kidney failure and overwhelming and out-of-control peritonitis and septicaemia.

The investigation changed from one of attempted murder to a full-blown murder inquiry.

CHAPTER 5 DI Anderson

Catherine and Eddie sat across from each other at the kitchen table in Eddie's flat. The remnants of a pizza bought in from the Italian restaurant a few doors away had been pushed to one side, and pads, pens and printouts covered most of the remainder of the table. It added to the general chaos and clutter that had taken over much of Eddie's place since it had become the incident room for their private investigation.

Eddie held up a copy of the Daily Record and pointed to the headline on the front page; he was becoming more than a little agitated.

"This is our man," he insisted, "it's got to be. He's moved on to killing people now, I'm positive!"

"We can't be sure of that, but I agree that it's a possibility."

"There's very little doubt in my mind. It's almost identical in every way to that last cat. The only difference is that it's a metal bar instead of a length of wood."

"Eddie, I'm with you on this to a certain degree, but we can't just go to my boss and say that we've been investigating their suspect for months, without something pretty concrete."

Eddie had a sudden thought. "At least get them to check for ethylene glycol. I mean, the guy died of kidney failure, didn't he? They talked about him being on dialysis before and after the operation to remove the pole."

"They're not saying the post-mortem showed that, but even if it did, there could have been organ failure just because of the infection, couldn't there?"

"Well, I suppose it's possible, but it seemed pretty quick. The reports say that he died twelve hours after they operated on him, and it usually takes longer than that, even for E. coli, or one of the similar infections."

"Couldn't the infection have started earlier, when the bar was shoved into him?"

"Yes, you're right, but I'd still love to see a toxicology report. If there's any ethylene glycol in there, I'd say it would make it certain that this is our suspect. Can you get a look at it?"

"I can't just walk into an ongoing murder inquiry and help myself to something like that. I'd be on a disciplinary for sure."

"We've got to do something. If it's the same guy, we have a hell of a lot of information that would be useful to the investigation, and they have all the resources necessary to follow up on it."

"It doesn't work that way, Eddie, and anyway, if I go to them with this, they'll know I've been working on the case after they pulled it."

"What if I went to them, and said that I'd carried on the investigation on my own?"

She thought about it for a few moments. "That might work. I could get you the right guy to speak to." She remained pensive. "You'll have to be tactful about it, though. If you go in too heavy handed, they'll just brush you off as some weirdo."

"OK, OK, so I'll be careful. Wouldn't want to damage their egos, eh?"

"See, that's the sort of attitude that will get their backs up. You're going to have to swallow your pride and pretend they're much cleverer than you."

He didn't know if she was having a dig at him. He wondered if he came across as arrogant, sometimes, so he asked her.

"Not really, not to me, but you could rub some people up the wrong way by being a bit too forthright." She grinned. "Just take it easy. Remember they've done hundreds of investigations over the years, and they won't take too kindly to what they see as outside interference."

Eddie held up his hands in surrender, and they sat for another half hour discussing the details of how he should put their case across.

"Are you going to be there?" he asked her.

"I think that would probably be OK, seeing as it's me who's getting you involved, but I'll not say much unless asked."

"That's fine. I think I'd rather you were there, for moral support, if nothing else."

She blushed slightly at that. It was probably the first time Eddie had said anything remotely personal. They got on really well, but he was always very businesslike there was never much small talk; she took the opportunity to ask him how work was, and how he was finding the time to fit all of the work on the investigation in.

"I'm getting the odd comment from the other partners about the amount of time I'm spending on this. It's nothing, really, and it's a bit bloody unfair of them, pardon the French. I put in more in clinical hours at the surgery than anyone else, and anyway, the SSPCA are paying for some of the hours I'm racking up. Most of the rest I'm doing in my spare time. It's not as if I've got anything else to do." It was Eddie's turn to blush. "Shit, that makes me look pretty sad, doesn't it?" He laughed. "It's not as awful as that, but you know what I mean, don't you?"

"Don't you have anything else other than work?" she asked him, taking advantage of the fact that for once he seemed happy to talk about something other than mutilated animals.

"Oh, don't get me wrong, I read a bit, watch TV, catch the occasional football match, do a bit of walking and cycling and play a game of fives once a week, but I love veterinary medicine, the real stuff, and I find that it fills a lot of my time. I read a lot of veterinary papers and textbooks, and I'm just as happy doing that as anything else.' He paused. "Christ, that sounds bad, doesn't it?"

"No, I'm much the same. I love my job and spend a lot of time studying to try and get better at it, and hopefully get promotion. And it does fascinate me, as well."

Suddenly realising that they were discussing their personal lives, a slight awkwardness came over them, then Eddie stood up and asked her when she would be able to organise a meeting with someone on the inquiry. She looked a little hurt by his abruptness, but knew it was just his way.

"I'll phone you as soon as I can talk to the DI in charge. Hopefully that should be tomorrow."

-o-

It took three days for Catherine to arrange a meeting with DI David Anderson and when Eddie arrived it was made clear that he could have ten minutes, and no more, of the Detective Inspector's valuable time. Catherine was already in the interview room when a young constable showed him in. There was another detective in the room, sitting beside the DI, leaving the seat next to Catherine the only one free.

He sat down, smiling rather nervously at first. "I feel like I've been arrested and that I'm sitting here next to my lawyer, being questioned." He looked sideways at Catherine, but she gave him a frown, and nodded at the opposite side of the table.

"Mr. Henderson, we are using this room because it's the most convenient for our discussion. Now, DC Douglas tells us that you have some information that might be pertinent to our investigation." The DI seemed unamused.

"Sorry, it was a crass comment. Put it down to nerves." He took a deep breath. "I believe that the person you are looking for is the same one who has been killing cats for the last four or five years."

"Right, Mr. Henderson, DC Douglas has already indicated to us that you are convinced of that. What we'd like to know is how you've come to that conclusion."

Eddie could hear the sarcasm dripping from every word. "Well, the last case we looked at had many similarities to your murder victim."

"Apart from the fact that it was a cat that was involved." The younger detective spoke for the first time.

"Yes, obviously, but in many other respects the crimes are the same, and there's a well-established link between people who abuse animals and then go on to abuse humans."

"We'll have to take your word on that last point, although it would be nice to see some evidence. Even then, we're sceptical. It's a big leap from torturing a cat to repeating it in a human."

"I'll have copies of scientific papers showing the link sent over to you, but in the meantime, have a read of these post-mortem results and see if they match up to your case."

Eddie took the report out from his laptop bag and handed it over. DI Anderson gave it a quick look and handed it to his colleague.

"As far as we're concerned, apart from being impaled by a pole or a rod, there's nothing specific to link these crimes. In any case, the victim was a known drug user who'd only recently been released from prison. He may well have been involved in the supply of narcotics. This murder has all the hallmarks of a gangland killing. They like to send out the message that if you cross them, you'll not only end up dead, it'll happen in a way that's generally not too pretty."

Eddie was beginning to get annoyed at their intransigence, but managed to keep a lid on his frustrations.

"Listen, your victim died of kidney failure, didn't he?"

It was the DI's turn to be annoyed. He made as if to stand up, and looked stonily at Catherine.

"Have you leaked the post-mortem report to this fruitcake, DC Douglas?" he said, explosively.

Taken aback, Catherine retorted, "No, sir, I would never do that. It's more than my job's worth, sir."

Eddie butted in. "Leave her alone. It doesn't take a genius to work out that someone who has to be put on dialysis has some degree of kidney failure. That was in the Daily Record."

The two policemen didn't appreciate the implied barb, but Eddie went on.

"All I ask is that someone looks at a toxicology report. If there's ethylene glycol in there, would you believe me then? Or will it take the next victim to turn up nailed to a barn door or to a raft, or hung from a tree, to convince you?"

"Mr Henderson, I'd appreciate it if you would keep yourself in check. I'm not sure that I like your tone, or your inference that we're not conducting this inquiry thoroughly."

Eddie sighed. "I'm not implying anything of the sort. But the method I think this guy is using is very unusual. I'm just trying to help. Please, just check the toxicology report. That's all I ask."

"I've seen a toxicology report. Heroin and alcohol, Mr. Henderson, that was all."

Eddie was shocked. He had convinced himself that he was right.

"No ethylene glycol? Are you sure?"

"No mention of it, no."

"Did they look for it? They might not have. Can you please check?"

"I'm sure if it needed to be done, it would have been."

"Not necessarily. I only did it because it's the most common poison in cats. I don't think it's found that often in humans."

"Mr Henderson, we've listened to what you had to say. We're getting nowhere with this." The DI stood up.

Eddie also stood up, livid, and overstepped the mark with his next comment.

"If you don't check for antifreeze, and it turns out that this is the same man, I'll let the papers know about this conversation."

The DI was now on his feet, and Catherine sat with her head in her hands, horrified at their behaviour. She could imagine the effect that this would have on her career prospects, but she knew that Eddie was right; she just wished he'd been a bit more diplomatic about it.

"Mr. Henderson, you've just crossed a line here. I will not be threatened by anybody. In your case, I can see that you are upset that we have decided not to pursue your animal cruelty investigation, and that you feel frustrated and annoyed, but that doesn't mean that we'll tolerate this sort of behaviour." He turned to Catherine. "Please show Mr. Henderson out, and I'd like to see you in my office when you've done that."

Eddie got the message. He gathered up his stuff, and went to reach over and pick up his report.

"Just leave that. We'll file it away in case more evidence ever comes to light concerning your cat killer."

As Eddie left, shown out by Catherine, he realised that it was going to be very hard for him to work with the police in the future, as word would get around about this. The SSPCA would probably dump him from their register of veterinary experts. He looked at Catherine, feeling guilty, knowing that he'd also made her position very difficult. He had probably risked her career on whether he was right or not.

In the foyer, he apologised to her for letting them get to him, and dropping her in it. She obviously wanted to avoid being seen to have any involvement with him, because she replied that she'd phone him later, and turned to go back upstairs.

-o-

Eddie went home, dropped his stuff off, and changed from his suit into his everyday work clothes – chinos and a polo shirt with the practice's name on it – and headed for the surgery.

When he arrived he saw that he'd a list of cases as long as his arm to deal with. In a way it helped, as it took his mind off what had happened. It was nearly five o'clock by the time the last of the patients he'd operated on had returned to the recovery ward, and he still had a number of phone calls to make, to update clients on the progress of their pets.

He flopped down in his chair in the partners' office, nodding to the other two partners who were there. Only Gavin and Ann were missing. He could sense that the two men had stopped talking when he'd entered, so he asked them what was up.

Embarrassed, Chris Stevens fidgeted awkwardly, glancing furtively at Campbell Armstrong, the oldest of the firm's five partners. It was Campbell who spoke.

"Eddie, we've been having a wee talk about it, and I've been asked to have a word on behalf of the other partners."

This was all Eddie needed; today of all days.

"What's the problem, guys? Something I need to know? Has one of the clients sued us?"

"No, no, nothing like that. It's just, well, it's a little awkward, but we think that you're taking this SSPCA stuff a little bit too seriously."

Eddie couldn't believe it. This was the last thing he'd expected.

"Campbell, I'm sorry, I don't quite understand. Are you saying that I'm not pulling my weight around here; that I'm swanning off, having a ball with this?"

The older man didn't look surprised at Eddie's reaction. Eddie was known for his straight talking and for being touchy at times.

"No, Eddie, that's not what we're saying. We're just a bit worried about you. You seem to be spending all your free time on this, and any odd ten minutes that you can squeeze in during working hours. You hardly stop for lunch and the nurses say it's sometimes after nine o'clock in the evening before you leave. It can't be good for you."

"Does anyone think that it's affected my work? Or that I'm not charging the SSPCA enough?"

"No, your work is the same as always, but there are one or two wondering if the SSPCA are getting a little too much of you for their money."

"Campbell, I can't believe you're saying this. What did we become vets for? Was it not because we cared for animals? There's a nutcase going round poisoning and skewering cats, or nailing them alive to pieces of wood, and you want me to take a step back?"

"That's not what I'm saying. Of course animal welfare comes first, but there's a fine line between thoroughness and obsession, Eddie, and we think you might be close to it."

"I appreciate your concern, but I'm quite capable of deciding how hard I can work, both on and off duty. It would be nice to have a little support instead of what appears to me to be a questioning of my commitment to the practice."

"Eddie, you're a bloody good vet, and an asset to this practice. We're just concerned that you're pushing yourself too hard, that's all."

Eddie calmed down a bit. He could see the genuine concern on the older man's face, but he knew that with some of the other partners, it would be the possibility of unbilled hours that would be the issue.

"Sorry, Campbell. It's been a bad day. I apologise, but I can't let this thing slip just now, it's too important."

He explained about his meeting today, and his suspicions about the link between his investigations and the recent murder.

Campbell looked aghast. "Christ, Eddie, you've really stuck your neck out on this one. I hope for your sake that you're right, or you'll be getting parking and speeding fines every day of the week from now on."

Eddie laughed. It felt good after the sort of day he'd had. It hadn't even crossed his mind that the police would make life uncomfortable for him, but he hoped that what his partner was saying was largely tongue-in-cheek.

"Look, Campbell, I'll take your concerns on board. I'll try and take it a little easier. And I will provide you with an accurate billing record for all the hours I've put in on this during work time, for the benefit of some of the others."

A slight smile twitched at the corner of the other man's mouth, and he could see Chris Stevens stiffen a little, but he said nothing.

Campbell finished by telling Eddie that he was taking him for a pint after work, no refusals. Eddie recognised and admired the skills the senior partner had with people, and was envious of his ability to handle awkward situations, and thought that it would be worth trying to learn from him.

He also knew that the resentment of some of the other partners would continue behind his back, and resolved to be a bit more discreet, doing more of his SSPCA work away from the practice, watching what he was saying while he was in the surgery and letting them think he'd taken their advice about overdoing it.

-o-

Catherine phoned him on his way back to the flat. He pulled over and arranged for her to come over later on, to sort out where they could go with the case. He had a feeling that she was going to have to cut him loose to save her career, and he wouldn't blame her if she did. He asked her if she'd eaten, and when she said she hadn't, he arranged to meet her at the Italian that they'd had the last carry-out pizza from. He quickly changed and headed for the bar where he'd arranged to have a pint with Campbell.

The senior partner, in the pub and away from the practice, told him that he admired Eddie's dedication and skill, but sometimes it was necessary to work with people who weren't quite up to his standards, but who had a different set of skills. He pointed out, for instance, that Chris Stevens, although he could be a penny pincher and a stickler for procedure, got the practice running a hell of a lot more smoothly within a couple of years of buying in as a partner. Gavin and Ann both had a tremendous rapport with the clients, and it was often one of these two that attracted new customers to the practice by word of mouth. As for himself, well, he was just the old guy with a lot of experience, with a talent for being able to smooth over any minor disagreements between staff members, or with the public. When it came to Eddie, Campbell said that he provided the practice with a gold standard in medical care, and a conscience.

Eddie felt relieved that Campbell was essentially on his side, but knew he'd have to take on board the points that the older man had made.

As a result of a pleasant hour in the pub, he just made it to the restaurant on time, where Catherine was already seated. She looked at her watch and smiled.

"You haven't been waiting long, have you?"

"No, five minutes at the most. You just made it, though."

"I had a pep talk in the pub from the senior partner. The rest of them think I'm obsessing about this case, and not charging enough for it."

He looked at her and saw her worried frown, then kicked himself for mentioning his own minor problems without asking how she was.

"Are you going to be OK?"

"Well, I'm feeling pretty down about it all and I think I've probably screwed up any chance of a quick promotion but, do you know, I think you're right, and I'm glad we tried to persuade them to listen."

He saw that she was close to tears and looked away to give her a little time to compose herself.

"I've been assigned to a team investigating fake designer goods on market stalls. I think it's their way of giving me a slap on the wrist." She smiled thinly. "Don't get me wrong, it's better than being sent back to uniform, but they can keep me sidelined for as long as they like and I can do very little about it."

"I can't begin to say how bad I feel about what happened. I shouldn't have let them goad me, and I definitely shouldn't have threatened them with the press. I am truly sorry, especially for putting you in a bad spot."

"Don't worry, Eddie, it will likely blow over. In the meantime, I'm not going to let the bastards stop me helping you with this, if that's all right with you."

"Of course it is." Eddie was surprised, and delighted. "I can't imagine doing this on my own, but are you not taking a big risk?"

"I don't care." She shook her head. "No, I do care, but I'm not giving in to them. What I do in my own time isn't any of their business!"

Tired and still upset, she left a short while after they'd eaten, and Eddie walked her to her car.

"Don't phone me at work or on my mobile. I don't think they will, but they can check up on my calls if they want. I'll phone you, or you can email me on my gmail account."

Eddie watched her drive away, glad that she was still involved, but knowing deep down it was slipping away from them.

CHAPTER 6 James

James Prentice had fucked up. Three times he'd had the rent money in his hands, and three times he'd blown it. And wee Dougie Houston wasn't somebody you wanted to owe money to.

He needed two things: money, fast; and a cheaper gaff to stay in. The thing was, the place he lived in at the moment was as big a shitehole as you got in Renfrew, so he was going to struggle to get anywhere less expensive, and he wasn't due his broo money for another two days. He had about twenty-five notes in his pocket, but he'd earmarked that for essentials, and just then, that meant drink.

James Prentice was thirty-two, and an alcoholic.

The woman in the Moorpark offy refused to serve him. Said he was fucken drunk, cheeky bitch. He'd show her drunk, if that's what she wanted, if only he could get some sauce.

He stood for a while, just round the corner, out of sight, waiting for someone he knew to pass by, but it was all old women, and they were never willing to help out a cunt like him.

He was just about to move on when he spotted somebody walking down the other side of the road, in a baseball cap and a Lacoste jacket. He squinted to see if he recognised him; he couldn't put his hand on his heart and say he did, but there was something familiar about him. *Hey, nothin' ventured*. He crossed the road, as casually as possible, aiming to intercept the man. At first he thought that the cunt was going to cross over to the side he had just left, to avoid him, but he seemed to change his mind, and slowed down as James spoke to him.

"Ah need a favour, man, any chance?"

The man looked him up and down. James's ill-kempt appearance, thin face, heavy eyes and blank expression marked him out as an alky or a junkie, and he knew the guy was going to tell him to fuck off.

"Aye, OK, whit d'ye want? Only it'll huv tae be quick."

"Nae bother, man, ah just need ye tae buy me a couple o' boattles o' White Lightnin', man. The crabbit auld bitch in there willnae serve me. Says ah'm too drunk awready, stupit cunt."

"Aw right, man, calm the beans, ah'll get it fur ye. Gie's the money."

For a moment James had doubts about trusting the guy; he'd agreed almost too easily. But he didn't have any choice; it was the only way he was going to get a drink. He handed over a tenner and paced around nervously while he waited for the stranger to reappear. Two minutes later, the guy came out with a blue carrier bag containing his bottles of extra strength cider. His hands shook as he took the bag from the stranger, and he mumbled his thanks over and over again.

"Yer change is in the bag, man. Enjoy yer drink."

He was just about to slink away round the corner, when the guy said something.

"Whit?" he asked.

"Ah wis just saying, wid ye be interested in some cheap booze?"

"Ah might," James said hesitantly, not familiar with the concept of someone doing him a favour. "Where did ye get it?"

"Ah cannae tell ye man, or ah'd huv tae kill ye. It's a fucken secret." He laughed, and James joined in, liking his new pal instantly, in the way only very drunk people can.

'Aye, okay then,' he said.

"Well, come wi' me, man, an' ah'll get ye some, at quarter the price o' that stuff ye huv there."

James could hardly believe it, and through an alcoholic haze, he could see an answer to all his problems – retail! Buy some stuff at rock-bottom prices from this guy, then sell it for twice that amount to his drinking pals. *That wid pay the rent, and ma ain drink wid be a fraction o' the cost that it is at the noo. Sorted!* The big thing now was to persuade this guy to part with enough to make it worthwhile, and get enough cash together as soon as he could to pay his debts off, so he'd have somewhere to store it, without getting hassled from Dougie Houston for the rent.

The pair walked briskly, although James's movement was somewhere between a shuffle and a trot. They passed into Wright Street and the row of houses ended, to be replaced by factories on both sides.

"How faur is it?" James whined, not liking this fast pace and the unfamiliar surroundings.

"Not much further noo, wur nearly therr."

"Wherr d'ye keep it man? Therr's nae hooses roon here."

"Don't you worry, ma friend, ye'll see wherr wur goin' in a second. Now, watch that wire disnae spring back on ye." The guy had stopped and pulled back a corner of the wire mesh fence from one of the concrete posts. He held it open for James to squeeze through, then slipped through himself, into the factory grounds. Well hidden by the scrub at the end of the factory yard near to the river, they made their way through the bushes and along the bank towards the old loading dock, where there was a small, windowless, rendered brick building with a concrete roof, just at the edge of the vegetation.

The door was fastened with a rusty old padlock so the building was obviously unused, but surprisingly, his new friend had a key for it, and much to James's astonishment, it opened easily. The guy grinned.

"Ah cut the auld yin aff an' put ma ain yin oan. Took ages tae get it tae look rusty though, an' still work. The factory disnae use this onyway; ah think it wis fur when boats used tae come here tae offload, an' that."

He pointed to the concrete loading dock nearby, like a square bite out of the riverbank.

James went over to the edge, and saw only mud on the bottom.

"Thae fucken boats must o' had wheels oan them. Therr's nae watter."

"Ya silly bam, ye, the tide's oot. An' onyway, it's no been dredged for twenty years."

James didn't take offence. He was used to people thinking he was a fuckwit. If this guy set him up with some booze to sell, he could call him just what the fuck he wanted.

His new pal opened the door and beckoned him in, closing the door behind them before switching the light on.

"Habit," he said, "in case some cunt sees the light. I've been usin' this for two years now, an' nae cunt's bothered me yet. They even supply the fucken electricity!"

James was fidgeting. Should he take a drink of White Lightning or wait for the guy to produce the promised alcohol for him to try? *Just whit is the fucken etiquette here?*

"Ah'll put you oot o' yer misery, wee man. Here."

The guy reached into one of a stack of cardboard boxes, lifted out a bottle, flipped off the top with a bottle opener that suddenly appeared in his hand, and gave it to James.

James's first reaction was that it was a bit poncey and not the sort of drink he'd imagined would be on offer, but he supposed it was OK, as long as it was cheap enough. As he took his first drink, he worried that it would be more difficult to shift the stuff to hardcore drinkers like himself or his pals, but on the other hand, there was a whole market out there among the groups of twelve to fifteen-year-old kids who hung about the street corners of the estates every night, looking for anything sweet with alcohol in it. *Thae young lassies especially wid like this.*

He'd never drank alcopops before, and the blue colour did nothing for him, but was pleasantly surprised at the kick he got from it, having heard that you'd have been better drinking piss.

"Hey man, that's no' bad. A bit fancy for me, like, but ah could do some if the price wis right." He paused, then broached the subject that he thought might piss the guy off. "Is it OK wi' you if a punt some to ma mates, man?"

"Personally, ah don't huv a problem wi' that, but ah might huv tae talk tae a man furst. Ah don't want tae huv ye step on onyone's shoes."

"Nae bother, ah just thought I should ask." He fidgeted again. "See before we talk aboot price, can ah try anither yin, just tae make sure it's OK?"

The man held his hands up. "Ye don't huv tae ask, these are on me. Just help yersel. Just take them oot the open box."

"You no' huvvin' wan?"

"Ah've goat wan here, man," he said, holding it up for James to see. James hadn't noticed the guy opening a bottle for himself. He looked around the building. There were a couple of old armchairs in the shed, and a wooden crate that served as a makeshift table. The pile of boxes against a wall, unmarked, contained the guy's stash of booze. *A ferr bit therr*, he thought. *Wance ah get ma broo money, ah'll be able to buy a stack o' it*. The only problem he could foresee was getting the stuff moved, and keeping Dougie Houston off his back until it was all sold.

"Aw right tae sit doon?" he asked. His host nodded, and they both settled comfortably in the armchairs, despite a slight dampness to the fabric, and discussed money. James wondered if he should barter a bit, but the price was so low that he didn't think he needed to. Anyway, he was shite at it. *Mair than likely ah'd negotiate the price up the fucken wey*.

They shook hands on a deal for six boxes to start with, with more to follow.

"It suits me this way. Ah don't want tae shift them tae punters masel'. Mair wholesale, if ye like. Whit's yer name wee man?"

"Ah'm Jamesey. Jamesey Prentice. Whit aboot yersel?"

"Just call me Jacko. Aw ma friends do."

-o-

"D'ye notice the tide's in noo, ya daft wee fucker?"

James couldn't miss it. Through the tears that nearly blinded him he could see, eight feet below him, the dark waters of the White Cart River as they swirled around the concrete walls of the loading dock. Agonising pain shot through his hands and feet with every movement. He knew why, or rather, he knew what was causing the pain, but he didn't want to look again, *'cos it was fucken horrible, man.* There were three big nails hammered through each of his hands, all at different angles, holding him firmly on to some form of rough building board, and he knew his feet were nailed on in a similar fashion, because of the pain.

He'd woken up in the darkness with the worst hangover he'd ever had, to the nightmare he now found himself in. As he'd let out a moan, the light had snapped on, and a familiar voice spoke to him.

"Jamesey boy, how's it goin'? Been better, huv ye?"

The only sound that he made was a loud groan. He'd tried a few times to pull his hands free but the searing pain had been too much, and he'd stopped trying. The first time he'd looked, he'd almost vomited when he'd seen the nails sticking out of his own flesh; the dry, caked blood on the backs of his hands and a coagulated pool on the board told him that the nails had been there for some time. When he tried to twist round to where Jacko's voice was coming from, the pain in his feet matched that of his hands.

He nearly passed out, but managed to fight it, as Jacko's legs appeared in front of him across the pitted concrete floor, followed by the rest of him as he flopped down on the armchair in front of him.

James struggled briefly and violently, but the pain in his hands and feet became unbearable and so he lay still, sobbing quietly.

"Well, well, well, Jamesy. A wee bit too much tae drink, eh? Maybe teach ye a wee lesson or two? Maybe yer thinking ye'll sober up if ye get out o' this, or maybe yer just gaggin fur a swallae."

James watched him, silent, apart from a low whimpering sound that escaped from his lips involuntarily.

"Ah'd gie ye wan, but it's aw finished." He showed him the box, full of the empty Blue Wicked bottles. He then kicked over the pile of boxes stacked against the wall. Empty. Not a bottle in them. Every last one. James didn't quite comprehend. He couldn't have drunk all that booze.

"Ah know what yer thinkin', man, an' naw, ye only drank one box. Why's the ithers aw empty? Well, ya stupit cunt. Therr wis never any mair. When ye finished that box last night, ah thought ah'd huv tae gie ye wan o' mine, but ye passed oot just before ah needed tae crack it open."

James finally managed to speak, but it was difficult, with his chin held firmly to the board by his outstretched hands. He turned his head to the side, so that he could open his mouth.

"What the fuck huv ye done this tae me fir? It's fucken cruel, man."

"Yer spot on James, ma man, but life sometimes is. That's just the way it is in the world these days."

"But why?" he pleaded.

Jacko laughed. "They aw say that, don't they, Spencey?"

"Aye, Jacko, Ah think yer right."

James jerked his head to the other side, hearing the new voice, scraping his chin raw on the abrasive surface of the board as he did.

He saw another pair of feet, then the bottom half of the new person, clothed in orange, as they sat down in the closer of the two armchairs. He could just see a pair of hands, belonging to a man by the look of them, and he held one of those modern compact video cameras.

"Don't worry Jamesy, ah'm no' gonnae hurt ye, ah'm just here tae record the proceedins fir posterity. You'll manage on your own, Jacko, won't ye?"

"Ah'll try ma best, Spencey, ah'll try ma best. But ah could dae wi' a wee hand here, if that's aw right."

Jacko disappeared behind him. He'd heard the door opening, and suddenly the board he was pinned to was being lifted, tilting sideways, the nails in his hands and feet tearing at his flesh as he bumped over the threshold. He could see the second man's arms holding the board, his midriff inches from his face. *Fuck, the guy has a hard-on.* He could see it poking at the cloth of what he now realised was an orange boiler suit. Then he was out the door and into the darkness. The guy with the cock dropped his end of the board onto the ground, then Jacko did the same. Pain swept through his body, and he heard his new tormentor speak once more.

"Yer on yer ain now, Jacko, the grun's a bit saft ower therr, an' ah don't want tae get ma trainers caked in shite."

"Nae bother Spencey, man, ah'll manage fine fae here."

James had felt himself being dragged backwards again, and he caught a glimpse of the second man holding the camera, illuminated by the light of the full moon. A little red beacon flashed on and off as the camera recorded James's plight.

He could hear the river getting closer, and realisation dawned on him as to what these bastards intended for him.

Through the excruciating pain in his kidney area, and the agony every bump or snag caused in his hands and feet, he made one last desperate plea to his attackers.

"Man, let me aff this, ah'll never say a fucken word, man. But sees if yehs disnae, an' ye throw me in there, an' ah survive, ah'm gonnae make sure the polis get you two cunts." He couldn't help adding the threat, but he doubted if they cared.

He was right. As Jacko turned the board round, and slid him face forwards towards the edge of the dock, both men laughed. It was Jacko who spoke, when he got his voice under control.

"James, sonny boy, ah forgot tae tell ye. See that stuff ye were drinkin' last night? Well, it wis maistly antifreeze, an' yer gonnae die. It's only a matter o' whit kills ye first. The river or yer liver."

The men burst into laughter again, until Spencey corrected his accomplice.

"It's no' his liver, ya silly bastard, it's his kidneys."

"Naw, it's his liver an' aw. They'rr baith fucked. But kidney disnae rhyme wi' river."

More laughter. Then silence. James mumbled the Lord's Prayer, of all things.

"Anither cunt prayin'. We must be daein' mair fir religion than maist ministers dae."

Spencey laughed, on his own this time, as Jacko had started to slide the board over the concrete edge of the dock, grunting as he pushed. The board started to slope downwards as it got beyond the halfway mark. James screamed as it tilted, partly from fear of the cold black water he could see directly below, partly from the pressure the nails were putting on the bones and sinews of his hands and feet. The board teetered as Jacko took the strain on the large loop of rope that passed through two holes at the back of the board, knotted at Jacko's end.

He gave the board a little kick with his foot, and it jerked over the side, falling three or four feet until the ropes held on the concrete lip, Jacko straining to hold it. James screamed again, the pain ripping through his limbs, as his full weight hung on them. Only Jacko's use of three nails in each limb prevented his feet from tearing off the board.

"Watch ye don't end up in therr wi' the silly cunt." There was concern in Spencey's voice and he went to help Jacko, but by that time Jacko had let the rope slide over the edge until the front of the board touched, and then entered, the water. James screamed even louder as the water came up to meet him, but with his face only inches away from the surface, the front of the board started to float out into the swirling current and it tilted gradually back towards the horizontal. With it almost level, the corner snagged on an iron ring that jutted out from the wall, and broke off, leaving the board suspended briefly from one corner. It tilted dangerously, until the second corner gave way and it splashed into the water.

The board, with its human cargo, slowly eased itself out from the wall of the dock, towards the river.

"Sorry, Spencey, that wisnae meant tae happen. A wanted tae hold the cunt therr for a while just tae hear him greet."

"Yer fine. We can follow him doon the river. C'mon."

They scrambled past their part-time store, with no further use for it. As they got to the fence, Spencey turned to Jacko.

"The hut, we forgot tae lock it."

"Ah'll go back. You just wait here."

Jacko sprinted back and squeezed the padlock shut, then made again for the fence. When he was halfway there, he realised he'd forgotten to turn the light off, but he carried on jogging to where Spencey was waiting to let him through. He didn't tell him about the light. They wouldn't be back, and Spencey need never know.

They rushed back to the car, and made for the first point where they could observe their recently launched craft's progress, the Inchinnan Swing Bridge. They parked the car a hundred yards away and walked towards it. Spencey jumped the fence and took the narrow path down towards the riverbank, where he could see round the bend in the river. He also got a good view of the bridge, and he could just see Jacko walking across it, slowing down as he got near to the middle. He was surprised when Jacko suddenly speeded up, passed over the centre, and disappeared across the other side, but he understood the reason for it when a car drove over it a few seconds later; a man walking across a bridge at four o'clock in the morning is hardly worth a passing comment; somebody standing looking over the side at that time of night might make a driver stop, or phone the police. *Good thinkin', Jacko*.

Sure enough, when the car had gone, Jacko reappeared on the bridge, just as the object of their interest floated into view, barely visible even with the moonlight, further upriver. Spencey could hear his cries for help almost before he could see him clearly. He started filming, and followed him with the camera as he drifted slowly by. As he approached, Jacko started taunting him. There was no way Jamesy could get his head up far enough to see Jacko, but he started to curse him back, all the way under the bridge. Jacko crossed over to the other side and continued to rip the pish out of his victim for as long as he could hear wee Jamesey shouting.

-o-

"Bastard. Cunt. Bastard. Bastard. Fucker. Cunt." He didn't know if Jacko or his mate could hear him, but he couldn't help it. How the fuck did he get here, when yesterday afternoon his biggest worry was Dougie Houston, the fucking rent money, and where his next drink was coming from? Well, he could murder a drink now, and no chance of getting any.

When he'd first gone into the water, the pain in his feet from the nails had made him black out for a few seconds, but the chill of the water lapping on to the board revived him. He'd been constantly shivering, from the cold, the shock and the pain, and probably the kidney damage, too.

He could turn his head to one side or the other and see both banks as dark shadows. Seeing the vague shape of buildings on the right hand side, he started to shout for help. It was difficult to tell, because the board he was nailed to rotated gently in the river's flow, but he gradually realised they were probably just empty factories.

Then that bastard Jacko had turned up again somewhere above him, goading him; he must have been on a bridge. Cursing back at him helped briefly, but the pain and the terror returned, making him weep silently.

There was a little light in the sky as it prepared for sunrise, and James's eyes, adjusted to the darkness, could make out more detail on the banks. He could see boats with masts on the left hand side of the river. *A fucking yacht club oan the Cart. Who knew?*

He had a new problem now. He couldn't believe, with his hands and feet nailed painfully to a board, his insides throbbing and his chin and face red raw from turning his head back and forth, that the sudden itch he could feel spreading out from the middle of his back could in any way add to his torture, but it did. The urge to scratch was made all the worse by his inability to move his hands even an inch. He wondered briefly if the two cunts had put something on his back to make him itch, just to add to the torture they'd already inflicted.

The river widened suddenly and he felt the board rock and turn faster in the current. He vaguely remembered that two rivers joined here, and the one he was on was the Cart, but that was as far as his geographical knowledge went. Oh, and the Cart opened into the Clyde further on. He realised that when that happened, there was even less chance of being rescued, so when he saw bright lights on both sides of the river, he started shouting again. *Surely the fuck some cunt would hear him.*

Just as that thought gave him a glimmer of hope, he became aware of a deep roaring, rumbling sound, building rapidly. *A ship! Hope to fuck it sees me.* He screamed louder and shouted for help, but knew that he'd never be heard above the noise, which was now deafening.

Suddenly it passed, and he knew what the bright lights and the rumbling sound were. He'd passed the end of Glasgow Airport's main runway, and the first plane of the day had just taken off. A brief hope that the pilot might have seen him died in an almost immediate acceptance of the reality of his position. Almost invisible from the land or the air, unless someone was looking for him. *An' who the fuck wid bother lookin' fir me, onyway?* That thought hurt him almost as much as the physical pain he was in.

Mostly resigned now to dying, he thought of his childhood, which hadn't been a bad one; people and places he'd known; and his first drink at sixteen years old. *If I'd knawn it wid lead tae this, eh? Maybees I wid o' stayed aff it. Too fucken late, noo.* He'd left school with a couple of highers and got an apprenticeship with the council as an electrician.

At first he'd kept the drinking under control, mostly weekends, just the odd evening during the week on a special occasion, but the weekend gradually stretched back to Thursday and he was off sick on more than a few Mondays, after all-day sessions watching football in the pub.

They'd sacked him after he turned up drunk one morning too often, and his life had gone downhill steadily from there. A couple of menial jobs also fell by the wayside and in time he became a registered alcoholic, totally supported by the state, and slowly killing himself.

His mind returned to his current situation. He floated by a golf course. He could see the tops of a few of the flags. *Too early for fucking golfers, though.* When he lived in Thornliebank as a youth it was a game he'd played badly for a while, with a hand-me-down set of clubs, on his local municipal golf course, Deacon's Bank.

He knew he'd entered the River Clyde without needing to look. There was a change to the water, which was more than just the width or the depth. He felt smaller, less significant, and it had a more purposeful character. Because the outgoing tide was now in full flow, it was faster. As the Cart spewed him out into the middle of the Clyde, he could see the abandoned docks on the far bank. The massive Titan dock crane, a remnant of the Clyde's glorious shipbuilding days saved for posterity, and a landmark that he'd often seen from a distance, spun slowly into view, dwarfing him and the river.

As he floated steadily downstream his hands still hurt, badly, but his feet had gone almost completely numb with the cold. He'd pished himself at some point, which briefly warmed him, but it was soon washed away by the brackish river water that occasionally washed over the sides of the board.

Drifting in and out of consciousness and vomiting from time to time, as the urea levels in his blood peaked due to a loss of kidney function, he noticed less and less the further downriver he travelled. At one point he was convinced he heard Jacko's voice taunting him one final time, but he thought he may have dreamed it. The smell of the river changed as the tide receded and exposed the mudflats and sandbanks, and the marshland at Newshot Island. The calls of thousands of birds, perhaps disturbed by his progress along the foreshore, surrounded him as they wheeled in flocks above his head. The sun, climbing across the sky, was beginning to warm up his back, but the front half of his body, in contact with the wet board, was still chilled.

How much time had passed he didn't know, but he was sure that he heard the sound of cars and lorries passing far overhead and, even in his numbed state, he realised he was passing under the Erskine Bridge, a hundred and fifty feet above. He wondered briefly why none of the people driving overhead noticed him.

The sun warming him up was a mixed blessing. As warmth came slowly back to his hands and feet, sensation returned with it. The torn and damaged tissue had now become inflamed and the first bacterial infection was just starting. He'd almost forgotten how bad the pain had been before, but it now returned, worse than ever. Dehydrated by the sun, the lack of water, and his failing kidneys, the tears he now shed were dry ones, and he knew that he just wanted it to end.

He hadn't noticed the wind getting up, but when he felt the warmth on his back fade and bigger waves beginning to break on to the board, he realised that it was strengthening and within fifteen minutes it had gone from a moderate breeze to a strong blow, the water calm to choppy. The board was now tilting alarmingly back and forth, each movement tearing at the wounds on his hands and feet. On a couple of occasions, he took cramps in his calf muscles, only adding to the agony he was in already.

Ready to die, and willing to try and make that happen, he tried rocking his little raft, but after several futile attempts, soon became exhausted. He lay panting on the board and allowed himself to rage against the world, himself, God and his torturers.

Gathering his final strength, he made one last effort. When the next large wave came he was almost completely side on to it, and he got his timing just perfect. He felt the edge of the board rise up on the wave and he threw his weight, as much as possible, away from it. The board became vertical, held for a second, then the whole thing flipped over and came down on top of him. His head fell away backwards from the board and the shock of the cold made him involuntarily hold his breath for a brief moment, his body still fighting to survive, but feeling the pain in his hands and feet, and the utter desolation of his situation, he took his last conscious decision and opened his mouth. Drawing in a lungful of cold, salty water, he felt a searing, burning pain in his throat and chest, and an acute terror at the sudden inability to breathe air, which lasted only seconds before he lost consciousness, and his life shortly afterwards.

-o-

James's body, suspended under the board, drifted on westwards, the River Clyde insensitive to the passing of a human life. Slowed down by the wind and the waves, but carried downstream by the flow of the river and the outgoing tide, the board and its cargo passed Bowling, the entrance point to the Forth and Clyde canal, a watery shortcut still used for boats to the east coast. Slowing as the tide started to turn, it reached Dumbarton Rock, a fortified volcanic plug guarding the mouth of the Leven, a short river disgorging the flow of water from Loch Lomond, four miles to the north.

Because of the tide and the wind the body took much longer to travel the few short miles along the river towards Greenock, until a wind shift to the south caused the board to leave the main shipping lane and follow the shallow channel running north west between Pillar Bank and Cockle Bank, well out of the way of being seen. Greenock was now nearly a mile off, on the south bank, and when the tide receded again James, hidden underneath his board, was left high and dry for a while on a small sandbank that almost blocked the channel at its seaward end.

A few hours later the incoming tide lifted the board again and pushed it back upriver for a while, but before long it was heading back out to the deep water beyond the sandbanks and shallows of the upper Clyde, driven westwards by tide, wind, and waves.

It briefly flirted with the mouth of the Gareloch, the base for Britain's nuclear submarine fleet, before a bit of north in the wind took it south and west to just off the Cloch lighthouse, where the board was spotted by a passing cargo ship which reported it to the coastguard as a danger to shipping. The changeable wind and small tidal currents pushed it around for a spell before it eventually entered the Holy Loch, coming to rest on the sandy shore, halfway between the Western Ferry pier at Hunter's Quay, and Whitefarland Point.

Only one person other than the murderers had seen the raft during its journey down what was still a moderately busy waterway.

CHAPTER 7 Vindication

"Eddie, it's Catherine Douglas here."

"Catherine, I know why you're phoning; I've just seen it on the news."

"Oh, you've heard about it then? I didn't realise it had been released to the press."

"Surely they must believe us now. We told them the next one could be someone dumped in a river, nailed to a board. I will go to the papers if the bastard doesn't listen."

"That's what I've got to see you about. Don't do anything rash. Can we meet up?"

"Yes, of course, where do you want to meet?"

They arranged to meet at the same restaurant as before, after work.

-o-

She slid a leaf of paper across the table to him. "I was told that I could let you see this."

Eddie picked it up and looked at it.

"Bloody hell! Toxicology. Positive for ethylene glycol. High levels."

"That's not all." She passed the next sheet over to him. "They've gone back and tested Craig Ferguson's tissues. He's positive as well."

Eddie was stunned and relieved. He felt like giving her a

big hug and a kiss, but realised that might be inappropriate. Instead, he thumped his fist into his hand and let out a loud "Yes!"

A few of the other diners looked round and he shrugged an apology. He waved to the waiter and ordered a bottle of wine, asking Catherine if white was OK for her.

"I've got my car, but why not? I'll get a taxi and collect it in the morning."

The news was beginning to hit home for Eddie.

"Fuck. This is dynamite. What's Anderson saying?"

"He's not saying too much. I think he's just trying to do some damage limitation. He wants to meet with you."

"I'm not surprised. If I went to the papers with this, he would be hung out to dry. I'm still astonished that he would give you those to show me; he must know that they give me more ammunition."

"I think that he's trying to appeal to your better nature; I suspect he hopes that you'll think of what's good for the investigation and sort the rest out afterwards."

"I'm not sure. He doesn't deserve a break. Why should I give a toss about what happens to him?"

"Well, think about it this way. If you don't drop him in it, you are in a great position to insist on being closely involved. If he goes, you're nothing to the new guy. And he's better than some. You've just seen the worst of him."

He thought about it for a while, and he could see that she made sense.

"There's more," she said, handing him another page. "Histopathology on Craig shows kidney damage consistent with antifreeze poisoning, but no deposits of oxalates. Might that have been because of the dialysis?"

He nodded.

They ordered food and chatted about the case, and she explained the events of the afternoon at the station.

"By four o'clock I was ready to go home, as I'd had a stinker of a day, when I got a call to go and see the DI. I honestly thought that I was finally getting shunted back to uniform, but Anderson couldn't have been nicer. He said that there had been another death and that it was similar to one of the cat killings, like you'd warned, and that toxicology was being urgently done on both cases. He apologised to me and said that you might be right."

She didn't tell him that Anderson's exact words were "… and your boyfriend was right," or that she'd blushed furiously and told him that there was nothing between her and Eddie, that they had just been working closely together, or that Anderson had then raised an eyebrow, looked at her, and carried on telling her about the case. The toxicology came back in just before five.

"I'm now back on this inquiry, with a remit to handle all the animal associated material within the larger murder investigation."

"That's great, you'll get all the resources you need. Now we can get this guy."

She noticed he'd said "we", and she told him the rest.

"They would also like you to be involved, as a veterinary consultant, and they are willing to set aside some funds for you. That means we can carry on working together on this."

She seemed to be inordinately pleased with this, and Eddie

found himself to be happier about it than seemed appropriate.

"So he's not such a dick after all, then?"

"Eddie! Behave. No, I think Anderson's all right. I suppose you have to see it from his point of view. Some smart-arsed vet comes in and tells him how to do his investigation, then threatens to go to the press if he doesn't agree. Can you blame him for being a bit hard on you?"

Eddie laughed. "Point taken, but it's no excuse. What does he want us to do that we aren't already doing?"

"First of all, he wants to have a meeting with you. He seems to think that you both got off to a bad start."

Eddie suddenly sat bolt upright. "Christ, I've just remembered. We have a possible DNA sample from the suspect in one of the cat cases, on the cat's claws. Mike and I joked about asking the police if they could use it to search their database for our suspect, but now that there are human victims, they would probably jump at it."

He was all for getting Catherine to phone the DI while he went and got the cat out of the freezer, but she managed to get him to see the sense in waiting until the next day.

"Anyway, it will give you something concrete to discuss when we have that meeting with him. I'll try and schedule it for tomorrow sometime. When would suit you best?"

He told her that mid-afternoon onwards would be the easiest for him, and had a quick run over the things that were likely to come up and how they might deal with them.

Business finished, Catherine steered the conversation away from the investigation, asking him about his work and how he'd got into investigating animal cruelty cases.

Once she got Eddie talking, it was easy for her to keep him going by asking the odd question when he ran out of words. On her part, she told him about some of the difficulties she had experienced in trying to break into what was still essentially a man's world. It had been especially difficult since her long-term relationship had broken up. As a reasonably attractive single woman, in her own words, it seemed fair game for every red-blooded male in the force, married or not, to make a move on her. When she didn't respond in the accepted manner she was described as frigid, and often found herself marginalised. She had considered faking a girlfriend to put herself in the gay camp, as while the few women she knew who were in same-sex relationships still got a bit of abuse, they didn't get nearly as much sexual harassment.

By the time the meal was over they had spent more than an hour talking about things other than work. As they left the restaurant, Eddie considered asking her up for a cup of coffee, but her tales of sexual harassment at work made him think twice. Again, there was an awkward moment when they split up to go home but, in keeping with the celebratory tone of the evening, she gave him a hug and a peck on the cheek before hailing a taxi and promising to phone him in the morning.

Eddie didn't feel like sleeping when he got up to the flat, so he took out all the case related stuff and put it all in order, making notes for the next day's meeting as he went along. He also decided that he would go in early the next morning and remove one of the claws from the frozen cat, to take to the police for DNA analysis of the material caught under it.

After he'd finished sorting everything, he was still wide awake. He fired up his laptop and started trawling through some of the cases on his spreadsheet that they hadn't already looked at. He concentrated on cases in the south side of Glasgow and Dundee, during the periods when the ones they'd already investigated had occurred. In the Glasgow area, he went back as far as the case of the bricked up cats. He went through the poisonings first, as it seemed to him that he could easily eliminate most of them, before moving on to the mutilated animals, which might throw up more questionable cases, flagging anything that he thought would fit in with those that they'd already found.

By the time he had gone through the poisoning cases, only one stood out as being different. Most of them seemed accidental, or were deliberate poisonings by cat haters who simply wanted to get rid of cats. The one that caught Eddie's eye was the report of a cat that had died of confirmed ethylene glycol poisoning, but it was found in an empty aquarium that had had its top sealed on tightly with black gaffer tape. From the report, the inside was a horrific mess of faeces, vomit, saliva, blood and urine, and the investigating SSPCA officer had estimated that the cat had been in the tank for at least a couple of days. The officer had done a very thorough report, but Eddie thought that it would be worthwhile phoning her the next day to see if she could flesh it out any more, so he added it to his morning's "to do" list.

-o-

The next morning Catherine phoned Eddie, catching him just as he'd finished putting one of the cat's claws in a little Ziploc bag and had popped the cat back in the freezer, to tell him that David Anderson had scheduled the meeting for 2.45 that afternoon. Eddie said he'd be there, then told her he'd found another case which he was following up, and gave her brief details.

He also phoned Mike at the SSPCA, who offered his full support to Eddie and the police. He mentioned the DNA to Mike, who laughed and said he would have bet any money against that ever happening.

He finally spoke with Campbell Armstrong about the latest developments with the police; Campbell said that he would square things up with the other partners to allow Eddie a bit of flexibility for his involvement with the investigation. He was absolutely fascinated by the whole affair, and asked Eddie to keep him posted on a daily basis. Eddie agreed, and realised that by keeping everyone informed, Campbell would also keep the rest of the practice on side.

"At least Chris will be happy that you are going to be paid for it. Just make sure that you negotiate a rate with the police that's acceptable to him."

Eddie smiled. "I'll try," he said. "Incidentally, I'm not sure how much detail I'll be able to give you on the murder cases. No doubt there will be restrictions, which I'll probably be told about today."

Eddie tried to cram as much work as possible into the morning, to allay any fears that the other vets might have about him pulling his weight. Just when he thought he was getting to the stage when he could run through the last few consults rapidly and be in plenty time to gather his thoughts before the afternoon meeting, a Mrs. Millar came in trailing George, a reluctant young springer spaniel, behind her.

Eddie could see from the note attached to the consult details on the computer screen that Gavin, one of the other vets, had been treating George.

"I usually see Mr Usher. He always deals with my dogs."

Great, thought Eddie, *a fussy client, multiple pets*.

"Hello, George," he said, talking to the dog first. He then turned to his owner, who had a fixed, stern expression on her face.

"Mrs. Millar, nice to meet you," he said, trying hard to keep his voice upbeat and friendly in the face of her hostility. "Mr Usher asked me to review George's records, just in case there was something going on with him that had been missed. Call it a second opinion, if you like. Did he not explain that to you?"

"Not really, but I suppose you may as well have a look at him."

With that grudging go-ahead ringing in his ears, Eddie told her that he was just going to read George's clinical history and then he would examine him. As he read, he could feel her quiet disapproval behind him, but he soon became engrossed in what was, for him, a refreshingly intriguing case. George had been having what his owner termed "wee turns". Every so often he would just collapse, and his body would jerk a bit. It seemed to be worse after exercise, and Gavin had noted down his possible diagnoses (or differential diagnoses, in medical parlance). The most obvious was epilepsy, with petit mal, or mild fits, rather than the full blown convulsions normally associated with the condition. It could also have been syncope, short "time-outs" where the heart misses a few beats due to a momentary aberration in the neurological control of the heart. Because he was a springer spaniel, exercise induced hypoglycaemia, or low blood sugar, could have been the problem, although this was less common; and indeed, when George had been blood tested, his glucose levels were at the low end of normal. When Gavin told Mrs Millar to feed him with carbohydrates before exercise, it had helped for a short while. The ECG, which measures the electrical function of the heart, was normal, ruling out an inflammatory disease of the heart called viral myocarditis.

Eddie then quizzed a by now fuming Mrs Millar about how exactly the dog acted when it took these turns. She told him tersely that she'd already explained his symptoms to Mr Usher; that the dog often took a few wobbly steps, then collapsed, sometimes jerking like a dog does when they're dreaming, and finally, coming round quickly and making a full recovery within minutes. For Eddie, none of this ruled out any of his likely candidates, and the blood tests that had been done so far didn't help eliminate anything.

"I'm going to admit George and induce another episode by withholding food, so that we can take a blood sample while his glucose is low, to check on his blood insulin. If that comes back as normal, we may have to refer George for an MRI scan. Is he insured?"

"Of course he's insured, the practice has filled out a claim form already."

Eddie should have spotted that George's record showed he was insured, but she'd only needed to answer yes or no to a simple bloody question. He asked a nurse to take George through, which further annoyed the old bag of an owner, and told her that they would phone her when he was ready for collection. Eddie warned her that the results wouldn't be back until later the next day and that someone from the practice would phone her.

He smiled when he heard her tell the receptionist on the way out that the vet they'd fobbed her off with this time wasn't a patch on Mr Usher, who normally made a point of seeing her personally.

Because of Mrs bloody Millar, and the much nicer George, he only just got finished in time, and that had meant having only a ten minute coffee break about eleven-ish and working through lunch.

It was during that break that he managed to talk to Barbara, the Glasgow-based SSPCA officer who had investigated the fish tank case.

She told him that the tank had been found in an empty industrial unit. An estate agent, surveying the property to put it on their commercial listings, discovered the gruesome object and had contacted the SSPCA to ask if they would deal with it, quickly.

She said that the state that the cat had been in was horrendous, and it had been hardly recognisable. Soaked in a mixture of its own bodily secretions, it had looked like a wet rag. All its nails had been worn down to the bone while it tried to claw its way out, and there was evidence of further trauma on its head where it had battered itself against the inside of the tank. The once clear glass sides and top of the aquarium were mostly opaque due the film of filth that coated its inner surface, and the bottom was nearly half an inch deep in slurry.

She also said that she had found it odd that the tank, and the metal stand it stood on, still had its tags and labels attached, and on the outside it looked brand new, except where there had been a little leakage of content from inside, mainly through the air holes in the top. Barbara was convinced that the perpetrator had deliberately used a clear tank so that he, or she, could observe the cat as it died, and Eddie agreed, having already come to the same conclusion himself.

She had taken photographs, including shots of the tags and labels, which she promised to send to him by email.

-o-

Eddie had the chance to talk to Catherine for about ten minutes before the meeting. He had brought along a couple of boxes containing the case files they'd amassed, but he'd kept copies of everything, so that he could also pass them on to the SSPCA. Catherine showed Eddie into the incident room and directed him to put the boxes down on the bench.

"Here," she said, handing him a form, "fill this in. It's for a civilian pass for the station. You'll be able to get in and out without one of us coming down to meet you every time, but your access will still be restricted."

He showed her his temporary SSPCA inspector's laminated ID badge. "Very fetching," she said as he blushed at her scrutiny of it; she took a photocopy of it for the files and handed it back. "We'll need another photo for your civilian pass, by the way."

He said he'd send her a copy, then filled her in on the details of the latest case he had discovered; they discussed the possibility that there could be others once he got a chance to go through the list of the animals with just mutilations.

When they entered David Anderson's office, he rose from his chair to greet them and had the grace to immediately apologise to Eddie.

"Eddie, I'm glad you could come. I know we got off on the wrong foot the last time, and that was my fault, but I'm hoping that we can put that behind us."

"Of course. I may have been a bit abrasive, but in my defence I was ninety-nine per cent certain that it was the same guy. I agree that the most important thing is to catch him before he kills again, whether the victim be human or animal."

The DI then proceeded to give them a brief update on the most recent case. A man's body, nailed to a large insulation board, had washed up on the shores of the Holy Loch, in the Clyde estuary, two days before. The "raft" was floating with the body suspended underneath, or it might have been noticed sooner. The local Dunoon CID officer was on leave, so officers from Greenock CID had initially attended the shout, crossing over to Dunoon on the ferry. They'd seen the broken corners at what looked like rope holes on the board and had assumed it had been a local gangland punishment killing that involved the victim being towed behind a fast boat until he drowned, and then abandoned as a message to others not to cross them. Because of this, it had taken another twenty-four hours for the news of the killing to reach the murder enquiry team in Paisley.

The post-mortem showed that the man had drowned, making him still alive when he entered the water. When the call came in, the DI knew right away that he'd been wrong, and the toxicology that he'd requested confirmed it immediately. He'd also asked for ethylene glycol levels to be done on the first murder victim.

He told them that he'd read the report that Eddie had left and was now convinced that all the cases, man and animal, were connected.

"That's where you come in. I'm hoping that Catherine can handle the non-human side of things, aided by you and the SSPCA, who have offered their assistance as well. It will allow the rest of the team to concentrate on the murder investigation. We're still keeping an open mind on the gangland angle, but we think that your information means that it's less likely. However, some of our team are still looking, just in case. What we need is for you to keep investigating your end of the case, but it is imperative that any information you find that could be useful to us is passed on immediately."

"I understand, and I'm happy to help." A slightly apologetic look reached Eddie's face. "My partners at the practice would need to know how much time this is going to take and, being pragmatic, how the remuneration will work."

"Those are fair questions. It's difficult to say exactly how

much we'll need you. DC Douglas will be working on ?
full time and will be able to call on further resources at my
discretion, so we should only need your input on
occasional veterinary matters, but I'm willing to be a bit
flexible and give the pair of you a little latitude, if you feel
you can add something to the investigation. As for being
paid, Strathclyde Police has a prescribed rate of pay agreed
with each of the professions for when their members are
acting as consultants, and that includes veterinary
surgeons. There is also a sliding scale in line with the
degree of expertise of the consultant. If you fill in one of
our external expenses sheets at the end of the month, and
give us your practice's bank details, you should get paid
within the following calendar month." He looked over the
top of his glasses at Eddie. "Have you any further
questions?"

Eddie thought for a moment, but shook his head.

"Right then," the DI said, "let's get started. What have you
got so far?"

"Well, other than the information we gave you the other
day, we've got a couple of new leads and some other areas
worth looking at that we feel could be productive. Can I
bring in DC Douglas on this, as she's worked on it with
me, and there are some aspects of the cases she knows
better than I do?"

Catherine and Eddie proceeded to fill DI Anderson in on
all their findings. They gave him the printout of all the
cases they'd investigated, showed him the work Eddie had
done on the computer, discussed how the cases were
linked, and pointed out all the information about the
perpetrator that could be taken from their research so far.
DI Anderson took short notes about all of it, and asked a
few questions where relevant.

When they got to the end, Eddie told him about the cat's

w, explained its significance, and the DI immediately lifted the telephone and ordered a motorcyclist to deliver it to the forensic laboratory as fast as he could.

Eddie asked if it would be possible to see detailed reports from the two murder investigations, in case there was anything in them that would lend more significance to their own enquiries. The DI had no problem with that, provided he didn't get in the way, nothing was removed from the incident room and full confidentiality was maintained at all times, to which Eddie agreed.

The DI was just about to conclude the meeting when Eddie told him about the latest case that they'd discovered. He asked if it would be possible for DC Douglas to search through the archives for any human cases that might mimic some of the animal ones.

The DI agreed to that, with similar provisos as before. He looked at the list they'd given him and shuddered. "Let's hope there are no more killings, but I have a horrible feeling that he's not going to stop. I know that for you, Eddie, it's as much about the animal cases as the human ones, but for us, the big priority is to prevent another murder." With that, he got up, shook Eddie's hand, and left the room.

-o-

Catherine had been allocated her own office, the smallest in the building, although all the files and photos the case had generated were in the main incident room to allow the other officers access to them, if they felt the need. As well as reporting on a daily basis to the DI, she was also expected to be present at the daily case conference and to produce a printed summary sheet showing any new developments on their side of the investigation, which was pinned up on the rear wall of the incident room.

Immediately after the meeting with the DI they sat down and produced the first two sheets summarising their investigation so far, printed them out and posted them up for the rest of the squad to read.

They then sat down to update the schedule they had made detailing the tasks that needed to be completed over the next few days. David Anderson had told them that there was a liaison officer within the Dundee CID working with the murder inquiry as a whole, and that within reason they could use him if they needed any resources on Tayside, so Catherine drew up a letter requesting information on construction projects during the period of the Dundee cases, any reports of stolen nail guns, a canvass of outlets that sold antifreeze, and a scan of their recent caseload for any deaths involving antifreeze.

"I'll get on to the PNC to check for murders similar to our cases." She jotted this down on the list as she spoke.

Eddie must have looked at her blankly.

"The PNC is the Police National Computer, which is the UK police database." She went on to explain, "It has four files on it: names, vehicles, property and drivers. I'll also look through the reports from both the murder investigations. Do you want to have a look at them, too?"

"No, probably not, there's no point in both of us doing that. I'll get on with looking at the rest of the animal cases on our list, and try and chase up on the antifreeze in the Glasgow area."

"Would it be worthwhile if I did a brief summary of each report? There'll be the post-mortem and the scene of crime reports, any interviews that they've done, and the results of the forensic analysis."

"That would be good." He checked his watch. "I suppose I should get going now, and let you get on. I can do what I need to do at home."

"Oh, all right then. Will you give me a phone if you find anything?"

"Aye, I will do, and likewise, get in touch if you come up with something. Do you want to meet up tomorrow, to keep everything moving, or would it be easier just to phone?"

"Well, it will depend on what's happening with the investigation; I'll let you know in the morning after the squad meeting."

Eddie picked up his laptop bag and left, but as he went down the station steps he was cursing himself for not finding a pretext to stay and work with Catherine, or having the balls to ask her out for something to eat again. After all, he had the perfect excuse to invite her for a celebratory drink, at least, having achieved their objective in persuading the police to take them seriously.

Grow a pair, you stupid twat, he thought, but it was too late. Even his offhand manner at suggesting that they should just keep in touch by phone made him cringe. *She must think that I'm a right arse; just using her to get the police involved.* He knew that he couldn't phone her and ask her to meet him; it would definitely look like he was asking her out on some kind of a date, and he knew that if he did that, it would risk spoiling the good working relationship they had.

As it turned out, they didn't have any need to meet up for the next three days. Nothing much happened on the investigation apart from a lot of leg work by the inquiry team, Catherine working her way through the PNC "names" file and Eddie finally getting to the end of the "mutilations" list. Frustratingly, nothing else jumped out at him, although there were a couple of cases that were mild possibilities; he added them to their action list with red question marks next to them. He wasn't having much success on the antifreeze front, either. Retailers just weren't interested in volunteering their sales figures to some random guy, even with his SSPCA credentials. He made a mental note to ask if Catherine or one of her "resources" could do it, as their requests might have a bit more weight behind them.

Eddie was more than happy to have little or no involvement in the investigation during this time, as there was no let-up in the practice workload and all the vets worked longer hours than usual just to get through it all.

He watched out for George Millar's results coming in, and was not surprised to find that his insulin levels were at the high end of normal. He phoned Mrs Millar, and told her that she would need to bring George in for an ultrasound scan, and possibly an X-ray, but that he was highly suspicious that he had an insulin-producing tumour of the pancreas called an insuloma.

Mrs Millar was distraught, and Eddie felt sorry for her because he knew that despite an early diagnosis, the outlook for George, even with surgery, was very guarded.

Eddie couldn't afford to dwell on their misfortune, but it was the sort of case he liked to be involved with, to offset the seventy-five per cent of the work he did that didn't tax his brain and sometimes numbed him with its tedium.

-o-

He spoke to Catherine every day on the phone, but with no real developments to speak of the calls were short, until she phoned him late on the Friday afternoon with some interesting news.

"The DI isn't all that excited about this but I've got a death here which could be worth looking at. Can you come over to the station?"

"I've got a surgery to finish up here; I'll be about an hour at the most. It's mainly expressing anal glands, and vaccinations, with the odd interesting case thrown in if I'm lucky!"

"That's OK, I've got plenty to do. Just ask for me when you get here, and I'll come down and get you. Your visitor's pass is here, ready, but I have to get you to sign for it. After today, you can come and go a little bit easier."

When she came down the stairs to collect him from the reception area, he realised how much he'd been looking forward to seeing her again. They didn't chat much as they climbed the stairs, but Eddie told her he was very intrigued about her news.

"It's just a possibility," she said, as they entered her tiny office and she handed him a folder containing a sheaf of papers. "I'll go and get us a coffee while you're reading it."

When she returned with two indifferent cups of coffee, she found him halfway through skimming the contents of the folder. He had a handy ability to speed read and extract the essentials from a document or book quickly, and go back later to read and digest the details. She handed him the coffee and sat down. He was concentrating and didn't notice her watching him. She thought that he wasn't bad looking, and improved a hell of a lot when he smiled or laughed. It was just that he was such a serious person in general, and didn't do it often enough; in fact, many people would have said he looked a bit dour. She knew that on a personal level he was very shy, in direct contrast to his confidence when working in a professional capacity. But she liked him. He didn't try to impress. What you got with Eddie was brutal honesty, and she enjoyed working with him because of that. In her world, where there were so many agendas and egos, it was quite refreshing.

When he was finished, Eddie looked up and nodded. "Steven Reilly is our cat in the aquarium, isn't he?"

"Well, that's what I thought. The victim died from ethylene glycol poisoning, and he was in a glass cubicle, but according to this, he wasn't forced to be in there. He also had heroin and alcohol in his system at the time of death. The Procurator Fiscal ruled that the death was due to the accidental ingestion of antifreeze."

Eddie had another quick glance through the scene of crime report.

"There's no report of an antifreeze container at the scene, so he's either deliberately stored or mixed it in another container, or someone else gave it to him."

"The DI doesn't think this is linked, but he's happy for us to re-examine the case."

"You'd have thought he would be less sceptical by now, wouldn't you?"

"Yes, but anyway, do you want to take a look at it with me?"

"You mean the crime scene? Is that allowed? "

"Yes; are you OK with that? There's no reason that we can't go up there tomorrow. Can you get some time off?"

"Yes, but it'll have to be in the afternoon. There are only two of us on tomorrow as it's a Saturday. We finish at one. What about sometime after that?"

They agreed that she would pick him up at the practice at one-thirty, and drop him back afterwards. Eddie said that he'd take a camera and asked her if they'd need anything else, but she said that the crime scene had been cleared and disinfected, so it was unlikely that they would find any useful forensics.

It was now well after seven and he hadn't eaten. It seemed reasonable to ask her if she fancied something to eat, but when he did, she said she had already agreed to meet a friend for a curry.

"No bother," Eddie said, disappointed. Then he remembered the problems he was having with the antifreeze retailers. "By the way, I'm struggling to get the antifreeze information from the garages and auto shops. They're just taking the piss. I've got no leverage with them. Can you or one of the team do it?"

"I can do that, but I might get some help. A couple of uniforms paying them a visit might persuade them to comply. What exactly do we want from them?"

"Can you request detailed monthly sales figures for as far back as they can go, and ask if they can remember any strange sales that stuck in their memory? You know, people that they wouldn't normally expect to buy antifreeze, for instance."

She said she'd get on to it in the next few days. It left Eddie with nothing to do, apart from accompanying her on her visit to the abandoned petrol garage where Steven Reilly had died, but when he got home, he was itching to do something constructive. He looked at the list of actions that they still had to complete and although, frustratingly, most of them needed to be done by the police, there were a couple of things he could do, and a few loose ends to tie up.

He thought it would be worthwhile asking some of his veterinary and personal contacts on the south side if there were any whispers flying around about the cats being tortured and killed, and he could do that over the weekend.

He phoned a few of his clients who were particularly obsessed with animals, and also a couple of welfare group contacts in the area, but the Cat Protection coordinator was away on holiday, and both the Cat Action Group and the local Dog Trust people had heard nothing.

He gave his pal Brian a phone, thinking that he would know more about the seedier side of the Paisley area.

"Whassup, Eddie?" Brian asked, when he answered Eddie's call.

"Oh, not much. Anyway, can't I just phone you for a catch up?"

"Naw, ye maist often phone tae burst ma baws aboot sumfin', or try and get me on some trainin' or other." He laughed.

"It's not that bad. I was just wondering how it was going. Anyway, I don't always give you a hard time; I'm just trying to help."

"Calm doon, Eddie, ah'm only ripping the pish, even though ye dae hand out mair than the odd sermon."

"Listen, to change the subject, you know that animal cruelty case I'm working on?"

"Aye, ye mentioned it. Huv ye got the sick bastard?"

"No; in fact, it's now a murder inquiry. We think he's moved on to killing people."

"Fuck man. Is that the wan that wis oan the telly? Are ye still involved?"

"Aye. I've been working with this woman detective on the cat cases for a while, until we discovered two murders that were almost identical to the way the cats were killed, so now both of us are part of the whole investigation."

"Fuck me. Ah cannae believe it, man. It's like fucken *Taggart*."

As he realised that Eddie was involved with the police, Brian saw the dangers, but also an upside.

"Ho, I'm no sure that ah can keep in contact wi' ye, now yer in wi' the rozzers, man. But on the ither hawn, ye might be able tae get me aff if ah get arrested by the cunts."

Eddie shook his head sadly, but with a smile to himself.

"Brian, fuck off. It won't make a bit of difference, and anyway, you're *not* getting arrested again, that's final, or I AM going to wash my hands of you."

"Aw right. Aw right. Ah'll try ma best. This new job's goin' OK, but the manager's a bit o' a prick. Gets right oan ma tits."

"Well, just keep your head down and don't let him get to you. You're not stupid, and if you stay in a job long enough, you never know what might happen. Go for any training courses they offer you. I'll give you a hand if there's any written work involved."

Brian always found a way of changing the subject when Eddie tried to better him, and this time was no exception.

"Hey, whit's this detective burd like, then? Auld boot, is she, or a wee stunner?"

"For fuck's sake Brian, I'm working on a murder case with her, what does her appearance have to do with anything?"

"Ah wis just wonderin', ye knaw, not that ah ever want tae

see her or nuthin'. Ah get nervous around thae cunts."

"Right, so back to these murders and the cat killings. You haven't heard anything, have you?"

"D'ye think ah'm yer snitch, is that it? Ye should knaw ah'm no' a grass."

Eddie knew Brian was just trying to wind him up.

"Brian, don't take the piss. For a start, I've not actually joined the police, I'm just acting as a consultant, and anyway, I wouldn't mention your name, I just wanted to find out if there was any talk doing the rounds about who might be responsible."

"Aw right, ah wis just jestin', but ah huvnae heard nuthin'. If folk did knaw anything, ah think they would tip the rozzers off, cos nae cunt likes this sort of thing, even yer mad violent bastards. Anyhow, it's all jakeys he's killin', isn't it, and nae drug dealer will want any o' his customers bumped aff."

With that pearl of wisdom ringing in his ear, Eddie asked Brian to keep his ears open for anything that might help, and ended the call.

-o-

The practice still did a significant amount of farm work, and even though there were three dedicated large animal vets in the practice, all the partners had to take a turn to be on call for farm emergencies at nights and over the weekends. As there were five partners, and two young large animal assistants, it was a one in seven rota, which meant that he had to cover less than one night per week and every seventh weekend. The small animal out-of-hours work was covered by one of the emergency clinics in the centre of Glasgow. Eddie, although he had chosen to concentrate on the small animal side, perversely enjoyed keeping his hand in with cattle and the odd sheep, and the coming weekend was his turn to be on call. The only thing that made being on duty onerous was the thought that he might have to attend to a sick or injured horse. They were his least favourite patients, and he wasn't keen on most of the owners, either, but, like the majority of the other vets in the practice, he just had to get on with it.

Apart from having to pack the on call kit box into his car and remembering to always carry his mobile, being on call wouldn't interfere much if he wanted to do some leg work on the investigation.

Feeling better for having sorted out his weekend's activities, he decided to work on something that had been niggling him for a while. He wanted to check that the Tayport cat had originated from Dundee, so he went online and looked up tide and weather records for the period prior to the animal being found.

From that, he confirmed that despite the tide coming in and going out twice a day, the ebb, or falling, tide was slightly stronger than the incoming, or flood, tide because of the flow of the river Tay. The prevailing wind in the three days before the cat washed up on the beach had been north-westerly, so the chances were reasonable that the board to which the cat was nailed was launched into the river somewhere along the Dundee foreshore, where the other cats had also been killed.

CHAPTER 8 Investigation

They found the disused petrol station easily. The industrial estate it was sited on was being redeveloped as "The Haven", a massive new housing development of "superior three to five bedroom villas and semi-detached homes in the countryside", so the factories and warehouses that had once surrounded it had all been demolished and the groundwork had started for the curving streets and cul-de-sacs that were the planner's vision of modern residential utopia.

The petrol garage was earmarked for resurrection now that a market for the fuel it once supplied had suddenly and miraculously re-appeared, and the oil company who had owned it fruitlessly for twenty years now had a prime location for a modern filling station without needing any planning consent. The whole site would need to be completely cleared and rebuilt from the ground up, but fortunately for Catherine and Eddie, that hadn't started yet.

Catherine had arranged for someone from the security company who looked after the place to meet them there at two o'clock, to let them in. The security had been beefed up since the incident with solid metal covers now firmly in place over all the windows and doors, but the skylight was only protected by a mesh of barbed wire over the glass and around the perimeter of the roof, so there was plenty natural light from a bright sun illuminating the sparse interior.

There was still some police tape across the door of the glass booth, but most of the rubbish had long been removed, and the whole place had at some point been power-washed down. Despite this, there was still some staining on the floor of the cubicle and discoloured areas on the counter. Eddie and Catherine took a good look inside the booth, imagining the sight that Jack the dog's owner must have found.

Eddie stood inside the booth and closed the door. He had difficulty in understanding why the original investigation had not questioned how a person who had scraped the ends of his fingers raw, almost to the bone, had not managed to get out of the booth, if he had inadvertently shut himself in. Even if his vision had been severely affected, as can happen in advanced ethylene glycol toxicity, Stevie surely would have been able to find the handle and get out.

"Hey, Eddie, come and see this." Catherine was looking at the large, curved stainless steel handle on the outside of the door of the booth. "There are some heavy scores on the inside of the handles; look, here, and under the other side too." She pointed to the damaged areas.

"It could just be wear and tear," said Eddie, peering at the area.

"That would be more likely on the outside of the handle. I think that something's been wedged in to stop this door from opening."

"That would fit in with our theory that the victim was held in the booth against his will. I still don't see why it wasn't mentioned in the original investigation."

"They weren't looking for it. This must have looked like a straightforward drug overdose at first, until the pathologist noticed something at post-mortem. When they got the toxicology back, it would have seemed to be a stupid accidental self-poisoning by a junkie who chose the wrong type of alcohol to drink."

Eddie looked round and saw the pile of burnished steel shop fittings in the corner. Picking through them, he noticed that one of the metal bars had similar signs of damage to the door handle. He picked it up and tried wedging it in the handle, and it fitted, the damaged areas on both surfaces matching.

"Go inside the booth and try to get out," he said.

"No way! You go in, seeing as it's your idea," Catherine said, looking a little uncomfortable.

"OK, lock me in, and I'll try and get out."

He stepped into the booth and she wedged the bar in when he had closed the door. Eddie rattled the inside handle four or five times and the bar fell loose. He came out from the booth and had another look round the shop area, but he couldn't find anything to wedge it with. *They must have used gaffer tape, or something*, he thought.

The light, which had been good until then, now faded suddenly as the sun slipped behind a dark cloud. Eddie glanced up at the skylight as if it was faulty. He noticed the cable hanging from the non-functioning light fitting and he finally realised how the door had been held closed to stop Steven Reilly escaping from his glass cage.

He searched around and found what he'd overlooked earlier; a twisted bundle of three-core cable discarded in the corner. He picked it up and took it over to the door, replaced the metal bar in the handle, wrapped the wire round it, and stood back.

"That's it." Eddie stood next to Catherine. He'd spoken, but they'd both had the identical thought at the same time. It was all circumstantial and there would be no chance of any forensic evidence by now, if indeed there ever had been any, but it was more confirmation for them that they were right, if such was needed.

Eddie took some photos of the "locked" door, and after

returning everything to its original position, he took pictures of the various component parts where they lay.

They thanked the security guard and Catherine headed back to drop Eddie off.

"I've just got a call to make on the way, is that OK? It'll only take five minutes." She glanced at the back seat and asked Eddie to grab the buff folder lying on it.

"Steven Reilly," he said, reading the label on the front, "What do you want with this?"

"Give me the first-of-kin contact address on the second page, will you?"

"Ah," he said, understanding, and thinking what a good person she was.

When they called in to see her, Stevie's mum was initially surprised, but when they sat her down and told her an abridged version of the whole story, she wept, and thanked them.

"I knew my Stevie wasn't as stupid as they made out. It wasn't his fault; it was just his bad luck that he bumped into a murdering bastard."

Catherine made her a promise. "We're going to get Steven's killer. We think that he's killed three people now, but it could be more. There's no doubt we *will* get him."

Stevie's mum hugged Catherine as they left. "It's a comfort, knowing the truth. You're an angel."

Eddie could see that Catherine was tired and emotionally drained, so he didn't suggest going for a drink or something to eat when she dropped him off at his flat.

-o-

At the station the next day they met with the DI, told him what they'd found, and showed him the photographs. He agreed that it was a good fit, but warned them that it would be difficult to link Stevie's death to the others, with limited forensic evidence and the passage of time.

He asked Eddie if he had enough time to stay for a meeting with his two Detective Sergeants, himself and the Detective Chief Inspector, as a press conference was scheduled for that afternoon and he wanted to pull all the areas of the investigation together and work on a strategy to move it forward. Catherine, although ranked only a DC, was also to be present, as she was in nominal charge of the animal cruelty end of the investigation.

Eddie agreed, looking at his watch and working out how much time he should allow to avoid any accusations of neglecting the practice. By the time he'd phoned his receptionist to tell her he would be another hour, the DCI and the two sergeants had arrived, along with a secretary to take notes if they were needed.

Eddie was introduced to the new arrivals and the DI got the meeting started without too much preamble.

The DI asked one of the sergeants, Tom Kelly, to summarise the Craig Ferguson murder case, more for the DCI's benefit than anything else, but it filled in a few gaps in Eddie's knowledge as well. The report by the first police officer on the scene stated that a member of the public had heard noises coming from the block of flats and had banged on the door and shouted. He couldn't see into the building because the windows and doors on the bottom three floors were completely boarded up. Still worried, he then phoned the number of the security company responsible for the building that was printed on the metal sheeted door guarding the entrance. The security company director had called by on his way home and had done a quick search of the building. Initially uneasy and unwilling to inspect each individual flat, he climbed the stairs and checked each landing, and wouldn't have found Craig if he hadn't heard a soft whimpering coming from one of the flats on that level. Thinking that a dog had been trapped in the flat, he let himself in, to be confronted with a sight that would give him nightmares for months.

When the police arrived the man was waiting in the hallway of the flat, visibly upset, a pool of vomit next to him.

As the sergeant detailed the extent and nature of the victim's injuries, everyone in the room, even those inured to some extent against violence, cringed noticeably. The only forensics recovered from the flat that could be linked to the killer were a few orange fibres from some commonly used construction workwear, probably a boiler suit, and the rope used to tie Craig up, which was a type sold in most builders' merchants and DIY superstores.

At this point, Catherine asked if there could be more than one killer.

"Unlikely. This type of killer nearly always works alone," said the DI, "and there's nothing specific so far that would indicate that more than one person was involved. What about your cases, Catherine?"

"There's nothing on our side that makes us think there's more than one, is there, Eddie?"

"Not really. I would have said it would have been difficult, if not impossible for one person to have done those things to a normal, healthy cat without sedation, but all these cats were severely compromised by ethylene glycol poisoning, so it is quite feasible that the person was acting alone."

Eddie noticed that the DCI was watching all his officers closely and he supposed that the man was constantly assessing the quality of his staff in these situations. He hoped that, after the setbacks, this case might be good for the career of Detective Constable Catherine Douglas.

There was even less to go on in the second murder case. Neil Thompson, the other sergeant, told them that the man had not yet been identified, but they expected to be able to do so shortly as an artist's impression of his face had been released to the media that morning. Again, the sheer coldness and brutal cruelty of the killing revealed by the post-mortem and scene of crime reports disturbed them all, and Eddie saw the secretary shudder as she listened while the sergeant read out his report.

"The man's hands and feet had been nailed to a piece of composite insulated fibreboard by a nail gun. The murderer used three nails for each limb, all fired in at different angles that made it impossible for the victim to rip his hands or his feet off his makeshift raft, and ultimately kept him attached to it when it presumably turned over and drowned him. Insulated fibreboard is a commonly used product in new residential and commercial builds, and consists of a dense and strong sheet of glass fibre held together with a modern hybrid cementitious material, glued to a thick layer of solid foam insulation. The sheet in question must have hit something pretty hard, as a six inch section had broken off from each of the two corners at the end of the board near the feet, and the break looked reasonably fresh."

He then detailed a few other documents, including the autopsy report.

Eddie was very impressed with the oceanographer's report on the likely track the body had taken before ending up at the mouth of the loch that the Americans had used as a naval base for over thirty years, until they left in ninety-two. He had worked backwards on an hourly basis, taking into account tidal flow, wind and wave data, and had come up with a few possible scenarios.

From the post-mortem, the pathologist had estimated that the man had been dead for about twenty-four hours, and realistically, even with the mild weather, could not have survived more than twelve hours nailed to a raft that was constantly awash with water at an average temperature of thirteen degrees centigrade. If wind chill from the moderate easterlies and the fact that the man was in terminal kidney failure were taken into account, plus the likelihood that he was put into the water at night time to avoid early discovery, he probably didn't last half that time. It wasn't known at what point exactly the "raft" capsized, but drowning was definitely the cause of his death. The vocal cords were noted as being inflamed at post-mortem, most likely caused by persistent and futile shouts for help. There were also signs of longstanding alcoholism.

There were no sightings of the upturned board with its underwater passenger in and around the upper Clyde estuary between Greenock and Dunoon, except for the one that was broadcast by the Clyde Coastguard during a maritime safety broadcast. The sergeant played a recording of the message, one of the many that were stored routinely at the Coastguard's headquarters at Greenock.

"... a bulk cargo vessel passing southwards has reported a sizeable object, possibly a large insulated box or fridge, floating in the main channel half a mile north west of the Cloch lighthouse at position 55°56.941' North 4°53.344' West. Vessels are warned that the object is partly awash and difficult to spot, but if seen it should be marked, if safe to do so, and reported to HM Clyde Coastguard."

Because of the wind blowing mostly from the east, the body couldn't have come from further down the Clyde, as tides are fairly weak south of where the body was found, and for the same reasons, the body would have had to fight against the wind to drift down from the sea lochs of the Gareloch and Loch Long. There were also deposits of sediment in the ears, nose and mouth, which matched samples taken from the sand banks just upriver of Greenock, so they knew that it had rested there at some point. The conclusion of the oceanographer was that the body on the board, if it had been put into the water twenty-four to forty-eight hours previously, must have entered the water on a stretch of the river Clyde between the River Kelvin and Dalmuir sewerage works, which included the lower stretches of the River Cart, and its two tributaries, the White and the Black Cart. As the White Cart flows through Paisley, Eddie wondered if, not more than a few miles from where he sat, the board with its sorry human cargo had been launched on an unbearable journey, until the merciful wake of a passing vessel or a white capped wave rolled its occupant underneath the cold and lethal waters of the Clyde and ended his pain and suffering.

After Neil Thompson had finished, the DI gave Catherine the nod and she, nervously but with gathering confidence, gave a thorough synopsis of their part of the investigation, but didn't mention the Steven Reilly case. Eddie thought that up until then none of her fellow officers had taken the work she had done too seriously, apart from the DI, who was already on board, admittedly after dragging his heels far too long. It came as a big shock to them all to learn just how many animals had been killed, and that there was such a degree of cruelty involved. It was a small leap of imagination for them to realise that they might be facing a long succession of murders if the series of animal killings was to be transposed onto the human side.

When she'd wound up her part of the proceedings, the DI asked Eddie if he wanted to add anything, but Eddie replied that Catherine had covered everything that he could think of.

"There's one more thing," said the DI, "before we start discussing where we go from here." He looked at Catherine and Eddie. "There is another possible death that might be down to our perp. DC Douglas and Mr Henderson discovered it by looking for recent cases that mimicked the animal killings. The death had been previously ruled as accidental, but with the evidence that has come to light during this inquiry we are reconsidering this verdict and reopening the case."

He went on to describe how similar the death was to one of the cat poisonings, and what DC Douglas had found when she had re-examined the scene of Steven Reilly's death. He finished by telling them that more killings were inevitable if the offender wasn't caught, and that he welcomed any proposals or suggestions from all those present that would help detain him.

DCI Alexander "Sandy" Edgar was the first to speak. He had risen to the rank of Detective Chief Inspector not only by being a good DI, but by having the ability to impress those above him in the force hierarchy, while retaining the loyalty and respect of his subordinates by being down to earth, and showing an uncanny ability to read internal police politics.

"First of all, we can't afford to slip up on this. I'm not saying this as any kind of threat, simply as a statement of fact. Once the press get hold of this it will run on the front pages for weeks." He looked at them all in turn. "Secondly, I'd like to take the chance to thank Eddie Henderson for getting us out of a hole, here."

The DI and the two sergeants almost fell off their seats, Catherine turned away to hide a quick smile, and Eddie had the good grace to look embarrassed.

"That said, I agree with DI Anderson that we all need to work together on this until we've got this killer in custody. What have we got to go on? Anything new?"

"We've got teams working on a number of leads, sir," said

Anderson, annoyed at the DCI. "We're looking at possible locations where the unidentified man could have been put into the river, but obviously that could be over a wide geographical area. The oceanographer's report, which in the past we've found to be reasonably reliable, narrows it down, but it still leaves a lot of riverbank to cover. Access isn't too bad on the south bank with the Clydeside Walkway, but there are long stretches of industrial complexes and farmland on both sides. We've got the Dive and Marine Unit involved in this, and they've already started searching. We also have two officers looking at PNC for any deaths in Scotland that we might need to add to our list."

Catherine interrupted with a question. "What about contacting our colleagues south of the border, and in Ireland, just in case he's been active anywhere else in the UK?"

"You're right, DC Douglas, but we've already been in touch, and we've also asked them to look out for animal killings similar to the ones on Eddie's list."

Eddie spoke, slightly unsure if it was acceptable just to butt in.

"I'll contact the RSPCA in England and Northern Ireland. I hadn't thought of doing that, but if he moved around Scotland, I don't suppose there's any reason he wouldn't have done stuff like this elsewhere."

Nobody reacted as if his contribution wasn't acceptable, so he continued.

"We have an up-to-date list of all the methods this guy has used to kill cats, and a few where we're unsure if he was responsible. If he's going to kill people in similar ways, we can expect a hanging, a crucifixion of some sort, and somebody being bricked up behind a wall and left to die, but there could be more."

"We're already canvassing all the property maintenance and security companies, demolition contractors, and building firms who have dealings with disused industrial or residential properties in Glasgow and in Dundee, about their employees' access to those buildings. We have also asked them to check for any new building works that have taken place inside those properties," said Tom Kelly. "And we've also asked them to notify us of any stolen or missing nail guns," he added.

"Was it the same nail gun in both cases?" Eddie asked.

Nobody answered, then the DI spoke. "Obviously, worth looking into. Do you have details of the one used on the cat, Eddie?"

"No, I don't, but we have pictures of the nails. I'll get them to you."

After a brief pause, the DCI spoke again.

"I'm reading through this file. An officer managed to speak to the first victim before he died. I can't see any report of what he said. Why not?

David Anderson apologised, saying. "It should have been made clearer. The victim was very weak, and almost completely inaudible, the officer told us. There was nothing worth noting."

"It will be well worth getting the officer back in and I'll give you a contact number for a speech specialist we've used on a few occasions; she's great at working on slurred or incoherent speech, with or without a tape recording." He looked on his phone, and read out the number. "Her name is Angela Robb."

The DI turned to make sure the secretary was noting

everything down.

"We're also following up on the rope and industrial clothing fibres found at the Craig Ferguson scene, and the fibreboard insulation our drowned victim was nailed to."

Eddie asked if he could make a couple of points.

"I've been trying to contact retailers and garages selling antifreeze, but I'm getting little or no cooperation. Can something be done about that?" Catherine had asked Eddie to bring this up, to try and get more resources allocated to the task. "Also, can we get access to records of juveniles who have committed animal cruelty crimes, as far back as we can go? There's very good evidence that children who torture animals continue to do this into adulthood, and often go on to abuse other humans."

The DI nodded and said he'd get someone on to it, and Eddie made one final point.

"The last thing I think we should be following up is checking hospital records for cat bite or scratch injuries, especially in the case where we have evidence that the cat managed to scratch its abuser."

The DI laughed. "You've got to be joking. I can't imagine that the hospitals would keep records of anything so trivial, and anyway, who would go to hospital for a cat scratch? Maybe if it was a dog bite, yes, but not a cat."

Eddie stifled a retort about people not having an open mind or a willingness to listen.

"You might not believe it, but cat bites and scratches can be lethal. People very rarely seek medical attention at the time, and cats carry a number of pathogens that can cause serious illness, and occasionally death, in humans. Cat bites or scratches can cause anything from cellulitis to septicaemia. If you go on the Internet and search for cat scratch disease, you'll see some pretty horrific pictures. There is a chance, albeit slim, that the suspect might have needed medical attention for something along those lines. We think at least one of the cats managed to scratch him, and it's worth checking."

"Eddie, we'll make sure we get some people on to both of those." The DCI was subtly, and without throwing his weight about too much, taking charge of the investigation. "Has anyone got anything else to add before David and I decide what to say to the press?"

Catherine had one last item of her own that she wanted to mention. "We're trying to trace the fish tank that was used when one of our cats was killed. We think the Steven Reilly killing was modelled on it, and the tank was brand new, with its labels, so we think it's important to chase it up."

"Very good, DC Douglas. Can you deal with that?" He gave her a smile, then rounded off the meeting. "OK, gents, ladies, let's call it a day at that. Just remember; every detail on this one, everybody." He turned to the DI. "David, can we sort out what we want to say, before this bloody press conference this afternoon."

-o-

Eddie watched the press conference on the Saturday evening news. What most impressed him was the way that Sandy Edgar gave away just enough to keep the press interested and maximise the amount of information that might be volunteered as a result of the publicity, without giving away to the killer how much knowledge the police had, or didn't have, about the crimes. He also came across with great empathy, and a steely determination to catch the person who was carrying out these crimes. He gave more details of the animal cruelty cases than Eddie had expected, and he told Eddie later, a little tongue-in-cheek, that some of the Scottish public would perhaps be more up-in-arms about the cats' torture than they would be about a group of junkies being killed.

The DI was nowhere near as comfortable in front of the cameras, and left most of the talking to his senior officer.

Just as the news item finished, the phone rang. It was Catherine. "The DNA is human," she said, "but there's no match on the database. Either this isn't our man, or he's not on the register."

"That's disappointing, but I would say that it almost certainly belonged to the person who killed the cat, because even with the effects of antifreeze, you'd expect that it would put up a fight. Also, cats are fastidious cleaners, and if the tissue had been from a previous encounter with someone else, the cat would have cleaned most or all of it from its claws. There was a fair amount of tissue present when I examined it."

"If you're sure of that, then our killer's a man, then," she said, explaining, "it's male DNA. At least we now know that."

"Of course, I forgot for a second. Still, if he ever gets a sample taken, we'll have him. Is anything else happening?"

"No, that's all, but this place is absolutely hectic now. They've put an extra twelve CID officers on the investigation today, and some uniforms, and I've heard that there's two boats out on the river, searching. I've been told to concentrate on finding where the aquarium came from, so I've been phoning up pet shops all afternoon. I've got a list of seven or eight to visit tomorrow that stock that make and model of fish tank; I'll show them the picture of the labels to see if they recognise them."

"Great, do you want a hand with that?"

"I'm OK, but if you're doing nothing, why not. You'll get to see how really exciting a police officer's job is, if nothing else."

"What time are you thinking of starting? I was going to follow up a few connections I have within the community, just to see if there are any silly rumours flying about that might just have a bit of truth in them."

"I've got the morning briefing at half past nine, which won't last more than an hour, so shall we say eleven o'clock?"

CHAPTER 9 Danielle

Danielle Simpson's friends, at least the ones that had a habit like hers, always assumed that it would be easy for her to get her hands on as many drugs as she wanted, because of who her uncle was. Quite the opposite was true. Most dealers were unwilling to pay the price of getting on the wrong side of Arthur "Muller" Simpson, one of the north side of Glasgow's most notorious gangsters, with a portfolio of business interests including security, massage parlours, a limo hire firm, video outlets, one casino, three nightclubs and a drug distribution network that utilised most of the other parts of his empire.

If you were a drug-taker in the half of Glasgow north of the river, there was a seventy-five per cent chance you would have bought your stash from someone controlled by Arthur, unless your name was Danielle Simpson. But somehow, despite his best efforts to preserve his own god-daughter from the miseries he inflicted on the remainder of Glasgow's lost youth, she was usually ingenious or persistent enough to acquire the heroin she needed to feed her habit. Her family had spent fortunes on psychologists, psychiatrists and expensive rehab clinics, but on every occasion, even though she would be clean for a while, she would always gravitate back to a life on the end of a needle.

It often meant relying on friends and acquaintances to buy her heroin, but many of them became nervous of helping her out after a few had been given physical demonstrations of how pissed off her uncle could be with someone who crossed him. She often travelled over to the other side of Glasgow, but even there he seemed to have some influence and she found herself to be one of the few people blacklisted by Glasgow's drug supply syndicates.

In spite of this, there was still the odd user who would deal a little to make ends meet, and while she obtained small amounts from them, it was an unreliable supply and she took more and more risks feeding her habit. Her forays for the little bags of brown powder took her into more and more dangerous places.

Drugs hadn't always been like that for her. She'd been a model pupil in a private all-girls' school up until the age of sixteen, financed by a family who, in their own circles, were respectable and wealthy, but whose financial underpinning was loansharking, a parasitic draining of the financial blood of the weak and vulnerable, and the provision of "security" to small companies and individuals worried that without protection, their lives and businesses could be at risk.

By the time Danielle and her wealthy girlfriends started experimenting with the odd spliff, her grandfather had passed away and the business had been taken over by his sons, Arthur and James, and had expanded into those other lucrative areas whose common values were preying on Glasgow's underclasses.

Before she had finished her first year at university, she had tried a gamut of new experiences, from her first sexual encounter with a fumbling sixteen-year-old at her last school dance, stoned on weed and alcohol, to an ecstasy-fuelled threesome in a caravan with two colourful and streetwise older men after a rave in a field near Balloch. She dropped out of university, got a job in a nightclub for a while until she was sacked for snorting cocaine in a toilet cubicle with a punter, sniffing the white powder from the top of the Shanks & McEwan cistern cover, her knickers round her ankles, as he banged away behind her.

Her parents disowned her, although her uncle Arthur tried

his best to keep an eye on his only niece. She moved into a squat in Pollokshaws, where she was introduced to heroin, and was prepared to put out for the guys who lived with her in return for her daily fix.

Even with occasional short periods off it, her life was ruled by her addiction, but in common with a surprising number of heroin addicts, and despite living in a squat, she managed to keep looking relatively normal, by being meticulous about looking after her appearance. She replaced her clothes regularly from charity shops, and had a daily routine that involved "wash-hand basin bathing" in department store and public toilets, always wearing make-up, and spending a little time on her hair every morning, the result being she could have passed for any ordinary young woman of her age. She always wore boots and long sleeved tops to hide the needle tracks on her ankles and arms, and the average guy in the street would invariably turn and check her out when she passed by.

Although she didn't consider herself a prostitute, she knew that she traded on her looks and her willingness to fuck to keep herself solvent. Most of the guys she went with, of her choosing, contributed something towards the fund that kept her drug habit going, with enough left over to live on. She took a job from time to time; mostly bar work, which she was good at, and the regulars usually liked her flirty style. But she was unreliable, and a few missed shifts on her part, or going too far with one of the punters often put paid to whatever short spell of employment was on the go at the time.

Her uncle had offered her bar work in the past, to keep an eye on her, but she balked at the proposal, resisting his desire to control her in any way.

She was working in the District Bar in Paisley Road West about three months short of her twenty-second birthday, and after two warnings about missed shifts she knew from experience that the job had just about run its course. The guys in the squat had been giving her grief about her not putting out any more and were threatening to throw her out. The truth was she was intensely bored with them and was thinking of moving on anyway.

She was dressed, as usual, in a low-cut blouse and a short skirt, which made her popular with the male punters and the bar owners.

It was the early afternoon shift and the bar was quiet for a Sunday; just a couple sitting at a table in the corner and a solitary drinker parked on a stool at the edge of the bar. He was quite well dressed, perhaps early thirties, and not bad looking, with worker's hands. On a couple of occasions he had gone outside, for a cigarette, she thought, but when she passed round the bar to collect a few glasses left from the lunchtime trade, she couldn't smell smoke from him, just the whiff of leather from his jacket and a rather attractive aftershave. *Possibilities.*

The next couple of times he went out, she watched him. On each occasion he checked his phone first. Through the frosted glass of the bar window, she could see that he was approached by another person who he talked to for a few moments before he returned to the bar. On the second occasion his phone had been on the bar and she'd heard it vibrate before he glanced at it.

When he sat down again, she went over and asked him if he wanted another drink.

"Yeah, gimme a still water again, pet," he said, giving her the once-over that she was used to, and expected. "Ah'm driving," he added, apologetically.

"That's OK, it's not compulsory to drink alcohol in a bar," she replied, grinning.

When she returned with his drink, she leaned on the bar

and gave him a view of her cleavage; it usually guaranteed a tip, at least.

"Not working today?" she asked, running her hand through the top of her hair.

"Well, sort o'. But no' at the moment. Why, whit do you huv in mind?"

"Cheeky bugger. Not shy, are you? What is it you do? Building?"

"Aye, a bit. How did ye knaw?"

"Your hands."

He looked at his hands and shrugged. "OK, so yer observant, darlin'. Whit else are ye good at?"

She laughed. A group of three women came into the bar, so she went to serve them. She smiled, but she could sense their dislike immediately. When they'd paid for their drinks and chosen a table, she returned to the other end of the bar. She could feel the women glancing over at her disapprovingly as she spoke to the guy.

"Fucking bitches. They don't like competition."

He laughed. "No competition, hen, they're no' in your league."

She casually touched his hand, and laughed. She knew the women were frowning and mumbling to each other reproachfully, so when one of them came to the bar a few minutes later, she undid another button on her blouse as she went to serve her.

When she returned, she could see that her builder friend had noticed that he could now see a glimpse of her bra.

"Whit time dae ye finish?" he asked her, trying to sound

matter-of-fact.

"Five o'clock. Why?"

"Thought ye might like tae go fir a drink, or somethin'."

"I suppose I might," she said, then, because of his behaviour earlier on, she took a punt. "I'll need to get some gear first, then I'll go with you."

His expression didn't change; there wasn't even a blink. "Nae bother, but ah think ah can help ye oot. Whit dae ye like, jellies, coke, or somethin' stronger?"

"I'll tell you later, I might be able to get away a bit early if Rhona or Davy arrive sharp for their shift. I'm just about through with this place anyway."

In the end, it was almost five by the time they left the bar, Danielle putting her hand on his backside as they passed the three women, just to see the expressions on their faces.

His car was parked round the corner, a dark grey BMW, not new, but half-decent. She got in, and asked him what his name was.

"Spencer," he replied, "but ah usually just get Spencey."

-o-

Catherine picked Eddie up at his flat and they spent the rest of the day visiting the pet supply outlets on her list. It was a long day, but ultimately their efforts paid off.

Two of the pet shops were closed, with it being a Sunday. Three shops and one pet superstore stocked the type of aquarium that they were interested in, but the labels were the manufacturer's, and not specific to any one shop. However, two of them only supplied tanks in the medium and larger sizes to order, and required a credit or debit card deposit. "Otherwise, we order the bloody things in, then people change their minds, don't buy them, and we're left with them," said one shop owner. In both cases, when they checked their records, the only people who had bought tanks of the size in question were regular customers. Catherine had taken a list of their names for completeness and would contact them, but she thought it unlikely that it would lead them to the killer.

The other pet shop stocked the right size of aquarium, but the shop owner said that he hadn't sold one solitary tank since purchasing them the previous year.

Eddie hadn't been hopeful that they would get any useful information from the pet superstore, figuring that it was too impersonal, with a large turnover of staff who didn't give a toss about anything other than their pay packet. He was pleasantly surprised when an earnest and very enthusiastic young man not only took them into the office and looked up the sales records for them, but also produced a printout of all the tank purchases, then called in every member of staff whose name was noted on the sales record and asked them if they remembered anything about the customers they'd sold them to. The young man's name badge identified him as Martin, and he even phoned a couple of staff members at home who were not on shift at the time.

Fifteen had been sold in total over the previous seven years, since the store had opened. Ten had been purchased with a card, and they could follow those up later. Of the five cash sales, three had been at the same time and Martin, who turned out to be the manager, remembered that they had been purchased for a new restaurant that was being opened in the town, the name of which Eddie recognised right away. The young manager specifically remembered the sale because he had negotiated a decent discount with the Greek owner for purchasing all three tanks.

One of the remaining tanks had been returned with a fault, and the staff member who had sold the tank went and found the return slip marked "Refunded in cash".

The final cash sale had been made back in March 2009 by Betty, the oldest staff member, a popular part-time woman of fifty-eight, who had applied for a job when her husband had died suddenly, and she'd needed to get out of the house and earn a little money to supplement her widow's pension. She found that she enjoyed the job more than she'd expected to and loved the banter with her fellow employees, and the shoppers. Because she liked to chat when they were making their purchases, she noticed more about the customers than some of the other staff, and this man had stuck in her mind for a few reasons.

"He was pleasant enough, but he didn't say one word about fish, and most people who buy an aquarium tell you what type of fish they have, and so on. The ones that want the tank for other things, such as terrapins or snakes, are even worse, asking you lots of questions you can't possibly know the answer to."

Eddie could see Martin and his staff nodding in agreement.

"Also, he had a little sack barrow with him, which struck me as odd, seeing as we have trolleys of our own and there's also a loading ramp out the back for large items. I told him that, but he just gave me the money and loaded it onto the barrow. By the time I came back with his change and the receipt, he had gone, with the tank. I looked out the front door to try and catch him, but he was driving off in a wee truck thing, like the council have, with the tank on the back."

Eddie and Catherine had looked at each other. *Someone has seen our suspect.*

Coolly, Catherine asked her if she would recognise him

again, and she replied, of course she would, and she agreed to come into the station to look at some pictures, and do an E-fit picture for them. Eddie thought that Betty was probably enjoying all the attention and excitement, and he couldn't really blame her.

He asked her if she had noticed any markings on the truck, or its registration number.

"Don't be silly. Why would I notice something like a number plate? But it was yellow and black at the back, and I think the rest of it was blue and silver. Yes, the sides of the truck were silver."

During all this one of the vets from the in-store practice had come into the office to find out what all the fuss was about, and because she'd heard that another vet was in asking questions about a fish tank. Eddie had to introduce himself and Catherine, and explain what the whole thing was about.

By the time this had all taken place, and Catherine had arranged for a car to collect her witness and take her to the station the following day, they were starving. She took him to a strange little diner she often grabbed a quick lunch in, before dropping him off and heading back to the station, both of them well pleased with their afternoon's work.

-o-

The call had come through less than an hour later, before she'd had a chance to write up her notes, known as actions in the force, for the day. She and Neil Thompson were the only two present at the time, so they jumped into her car and headed out to the murder scene, where a young woman had been nailed to the inside of a garage door in an empty 1930s bungalow in Giffnock. It was due to be sold as part of the estate of the owner, an old woman, who had died two months earlier.

One of the lay staff from the law firm handling the estate, and the surveyor who was with her, discovered the body. The surveyor, puzzled as to why the points of four large nails were sticking through the wood and why the door was so heavy to lift up, almost collapsed when he saw the reason for it. The garage door had swung open to reveal the naked woman, now suspended from the door above them. The young woman with him had been little help, standing and screaming hysterically, but between them they had managed to dial 999 and as a result two uniformed officers in a squad car that was in the area arrived in minutes, followed not long after by the two CID officers.

The cause of death needed to be confirmed by the pathologist, but it was clear to the four police officers present that there were two substantial head injuries, either of which could have been fatal. Apart from that, and the obvious wounds on her hands and feet caused by the nails being hammered through them into the thick wood of the substantial garage door, there weren't any other major injuries present on the body, although she had the tell-tale needle tracks of a habitual drug user on her feet, arms and inner thigh. There were also some bruises and abrasions in a line around her upper body; underneath her breasts, and in her armpits.

"For Christ's sake, I hope the doctor and the photographer get here soon, before the body falls off. It's only the nails that are holding it up."

The body was sagging horribly, and Catherine could only agree with the sentiment voiced by her colleague.

"Maybe we could just close the garage door, sir. There would be less pressure on the nails, and the body would be hidden from the street.

"It's tempting, but we'd get our balls kicked if we tamper

with it, pardon my language."

In the meantime they established that the killer had probably gained access by the rear door of the garage, which was unlocked, but no key was present. The lock was of a two lever type, easily circumvented by even a moderately competent house-breaker. The window was closed and unbroken, and a thick tarpaulin had been nailed over it to act as a blind. The floor was covered with a sheet of heavy duty polythene. A hammer with blood and other tissue on its head lay on the floor in the corner away from both doors. The young woman's clothes were in a heap near the rear door, and an open handbag sat next to it.

Neil Thompson pulled a pair of plastic gloves from his pocket and put them on, followed by a pair of plastic boot covers. He walked round the outside of the garage, reached in through the back door and lifted the purse from the woman's handbag. He opened it, and checked its contents.

"Danielle Simpson, it says here. I'm surprised she has a credit card, being a user. No debit cards though, or driving licence." He paused thoughtfully. "That name rings a bell, but I'm not sure where I've seen it before. Phone in and see if she's been reported missing. If not, get someone at the station to check with the issuing bank for the card, Cashplus. I think it's one of these prepaid ones that you can load up with funds at Post Offices, or online."

Catherine got on the phone to the station. There were no reports of the woman being registered as missing. She gave them the bank details and asked if they could run a check as a priority. She also told them to make sure the DI had been told about the body, and asked if the doctor and the photographer were on their way.

She found her sergeant looking around the outside of the bungalow. All the houses in the well-to-do area were detached, with large gardens. This one was the end house in a secluded cul-de-sac, backing on to a small area of heavily wooded parkland. There was only one neighbour, another elderly woman, who was an early bedder with poor hearing, and who'd already appeared at the top of the driveway, curious after she'd seen the police car arriving. She was told to go back home and that an officer would come and have a chat with her at some point later that day.

The DI, the police photographer and the doctor arrived within a few minutes of each other, and after the photographer had taken enough pictures of the suspended naked body in situ, the door was pulled down and the body returned to a vertical position, hidden from outside view. More pictures were taken. The doctor pronounced death, took the body's temperature, and the corpse was removed from the door as carefully as possible, placed in a body bag and removed in the ambulance. The scene of crime officers, or SOC team, spent the rest of the evening covering every square inch of the garage. There was no visible sign of entry, and no key present. It wasn't a very secure lock, and it wouldn't have taken much to gain access. The door from the garage through to the house was locked, and there was no evidence that the killer had been inside the house.

Because the killer had laid polythene on the floor and folded it up onto the main door, no blood had reached the driveway; it was all contained on the plastic sheet, although there wasn't a massive amount of it.

There was a little blood spatter on the garage door and the polythene from the nail wounds, and also from the blows to the head, but not much else until they turned the black light on. By the back door of the garage, on the concrete, a very small fluorescing spot showed up in the sweep of ultraviolet light from the lamp. They photographed it, and swabbed it for DNA testing. The hammer was photographed where it lay, and removed by the SOC team.

David Anderson stayed at the scene and sent Catherine and the sergeant to interview the neighbours. It was a thankless task, and there wasn't much to be gleaned from it. One of the other residents of the quiet street said that they'd heard a car at some point during the night, but when they looked out they'd seen nothing out of the ordinary, so had gone back to bed.

By the time the two detectives returned to the house the DCI had turned up, emphasising the profile that this investigation now had. Not since Peter Tobin's arrest had the press been able to get their claws into a serial murderer story in Scotland.

The DCI was also able to tell them, when they mentioned her name, that he knew who the deceased woman was.

"Somebody's killed the wrong person," he said. "Do none of you know who she is?"

"I vaguely recognise the name," replied Sergeant Thompson, "but I can't remember the context I've heard it in."

"Arthur Simpson. Ring any bells?"

"Oh shit, that's it. His niece. She was arrested once for soliciting\prostitution and possession. Arthur Simpson got her some shit hot defence lawyer, and it never stuck."

"Yes, we got our fingers burnt over that one. Having said that, I was never all that sure she was on the game, as such. Big Arthur was livid, but in the end all he could do was his best to get her off. Since then she's kept a low profile but, if you say she still has needle tracks on her arms and legs she's definitely still a user."

"Please say I don't have to go and tell Arthur Simpson that his niece was murdered, and like this." The sergeant looked worried.

"No, I think DI Anderson and I will do that. We may as well head off now and get it over with, before the press get whiff of it."

They left, leaving the two younger CID officers to secure the scene and arrange for a couple of uniformed police to be present overnight.

-o-

Catherine accompanied the DI to the mortuary for the post-mortem. This was her first.

"You'll be all right once you've seen a few dozen," he said.

She wished he wouldn't be such a patronising arsehole. She wasn't at all nervous, thinking that it couldn't be any more horrendous than seeing the body at the crime scene.

They parked outside the morgue and walked into the reception area. The reception staff recognised David Anderson, and a porter took them through. There were three other people present; the pathologist undertaking the post-mortem, a second pathologist, required to be present in any case of unlawful death, who noted down the findings as the autopsy progressed, and an orderly, who photographed every stage of the procedure.

The pathologist knew that the DI had brought a first timer to observe and so he took the time to list what had already been done with the body. "X-rays and an MRI scan have been taken of the head, and of all four limbs."

Mostly for Catherine's benefit, the pathologist explained what he was doing as he went through the autopsy and she watched, fascinated, as the woman's body yielded up its secrets.

He noted the external damage to the cadaver first.

"There are two substantial depression fractures of the skull, one in the left frontal area, with significant contusion and haemorrhage. The second wound is in the right frontal area and, although more deeply indented, there is much less bruising present, which probably means that this was the second blow. The shape and size of both injuries are consistent with trauma caused by blows from a blunt instrument. The circular nature of the wounds and the size of the depression, approximately two-point-five centimetres, would fit in with the weapon being a standard joiner's hammer, or similar."

The examination moved on to the extremities, and the obvious wounds to the hands and feet.

"The wounds in both wrists are full depth, proximal to the carpal bones, with some degree of tearing of the soft tissues, but there's no damage to any of the major blood vessels. There is a little local haemorrhage, and extensive bruising around the wounds, especially distally. Both these wounds are consistent with the passage of a standard six inch nail being driven through each wrist."

"The wounds in the lower limbs are very similar, but they're in the tarsal area. The nails have been driven through the transverse tarsal joints between the talus, the calcaneus and the navicular bone." He turned to Catherine. "That is straight through the ankle, in everyday language. The killer knew to nail the hands and feet above the metacarpal and metatarsal areas to avoid them tearing out. It's interesting when you see all those religious images of the crucifixion, with the nails through the hands and the feet. It's much more likely that the wounds would have been in the wrists and ankles."

He demonstrated to Catherine that there were strongly interconnected bones across those areas that supported the weight of the body.

"There are extensive needle tracks and phlebitis in both arms and legs, consistent with the victim being a habitual intravenous drug user."

He took swabs from underneath the woman's fingernails, then moved on to examine the trunk of the body.

"There are rope marks around the chest and armpits, a finding easily explained by the murderer hoisting her up using a rope looped around her upper body, before nailing her to the door."

Catherine made a mental note to check if there was somewhere in the garage where the killer could have rigged some sort of pulley system to lift her up.

"Moving on to the external genitalia, there is some bruising of the vulval labia."

The pathologist picked up a speculum from the tray and examined the vagina.

"There is also significant bruising of the vaginal tissues, and there are some abrasions present in the vaginal wall. This woman has been raped, and my guess is that it was done a short while prior to death. Histology should confirm this."

He swabbed the vulva and vagina for DNA and chemical analysis. The pubic area was vacuumed, and the few hairs retrieved were placed in an evidence bag. The pathologist explained that the attacker might have shed some of his own pubic hair during the sexual assault.

With the external examination complete, a "Y" incision was made in the trunk and, using bone cutters and retractors, the thorax and abdomen were exposed.

"Nothing remarkable in the chest cavity, but the woman was obviously a moderate smoker from the condition of the lungs. The liver shows some degree of fibrosis. This comes as no surprise, as we already know from blood samples that the victim is positive for hepatitis C infection. Incidentally, she was negative for HIV. The kidneys look a little enlarged and have an abnormal texture."

The organs were all removed and weighed, and samples were taken from all the major organs for histology and toxicology.

The brain was then extracted carefully from the cranium. It was the only part of the autopsy that Catherine found a little disturbing, but it did reveal, as expected, the likely cause of death. There were two large haemorrhages on either side of the brain at the sites of the depression fractures, the one on the right being more extensive. The increased intracranial pressure had forced the brain stem down through the foramen magnum, the opening at the back of the cranium, into the spinal canal. This effectively crushed this crucial part of the brain, vital for the basic bodily functions including breathing. Danielle would have been unconscious from the point of the first hammer blow, and death would have been fairly quick, probably within a few minutes of the second strike. The pathologist spoke to the two CID officers when he had washed and changed.

"No surprises here, then. Death almost certainly was due to the cranial trauma, but there was an extensive and probably lengthy period of torture beforehand, and a sexual assault. We will run toxicology for ethylene glycol as requested and do histology on the kidneys, which we would have done anyway."

Catherine filled him in on the reasons they needed the toxicology, explaining that what had started as a small scale investigation into animal cruelty cases had developed into one of the largest murder inquiries in Scotland in recent years.

-o-

The SOC report and both the histology and pathology results from the post-mortem examination arrived on David Anderson's desk almost simultaneously.

All the blood spatters and tissue found in the garage matched the victim's DNA. Few fingerprints were present, other than a few prints from the victim, and the old lady's: these matched the widespread prints in all corners of the house, and could only have been left by someone living in it. The only other prints were those of her gardener-cum-handyman. He was ruled out on the grounds that he was nearly the same age as the elderly owner had been, and very frail. Furthermore, he had been at home with his wife the whole of the night in question.

There was no semen, blood, or other bodily material from the attacker in the vagina, but it did contain some spermicidal lubricant with a chemical composition similar to that commonly used on condoms. All of the pubic hairs vacuumed from her genital area were Danielle's, and there was no tissue from under her fingernails.

As expected, the toxicology was positive for ethylene glycol, and there was the now familiar kidney pathology associated with it. She also had a level of opioids present in the blood consistent with intravenous use of heroin a few hours before her demise.

The small spot on the garage floor highlighted by the black lamp turned out to be the breakthrough the inquiry team were looking for. Spermatic DNA was isolated from the swab, and it matched the DNA from the tissue that had been found by Eddie under the cat's claws.

The only other finding by the SOC team was a solitary orange fibre, identical to the ones found near the other victims.

Since news of Danielle Simpson's murder had appeared on the national TV news, there had been a good public response. The staff at the District Bar phoned in and told police that she worked there, and that she'd left the bar with a man on the night she died, when they came on shift. They hadn't paid much attention to him, as she was often seen leaving with men after work, so they couldn't give a useful description. Detectives from the squad, knowing that there were likely to be surveillance cameras in the local area, contacted CCTV control and were told that there was indeed a camera with a view of the critical part of Paisley Road, but that it might be some distance away. Holding good to their promise, they copied the whole day's tapes and sent them over.

Some of the customers who'd been in the bar that day also contacted the incident room, and were confident that they would recognise the man who had left with Danielle if they saw him again. They were asked to come in and look at some mug-shots, and possibly attend an ID parade if the offender was arrested.

The CCTV tape showed Danielle getting into a car, almost certainly a BMW, with a man who looked like the one described by the bar's customers. It was too far away to be sure, but the car could have been a five or a seven series. Attempts were being made to enhance the video to make it possible to read the car's registration number.

CHAPTER 10 Manhunt

David Anderson stood at the door of Catherine's small office. She was spending a decreasing amount of time on the animal cruelty strand of the investigation as most of the groundwork had been done, and the focus had moved very much to the human cases. She was still chasing up the last of the antifreeze retailers, and she had been asked to phone round all the hospital casualty departments for information of patients who had symptoms related to cat bites or scratches. She'd almost completed that task, too, and with no return on her effort. She had widened her enquiries to include all GP surgeries in the area and was waiting for quite a few practices to get back to her; some were very reluctant to give out confidential information about their patients but had no choice when she'd produced the required warrants.

"Catherine, can Angela Robb use your room to interview PC Hamilton?"

It wasn't really a request, more of an order, but politely put.

"No bother, sir. Who is she?"

"She's the speech specialist the DCI sent over, to see if we can make anything of what Craig Ferguson was trying to tell us before he died. I'm not sure it will do any good."

"I remember now, sir. That sounds quite interesting. Would it be OK for me to sit in on it? I'd like to see how she goes about it."

"I don't have a problem with that. It's good to see a bright girl like you being willing to learn, although I'm not sure

Ms Robb will further your knowledge much."

He started to walk away, then turned back. "I meant to say. She's due at reception in ten minutes. Can you go down and get her, and tell the front desk to page Constable Hamilton?"

"No bother, sir, and thanks."

-o-

Catherine collected the speech specialist from reception and they chatted about the generalities of the investigation on the way up the stairs. PC Hamilton was waiting for them in the corridor when they reached Catherine's office.

"Sorry it's such a cubicle," she said, "but DI Anderson thought it would be quieter than the incident room."

"This is ideal," said Angela Robb. "I just have to set up a few things. Is there a mains socket?"

Catherine showed her where she could plug in what looked like some sort of dictation machine, with a foot control. The young policeman was told to take a seat and Angela explained what she was going to do.

"We just want to try and get the sounds that your victim made first, and write them down phonetically; that's when what is being said is written down as it sounds. You might have seen this in a dictionary."

Catherine looked at PC Hamilton's earnest face and gave him the benefit of the doubt. Perhaps he was more intelligent than he looked.

"After that, we will concentrate on how your victim made those sounds, and see if we can get some clarity by putting them both together. Don't feel embarrassed about making noises that don't sound like words."

Angela switched on the dictation machine and, using her foot controls, recorded each of the sounds that the young man thought Craig had made. After each, she would play it back and ask him if that was correct. He repeated a few of them over and over again until he was satisfied that the sounds on the tape were as close as possible to what he thought he'd heard."

She then switched the machine off, set up a small webcam on the desk, and plugged it into her laptop. She told him to close his eyes.

"I want you to imagine that you are back in the room with Craig. Try and picture his face as he says each word, and show me what you think his facial expression was, especially around the mouth. Again, don't be embarrassed about looking stupid. I assure you that you won't."

"I didn't see his face full on; he was tied face down to an exercise bench, but he did try and turn towards me as if he was desperate to see another human face. Sorry." His voice had a slight catch in it.

"That's OK, we know it must have been a hard thing to watch, but what you're doing here could help catch his killer."

She ran him through all the words he'd previously recorded, playing them back on the tape as he tried to mouth them. Again, he tried a few of them more than once until he was convinced he'd done all he could to give them an accurate picture of what he'd seen and heard.

She thanked him, and he left, relieved that it was over.

When he'd gone, Angela showed Catherine how she made the phonetic notation for each word, and described the mouth shape and the type of sound that it would normally generate. On a separate page for each word she made a number of suggestions as to what Craig was trying to say.

"I'll be advising your boss to use this sheet as a last resort. It's usually better to come to your own conclusions about what each word means because you have local knowledge and are familiar with the case. My suggestions might lead you away from your own choices. The best tool is to watch the video, with sound, as humans very much rely on the visual as well as the aural input when processing spoken language. The chances of getting all the correct words in this case are probably not great, considering how incoherent the victim was."

Angela opened up a video editor on her laptop and quickly edited the files into one short film showing PC Hamilton, eyes tight closed, recreating the words spoken last by a dying man. She saved it on to a USB stick marked with a logo, her name and "Speech Consultant", and gave it to Catherine, along with all the paperwork.

"Everybody thinks that I write speeches for politicians. I really must change that."

Angela smiled, shook Catherine's hand, and walked off down the corridor. Catherine should have walked her out, but she was too interested in the film to waste any time. She put a copy on to her own computer and, plugging her phone in, copied the file to it as well, to show Eddie later. She also emailed a copy to the DI, along with a message telling him that she had left all the paperwork in the incident room. She ran along and dropped it off, then returned to her room and her computer.

Taking Angela's advice, she wanted to watch the video first and make up her own mind. She listened to it five or six times, and on each occasion wrote down any words that could fit the sounds. After she'd finished, she looked at her list.

Anger, state, start the end of you, early in March, Blue Wicked, antifreeze, mama sis, friend, oh well, 2 a.m., hood fail dive.

-o-

That evening she phoned Eddie and told him that she had a video to show him. He presumed that it was CCTV footage and suggested that she came round to the flat.

When Catherine arrived she had the video loaded up on the screen of her smartphone. She explained how it was made, and told Eddie to write down the words he thought were being said as he watched it. She fetched him a pen and some paper from her briefcase, and went to make a cup of coffee. By the time she came back, Eddie had already watched it twice and had come up with a couple of the same words that she had, but he'd also written down a few that she didn't have, and when she glanced at them, she knew that he was right. *He must have a good ear for this.* Why hadn't she seen them? They were obvious once you knew.

She sat down, took the page from him, and replayed the film, reading the list again as she did.

Hackle, mistake, dark BMW, paisley back, Blue Wicked, antifreeze, my missus, other end, so unwell, do him, food hell dive.

Then she compared it to hers.

Anger, state, start the end of you, early in March, Blue Wicked, antifreeze, mama sis, friend, oh well, 2 a.m., hood fail dive.

"I think you're right with these two," she told him, pointing at the BMW reference and "the other end". "I didn't get either, but when I read them and played the tape, I'm sure they can't be anything else. I got the Blue Wicked and the antifreeze, but they're straightforward in the context of the enquiry."

"The dark BMW was straightforward, the CCTV footage shows Danielle getting into a car like that near the bar she worked in, and I don't know what 'other end' means, but I thought that was as clear as day."

She looked at his list again, but the other words made no sense. She looked at Eddie.

"I'm not so sure about 'so unwell', although we both thought it was that. It doesn't quite fit, but it was close enough to write down."

"Maybe he was just saying how he was feeling – he was dying at that point," Eddie answered.

"No, I don't think so. If you were in his position, you would say something like 'I'm fucking dying', wouldn't you, not 'I'm so unwell'." She went on. "Also, he wasn't married, and he didn't seem to have a partner, so why 'ma missus'?"

"I don't know. It will be worth coming back to. Bluetooth a copy of the video to my laptop, will you?"

She paused, looking slightly concerned. "I'm not sure I should; I'm not even meant to have it on my phone."

"I've got an encrypted directory on the hard disk for all the stuff associated with this case. It's probably safer here than it is in Paisley police station, but only let me have a copy if you're OK with it."

Reluctantly, she agreed to send it to Eddie, if he promised to keep it absolutely safe.

"We'll see what the others think he was trying to say," she said as she got up to leave.

Eddie couldn't think of a good reason on the spur of the moment to ask her to stay for a while, so he showed her out. She seemed to hesitate at the door, as if she'd forgotten something, but carried on down the path to her car, giving him a wave over her shoulder.

-o-

On her way home, Catherine called round to have a look in the garage where Danielle Simpson had been murdered. She found a block, with a pulley wheel in it, clipped on to a bracket on the garage roof which anchored the door opening mechanism. She took a photograph on her phone, then unclipped it and popped it into an evidence bag, for handing into forensics the next morning.

-o-

There were no messages from Catherine on Eddie's voicemail after he'd finished his late clinic, three days later. Even two promising medical cases that evening hadn't lifted his spirits, blunted by a spate of anal gland emptying and nail clipping, both of which he so detested. When he got into the flat he thought he'd try and tax his brain by taking another look at the investigation, which had stalled a little, although there was still plenty of legwork going on.

Eddie tried a trick that he sometimes used for complex medical cases. He wrote each fact he knew about the suspect on an individual Post-it note and stuck all of them at random to the glass of the kitchen door. Then he stepped back, perched on the edge of the kitchen table, and stared at his makeshift noticeboard.

Every so often he would walk over and move a note or two, seeing a connection here and an association there. In clinical cases, he was often looking for cause and effect and he tried to think of the police investigation in the same way, but there were too many threads and it was always just out of his grasp.

He had just decided to take a break and had opened a bottle of beer when the doorbell rang. He looked down from the large bay window that dominated his living room and could see Catherine standing at the front door of the building. She paced impatiently and took out her mobile phone, presumably to call him and ask him why he wasn't answering the door. He swung open one of the side windows of the bay and shouted down that the door was open, and she should just come up. She tried the door as if she didn't believe him, then disappeared inside. He walked through to unlock the flat door for her, leaving it a little ajar, and headed back through to the kitchen to switch the kettle on. He heard the door closing behind her, and her footsteps coming down the hallway. He looked round as she came into the kitchen. She must have come over straight from a late shift at work, because she was dressed in her usual dark skirt and jacket, and a plain blouse, the only clothes he had ever seen her in. *Perhaps she never wears anything else.*

"Tea or coffee? Or something stronger? I'm having a beer."

"Beer's fine, or I'll have a glass of wine if you've got a bottle open? I left my car at the station and walked here to clear my head. I'll get a taxi home. It's getting a little fraught over there."

"I've a bottle of red open. I think it's a Syrah." He found a glass and got the bottle from his small pantry, and poured her a glass.

"Have you eaten? I could put some pasta together for you."

"No, thanks, you're all right, I had some fast food earlier." She screwed up her face.

She suddenly noticed all the Post-its on the open kitchen

door. She could only see the back of them.

"Shopping list?" she asked.

He walked over and closed the kitchen door, and stood back.

"Ah," she said, "and here I was thinking I was getting away from it all for a bit." She smiled.

"Oh. Right. I suppose you must get fed up with the case after a while. I had a bit of a tedious day at work, and this is a little more interesting for me."

"I'm only joking. I did come over to talk about work; I just had to get out of the way of all those jocks over there. The more I work with them, the harder it is for me to like them, or even respect them in some cases."

"You're still getting some hassle then?"

"Nothing I can't handle, but it wears you down after a while. Anyway, enough about me. Have you got anywhere with this?"

"Not really, I was just mucking about to see if anything came up. I had just about packed it in when you arrived."

"Nice way to do it. Where did you pick this up?"

He explained that he'd adapted it from something he'd seen at a management seminar the practice had insisted he attend when he became a partner, and that he'd found it invaluable in difficult cases.

She wandered over to the door and, picking up a pad of notes, wrote five titles in large letters on individual sheets: LOCATION, MOTIVE, EVIDENCE, IDENTITY, HISTORY. She then stuck them on to the glass, clearing a space for each by moving a few of the other notes to the periphery.

She then started to rearrange Eddie's notes around these "headings". Where a note fitted in two categories, she copied it out, wrote the same number on both, and stuck them in the appropriate place. Eddie watched her with interest, not necessarily all professional. When she was finished there were only three or four notes that didn't fit in anywhere.

"You should have a 'miscellaneous' tab," Eddie said jokingly and got a stern look for his troubles. He went up to the door and moved a couple of Post-its.

"See anything?" she asked.

"No, but every so often I'll come back and have a look at it. It's surprising how often when I do that with medical problems, an idea just falls into place."

"I have a couple of things you can add. There were no prints or DNA on the pulley I found in the garage, but there were some blue polypropylene fibres stuck in the wheel, identical to the ones from the rope at the other murder scenes." She'd told Eddie about the pulley, and they knew that finding it explained how the killer had managed to lift Danielle Simpson while he nailed her to the door.

They sat down at the kitchen table, Eddie drinking his beer, Catherine sipping her glass of wine. They mulled over some aspects of the case; why rape Danielle using a condom, leaving only traces of lubricant but no semen, but then spill some semen on the floor? And why kill her with two blows from a hammer, when he had seemed to deliberately prolong the other deaths? Had he been disturbed? Had he panicked? It definitely seemed to be a mistake.

There was nothing new, but it sometimes helped to keep

stuff fresh. The conversation got round to the officers on the investigation. She said he had been right, David Anderson was a dick; sexist, patronising, a poor listener, with an ego out of balance with his abilities. The two sergeants were good, she had no issues with either of them, and the DCI was more than capable, but scattered through the rest of the squad were a collection of bigots, male chauvinists and bullies.

She told Eddie of the constant leering and accidental brushings, the way they assumed that they were better than her, the casually offensive language in relation to women and sex, and their unapologetic habit of putting her and other women down.

"But surely you could complain; have these guys pulled up for it?"

"It's not as simple as that. A friend of mine, Maureen Gilmore, complained about three officers in her squad. They got a slap on the wrist, but she's been off work for a month because of the undercurrent of abuse she was getting, and not just from the male officers!"

"So you've just got to get your head down and get on with it. Or get out."

"No way! I wouldn't give them the satisfaction."

The conversation drifted on to Eddie's career. She was as fascinated by his day-to-day work as he was with hers. He told her of his upbringing, and his determination from a very early age to become a vet, somewhat underplaying the difficulties he had overcome to succeed and the background he had come from. Having policed the south side of Glasgow for a number of years, and knowing the tough areas, she could understand how hard it must have been for Eddie to get to where he was, and why he took life a little too seriously at times.

As they relaxed into each other's company, Eddie couldn't help sneaking little surreptitious glances at her. He wished that he could think of a way to tell her how attractive she was without sounding like a letch. When he rose for another beer, and to fill her glass from the wine bottle chilling in the fridge, he suggested moving through to the lounge for a soft seat, trying to sound as off-hand as possible. She followed him through, and when he sat at one end of the couch, nursing his bottle like a comforter, he was surprised when she chose the other end to sit on, instead of one of the chairs. She made herself at home, pulling her legs up under her. Eddie could never understand how women could be comfortable in that position, but he wasn't complaining, as it gave him an excellent view of her legs.

Since the first day they met, an increasing fondness for Catherine had crept up on Eddie and he found that he enjoyed her company immensely. While at the beginning he was aware in an abstract sort of way that she was a good looking woman, he was finding her more attractive as time went on. He thought it unlikely that she had changed her appearance, so he presumed that he was now noticing something about her that had been in front of his nose all the time.

The truth was somewhere in between the two. For a long time, she had maintained a deliberately severe look to try and reduce the unwanted attentions from the "cavemen" on the force. It was accomplished by an almost painful tying back of her hair, very little make-up, and plain and efficient clothing, but it was only partially successful, evidenced by the levels of harassment she still received. When she has been the fiancée of one of the "boys" on the force, this had been much less of a problem. There was almost an unwritten rule that a woman "belonging" to one of their own was untouchable.

Despite the risk of encouraging unwanted attention at

work, she had gradually softened her appearance in the last few weeks. The tight bun was slackened a little, a few stray hairs were allowed to escape, to fall over her cheek, and one of the other female officers observed that Catherine had started using small amounts of mascara, eyeshadow and lipstick.

While Eddie pondered on a safe strategy to let Catherine know that he found her attractive without screwing up their friendship, Catherine asked herself if she was right about him and the looks he'd been giving her. He certainly wasn't making any moves, and she wondered if he was frightened of the fact that she was a policewoman. She decided he was just shy, and that she would have to do something about it.

"What are we going to do about all this sexual tension, Eddie?" she asked.

The momentary shock on Eddie's face made her think that she'd gone too far. She felt a flush coming to her cheeks and she started to get up, mumbling her apologies, but his expression changed rapidly to one of concern, and he reached out to stop her leaving.

"I'm sorry, I never realised," he mumbled. He didn't know quite how it happened, but she was suddenly tight in his arms, half-on and half-off the couch, kissing furiously. He could smell her perfume and taste the wine in her mouth. All sorts of wonderful sensations were happening to his body where she pressed against him. He now knew that she was just as keen on him as he was on her, but that didn't mean that he was going to start ripping her clothes off. He was envious of men who could read what women wanted, but he wondered sometimes if they just didn't give a fuck, and *that* was what some women wanted in a man.

After what seemed a long time without breathing, they both came up for air, and looked at each other.

"How did we get here?" asked Eddie, smiling as he did.

"You really don't know, do you? I think that's what I like about you. You've got no agenda."

He grinned. "How do you know I've no agenda? Maybe I planned this seduction all along."

She laughed. He could feel the whole settee shaking, she was giggling so much. She managed to pull herself together long enough to speak.

"Eddie, even now, when I've practically jumped on top of you, you're still wondering how far you can go without upsetting me."

Eddie blushed, and tried to look annoyed, but just succeeded in looking embarrassed. He sputtered a reply that she didn't quite catch. She continued.

"I like that you're not sure. And, by the way, I don't mind how far you go, if that's what you want."

Again, she'd reduced Eddie to incoherent mumbling. He finally managed to spit out that he'd been thinking of asking her out for a while, but he didn't want to do anything that would spoil their friendship.

She took his hand, and placed it on one of her breasts and kissed him, more softly this time, but with her tongue playfully touching his teeth. He could feel her nipple, hard, even through the material of her bra and her blouse.

This time, they kissed for much longer; she felt Eddie's hands everywhere on her body and she knew he wouldn't be able to stop now, unless she asked him to. And she wasn't going to do that. She managed to undo his shirt buttons and she could feel his clumsy attempts at trying to undo her bra fastener. Eddie somehow managed to speak, even now seeing the practical aspects of where this was leading.

"Bugger, have you got any condoms? I'm afraid it's been a long time since I've needed any."

"No, but I'm on the pill."

Eddie almost made the fatal error of asking one of a number of questions that came into his head, prompted by this piece of information, but did the correct thing by saying nothing and looking confused.

She saw his puzzled frown and elaborated further. "I started taking it three weeks ago. I wasn't sure how long it would be before you plucked up the courage to take me to bed." She laughed, stood up, took his hand and led him through to the bedroom.

-o-

Eddie woke up to the sound of an unfamiliar phone ringing. He automatically reached for his own mobile, but soon realised that it was Catherine's phone that was buzzing furiously on the bedside cabinet. She answered it and talked quietly to someone on the other end.

It all came flooding back to him in a warm glow of contentment. Catherine and he were now lovers, and the night before had been without question the best night of his life. Being with Catherine had been unlike any of the few other sexual relationships he'd had, and he wondered if it had been because they had become friends before he'd fallen for her in such a big way. She looked fantastic, dressed or naked, and she was uninhibited and exciting in bed; playful, adventurous, and the way she looked at him! He couldn't believe that someone like her could be into him so much.

After the first time, they'd talked for hours, and then made love again, before falling asleep wrapped round each other, entwined with the bedclothes. He'd woken once during the night and gently disentangled himself, before instantly falling back to sleep.

Now, watching her naked back as she talked on the phone, he had the urge to touch her, but he could hear the seriousness of her tone and knew it was work related. She spoke for about five minutes, then hung up and turned to him.

"They've found the crime scene for the body in the water, and they think they've identified the victim." She stood up, still naked, and started gathering her clothes from the floor, where they'd been discarded carelessly a few hours before. She dressed while he watched, knowing that he was looking, and not minding. Turning to him, she smiled apologetically.

"You're going to have to run me to the station to pick up my car."

Eddie jumped up, throwing on clothes in an ad-hoc manner, not wanting to hold her back.

"I'm sorry, I should have remembered that you don't have your car. Do you want me to come with you?"

"No, I'm not ready for everybody to know about us yet; I think it would be better if you dropped me off a couple of streets from the station. I'll tell you all about it later on."

If Eddie was disappointed, he hid it well. They spoke little in the car, both wrapped up in their own thoughts about their new relationship, and what impact the current development could have on the investigation.

-o-

Catherine didn't even manage a cup of coffee at the station. As soon as she had arrived, she'd been told to get her arse into the car with Sergeant Thompson and two other DCs; that they were going to the old Babcock factory on the banks of the White Cart River in Renfrew.

A night watchman patrolling the periphery of the factory grounds in the early hours of the morning had noticed a chink of light coming from the bottom of the door of the disused store, near to the river. By the time he'd discovered that the key that should have unlocked the padlock didn't fit and had found a hacksaw and cut the hasp, the dawn was beginning to lighten the morning sky. He had phoned the police on discovering the dried blood stains on the floor of the building, and its unexpected contents.

The scene of crime team were already working inside the building when Catherine arrived with her CID colleagues.

The DI pulled them all together, split them into units of three or four, and allocated a task to each group. Catherine, DS Thompson and another DC were to painstakingly search the ground between the store and the road, while the two other groups were split between the immediate dock area, and the rest of the factory. The DI had a word with them all before they started.

"The weather has been dry since the body was found, so there's a good chance we'll get some evidence from this site. No cock-ups, please, and sharp eyes, everybody. We're looking for anything at all that could identify the suspect, or something that will tie him to the other crimes, no matter how small or insignificant."

He paused to see if they were all paying attention.

"We also have a name for the victim. James Prentice, thirty-two, unemployed, and a registered alcoholic, lived not far from here in Mitchell Avenue, Renfrew. We've got a team over there now finding out as much as possible about him, and tracing his movements prior to his death.

All our victims so far have had drug or alcohol issues, and would have been vulnerable and easily targeted. They also wouldn't have been reported missing for a considerable time, and we think all these factors were important in the killer's choice of targets."

It was an arduous day for everybody, broken only when the DCI arrived, accompanied by a uniformed driver carrying a box of sandwiches, teas and coffees, and bottles of chilled water for the teams. Catherine vowed to remember the DCI's clever personal touches if she ever got promoted, as his act of kindness seemed to markedly improve everyone's morale.

Her group found very little; A few old cigarette ends and a condom that had obviously been there for some while. Catherine recovered a few orange fibres, similar to those found in the flat where Craig Ferguson had been assaulted. She spotted them on the broken piece of fence that the murderer had presumably used as an entrance into the grounds of the factory and she bagged them up for forensic analysis.

The other teams had mixed fortunes. The factory buildings closest to the dock were a now disused part of the once massive Babcock & Wilcox boiler factory, which employed up to ten thousand men at the height of its production, but was now a shadow of its former self. The group who searched the factory found nothing at all that they could link to the crime.

The dock had been the route by which many of the large boilers, other industrial machinery and armaments manufactured over the years at Babcock's had left the factory by ship to destinations all over Europe. Even into the twenty-first century, it was still occasionally used, mostly for components for the nuclear industry, which is why the Inchinnan Swing Bridge just downstream was still functional, allowing large barges to pass to and from the

Clyde and further afield. The officers who scoured this dock area were much more productive.

There were distinctive drag marks where the fibreboard sheet had been dragged across the softer ground, and some polystyrene material had crumbled off the insulation board, falling in between the cracks at the edge of the docks, along with a few blue polypropylene rope fibres. They also found a series of footprints in the softer ground between the jetty and the store. The photographer with the forensics team took a series of pictures of them, and a cast was made of two of the more complete prints. When Catherine's colleagues found a large number of indistinct but similar footprints in the scrub near the fence, these were also photographed.

The store gave up less information than they'd hoped. All of the blood was James's, and the empty bottles all contained ethylene glycol, apart from one. Strangely, there were only two that had no prints on them, and the non-poisoned bottle was one of them. More rope fibres, polystyrene and some of the fibreboard itself were found on the floor, along with a couple of discarded air gun nails and residue from the firing caps.

In the river just below the dock a fallen tree branch caught in one of the piles that lined the jetty formed a trap which collected a variety of flotsam which had ended up in the water. There were plastic containers of all shapes and sizes, an old football, a variety of carrier bags and part of a wooden pallet, all floating in a froth of brown foam.

Using a RIB, a rigid-hulled inflatable boat, the Dive and Marine Unit made a detailed search of both banks of the river near to the dock and downriver of it. They scooped up the contents of this eddy and bagged it for further examination. Of the items they picked up, the most significant were two small broken-off corner pieces of insulated fibreboard. Each had a distinctive groove on the rough surface which the CID officers suspected would exactly match the ones on the board that James Prentice had been nailed to.

-o-

David Anderson invited Eddie to the Friday morning briefing, albeit in a roundabout way. When he told the squad on Thursday that he wanted everyone involved in the investigation to be at the meeting, Catherine asked him if he expected Eddie to be present. He agreed reluctantly, but in the light of Eddie's contribution to the investigation, and with his official SSPCA rank, it would have looked churlish to refuse.

Catherine wondered if she'd done the right thing. She quickly sent him a text to allow him to organise an hour or so away from work the following day.

-o-

Eddie had known Margaret Taylor since joining the practice in Paisley. Every practice has a Cats Protection lady or, less commonly, man. Fruitcakes in the nicest way possible, they are ferociously fond of anything feline and will do anything necessary to prevent cruelty to cats, or improve the lives of the local felidae. Margaret had been the local coordinator of Cats Protection for over thirty years, and Eddie figured that if anyone had heard about somebody torturing cats, she would have, but he suspected that if she knew who was carrying out the crimes they were dealing with, she would have hung the bugger up by the ears for a week. He still thought it was worth having a word with her, and she was quite willing to talk to him if it could save cats from being abused.

He met her on Thursday, after work, at her home in Dean Park. It was a shrine to cats inside and out. Cat ornaments and pictures covered the interior walls, and outside her garage and garden shed were full of pens holding cats waiting to be re-homed.

He explained the background of their investigation, describing all the tortured cat cases he'd investigated and the links to the spate of murders that were taking place. Surprisingly, she was equally concerned about both. He told her about their suspicions.

"We think this man lives in the Paisley or Renfrew area, or knows it very well; perhaps he even grew up here. I know you've been looking after cat welfare here for a long time, and I'm hoping you might have heard some rumours about this guy."

"Eddie, I'm not sure I can help. I'm afraid I haven't heard much, only what's been in the press, and that was mainly about the murders."

"Nothing at all? Even daft gossip?"

"Och, there's been one or two stories flying about, but none that make sense when you think about it, and none that concern the cats, which I presume is what you have come to see me about, yes?"

"Well, yes, I suppose it was, really, but what stories have you heard?"

"Oh, there are rumours doing the rounds that it's just someone who hates junkies and drunks, or that there is a gang war going on, or that there is a coven of devil worshippers in the area. There's even been a few names bandied about, but they just feed on people's prejudices and fears."

Eddie didn't show his disappointment at this, and changed tack.

"What about cases of cat cruelty and kids, say about ten to

twenty years ago?"

"Ah, that's a different story. Kids can sometimes be even crueller than adults."

"And it's been shown that cruelty to animals by young children often carries on to adulthood; there's a proven connection between the abuse of animals and violence towards humans in some people, so that's why this is so important, aside from the fact that this brutal fiend is torturing cats," Eddie replied.

"I do remember a couple of incidents. Both were about twenty years ago. One was a teenage girl who tied her own dog to a pier at low tide somewhere on Clydeside, near the Renfrew ferry, and watched as the tide came in. The poor dog was swimming desperately for hours until the lead became too tight and pulled it under."

"It's a man we are looking for here. We have DNA from one of the cat's claws and from one of the murder scenes. How did you get involved with that case?"

"The girl in that case has some mental health issues. I believe she was admitted to hospital and received treatment, but I'm not sure what became of her. The reason I knew a little about it is that my husband was an SSPCA officer for about ten years back then, and it was one of the cases he dealt with. He died very young, you know. A heart attack."

"I'm very sorry. I knew you were a widow but I didn't know the circumstances."

"Oh, it was a long time ago. I just had to soldier on. That's why I put so much into the CPL over the years. I know you vets think we're all barmy and have a laugh at us, but we don't mind, really."

Eddie noticed that she used the old name for the charity,

the Cats Protection League.

"Not at all, Margaret. We sometimes have a quiet smile," he admitted, "but we all know you do a great job."

He waited a moment, then continued.

"What about the other case?"

"Now that was just plain nasty. A horrible little boy, about six or seven, whose neighbour's cat had a litter of kittens. One day the neighbour came home and found all the kittens had been killed, impaled on the fence spikes around the garden. At first, they didn't know who had done it, but someone had seen him. They confronted the boy's parents and the boy's father, who was apparently often violent, beat the truth out of the boy and made him promise that it would never happen again."

"Were the police involved, or the SSPCA?" Eddie hoped that there might be a record of it.

"No, the neighbour was too frightened of the boy's father to take it further, and hoped the boy had learned his lesson."

"How were you involved?"

"I was only involved because the owners of the cat, who had pretty restricted finances, came to us for help to get the cat neutered, so that there would never be any more kittens for the boy to kill. They told me the whole story and we agreed to get it done for them. I think it may have been your practice that did the operation."

"I don't think we keep records for that far back. Can you remember any of the details?"

"I can't remember a name or specific address, and we don't keep records for that long either, but it was definitely

Ferguslie Park, and I think it might have been the bottom end, maybe Woodvale Drive or Dalkeith Avenue."

Eddie wrote the names down, along with the age of the boy.

"Can you remember when it happened; what year it was?"

"Well, Tom's been dead eighteen years, and I think it was the year before he died, so that would make it just about nineteen years ago."

"The boy would be about twenty-five now, or thereabouts. That's certainly possible."

He chatted to Margaret about the case for another few minutes, thanked her for her help, and told her that he'd keep her updated if anything came of it.

-o-

Back at the flat, Eddie booted up his computer, waited for the desktop to appear, then clicked on Angela Robb's film. There it was. Ferguslie Park, and Woodvale Drive, one of the streets Margaret had mentioned, and the housing estate it was part of.

He nearly grabbed Catherine as she came in the door, he was so excited.

"Whoa cowboy, what did we say about showing restraint. Give me a chance to get my coat off before you ravish me." She laughed and kissed him on the mouth, wrapping herself around him at the same time.

Eddie, trapped by her embrace, could do nothing but reciprocate, but as soon as he felt it was appropriate to stop, he disengaged and led her over to his computer.

He told her about his conversation with Margaret. "Now

listen to this." He clicked on the button to play the film.

When it came to the fourth word, she gasped. "You're right, Eddie; Ferguslie Park."

"I know, keep listening. The last one on the film."

When the video had finished, he turned to look at her. She was nodding her head. "Woodvale Drive. That's it! I can make it out clearly now. It's one of the streets that Margaret named."

"The only thing is, the address Craig used was his mother's, and that's in Ferguslie Park, too. Mightn't he have just been telling the policeman to contact his mother?"

"I don't think so. He would have used his mother's address." She pointed at the screen. "Let me watch that again."

Eddie played it back once more.

"Ma ma's hoose, that's what he's saying. It's at *the other end* of Ferguslie Park from his mother's house, the bottom end. Eddie, I think he might be telling us that he'd seen the murderer around, and he was trying to tell PC Hamilton where to look for him."

Eddie knew that Ferguslie Park in Paisley was one of the most deprived areas in Scotland, and despite efforts to regenerate the housing scheme from the way it looked in the seventies and eighties, it still ranked in the top five along with other notorious housing schemes like Possilpark and Eddie's own birthplace, Castlemilk, with poverty levels competing with the highest in the country, and life expectancy amongst the lowest. Although it was just a chance, the thought that they had a positive lead gave them hope that they were finally getting somewhere.

He grabbed hold of Catherine and danced her around the room, telling her they were a brilliant team. "Phone David Anderson," he told her, desperate to put their findings to good use.

That brought her back to reality. She told him that the thought of going to the DI with something as tenuous as this was not appealing.

"But what if this killer strikes again, and you haven't said anything? How will you feel then?"

She slumped her shoulders and conceded that he was probably right.

They had another go at trying to unravel the rest of Craig's words, but failed.

David Anderson spoke with Catherine for all of thirty seconds when she phoned him and explained Eddie's and her own conclusions about what the dying Craig was trying to tell them. His reaction disappointed her on a number of levels; she had anticipated his scepticism and closed mindedness, but wasn't ready for his unwillingness to listen to them when they had been proved right on a number of previous occasions. He had a complete inability to learn from his mistakes. In the end, she knew he'd agreed to talk to her in the morning simply to get her off the phone. He had, however, brought forward the morning briefing to eight-thirty, and told her they would discuss her findings afterwards.

Eddie was fuming when she told him, and she thought it would be advisable to warn him about his behaviour.

"For God's sake, don't wind him up, even if he can be a jerk. And for now, remember that you and I aren't officially together, so no little looks or smiles, or comments. And definitely no touching!"

Eddie tried to look hurt, but there was a smile at the corners of his mouth which ruined the effect.

"I'm not stupid, and I do understand why you'd want to keep your private life separate, so you can trust me to be discreet. You'll just have to keep on my good side, though …"

Since that first night, they'd spent every night together, apart from one, when she had a course the next day at Tulliallan and was being picked up early in the morning by a fellow female DC who was also attending the course. Eddie hadn't so much as stepped inside her flat, as his was larger and more convenient. Besides, he felt that she needed a bit of time to fully trust their relationship and to find a suitable moment to let the world know about it. Keeping her own flat outwith their existence as a couple gave her an identity of her own, and for a while it worked, and nobody guessed.

Eddie did tell Brian, after checking with Catherine that she didn't mind. He assured her that Brian was surprisingly discreet, and also that he was unlikely to bump into anyone socially that she knew or worked with, apart from the slim chance of him being arrested by one of them.

Although it varied, Brian and Eddie were usually in contact about once a month. Eddie would phone Brian and find out how he was behaving, and if he currently was holding down a job. Sometimes he felt like Brian's parole officer.

They would occasionally meet up, although rarely more than two or three times a year, when Eddie would inquire about Brian's latest life disasters, and Brian would feign disinterest in what Eddie was doing, while clandestinely probing to see what Eddie's latest achievements were. Secretly proud of his friend, he would never show it.

Eddie smiled afterwards when he thought about Brian's reaction when he'd told him, sitting in the Abbey Bar in Paisley, just round the corner from the police station.

"Yer shagging the fuzz! Fur fuck's sake man. That's us finished. Ah cannae be seen wi' someone who's doin' a polis wummin'."

"Brian, give it a break, I told you we were together, I'd prefer it if you weren't quite so fucking graphic about it, and a bit less of the fuzz, filth, rozzer or pig, if that's OK."

"Aye, sorry, mate, just a natural reaction, like. Nae offence meant. But fuck, man, it's a bit much fur me tae take in."

"It's all right, I'll let you away with it, but promise me you'll not call her anything bad when you meet her."

"Nae way. Nae chance. Ah draw the line at meetin' her."

"No, seriously, she's really nice, and I've told her all about you, and she wants to meet you." Not strictly true, but she had agreed to meet the guy who was Eddie's oldest friend, and in truth, she was intrigued by the relationship between the two men who, on paper, were poles apart.

"Ah cannae, Eddie, ah'm no comfortable near ony polis. Ah wid just show ye up."

"Look Brian, we've been friends since we were both in nappies, just about, and sad as it might be," Eddie said, grinning, "you're the only *real* friend I have, so it's important to me that you two meet each other."

Brian was quite touched by Eddie's admission, despite him saying that it was a bit sad.

"Christ, you must be serious aboot this polis burd. Ah wondered when ye would eventually get a wummin, right enough, but a fucken …"

He stopped himself just in time, seeing Eddie's disapproving look.

"When dae ye want me tae meet her, so's ah can be on holiday or sumfin'?"

"Aye, right. No chance you're getting away with that. Anyway, there's no time like the present. She'll be here in five minutes for a drink."

"Ya sleekit bastard, ye." Brian looked round frantically, as if there was about to be a police raid and he was looking for an escape route.

"Calm down, she's probably just as worried about meeting you."

Brian chuntered and fidgeted nervously, taking frequent drinks from his glass, bemoaning the fact that Eddie had pulled a stunt on him. Eddie bought him another pint, as he had almost finished the one he had, whilst his own was still three-quarters full.

When Catherine came in she waved over to Eddie and went to the bar to buy herself a drink. She'd come straight from work, so she was dressed in her usual grey and black, but she'd let her hair down before entering the pub and most of the men in the bar took the time to have good, long look at her. As she stood waiting to be served, Brian whispered to Eddie.

"Ye knaw ye'll get ten years fur that, don't ye?"

"What are you talking about?"

"Kidnappin' a polis wummin, ye'll get the jail fur that. Don't try and tell me there's ony ither way ye'd get a wummin that looks like thon."

Eddie laughed. The blunt humour was part of the reason

they were friends. Brian thought Catherine was "well fit" and was giving him a bit of respect, but letting him know that he thought Eddie was punching well above his weight. And he could only agree with him. Every time he saw Catherine, he thought the same.

"Twat. I'm not the worst looking at this table, and don't underestimate the effect saving the lives of little furry animals has on women, you philistine."

"Bollocks. Women like a man wi' a sense o' humour, and yer too fucken serious. On the other hand, ah'm an ugly cunt, but I get plenty o' poontang 'cos ah'm a funny bastard when ah need tae be. Aw right, they're no quality like your burd, but yeh've had tae wait aboot twenty years fur wan."

Eddie couldn't help but laugh again at the brutal summary of their respective love lives, but Brian wasn't finished.

"Anyhow, ah still don't know fur sure that she is yer burd, ah've only yer word fur it."

Eddie stifled more laughter as Catherine came over to the table. She sat down next to Eddie and touched his hand only briefly, an act which wasn't missed by Brian and that somehow told him more about their relationship than any overt display of affection.

Eddie had warned Catherine about Brian, but to be fair, he was a pussy, behaving far better than Eddie could have expected, and the pair of them, much to his surprise and relief, hit it off. They had very little in common except that they were both very fond of Eddie, but Brian could, when he wanted, turn on a bit of rough charm and be very amusing, and Catherine, in Eddie's eyes, was warmhearted, good company, and beautiful, a combination that had Eddie's childhood pal completely forgetting she was a member of the Scottish constabulary, a group of people he would do anything to avoid.

She teased him at one point, by saying that she was sure that they'd met before, resulting in him vehemently protesting that they hadn't, beads of sweat appearing on his forehead. Eddie stifled a laugh as Catherine made Brian squirm, knowing full well that she'd never come across his friend in a professional capacity.

After an hour they parted company, but not before Brian had a last chance to have a word in Eddie's ear to tell him that "Ye really shouldn't fuck this yin up 'cos ye'll never get anither wummin like Catherine again if ye live tae be a hunner," which Eddie took to be a qualified endorsement of his "bidey-in".

CHAPTER 11 Jacko

Eddie had never seen so many police officers in one place since he'd been invited by a client to the New Year's Day Old Firm fixture. It was standing room only, but Eddie, as a guest, was given a seat in the front row.

The DCI chaired the meeting, sitting next to the DI and flanked by sergeants Kelly and Thompson. They sat behind a table facing the rest of the squad, who crowded in front of them.

The DCI started off by praising everyone for their efforts, and impressed on them the need to keep focused on getting the job finished. He then ran through a brief outline of all the murders, surprising Eddie by including Steven Reilly's death with the other three. Eddie learned nothing new, but it was a useful overview of the investigation so far. Beside him, in front of a large blank whiteboard, a WPC stood patiently, ready to record anything he deemed significant.

"Right, what have we got that is going to nail this suspect?" he looked around the room. "Anybody? Tom, what physical evidence do we have?"

Sergeant Kelly had been assigned to be the Productions Officer for this enquiry, responsible for all the material evidence relating to the investigation.

"The DNA from the Danielle Simpson scene, and from Eddie's pussy, is critical." He paused while laughter swept across the room, relieving the tension a little, and then carried on.

"But only if we can get him into custody, because we have

no match on the database for him. We have the polypropylene rope and boiler suit fibres that link the Craig Ferguson, Danielle Simpson and James Prentice murders, and all the evidence from the factory loading dock that confirms that it's the place where he nailed James Prentice to the board and dumped him into the river, but we have no forensics that tie the killer to either of those murders. The footprints weren't much help; they were Nike Air Max 90s."

A collective groan came from the room. This was the most common footwear worn by those arrested by the Strathclyde Police Force.

"All the forensic traces at the scene were from the victim, including a fair bit of blood, naturally. From its distribution, James was nailed to the insulated fibreboard in the store, and he must have been almost unconscious at the time as there were no signs of a struggle. The blood was more or less in four neat pools, and there was surprisingly little of it."

He hesitated, as everybody took a second or two to consider the cold brutality of the act. He then moved on to the other items of evidence.

"There were thirteen bottles of Blue Wicked in the building beside the dock, twelve of which held various concentrations of ethylene glycol. Eleven of these had James Prentice's fingerprints on them, but one had been wiped clean, as had the only bottle not containing the toxin."

One of the DCs interrupted. "Why would he wipe some of the bottles clean and leave them there? Why not just take them away?"

"This guy knows how to leave little or no forensic evidence. He must wear gloves for most of the time, but his victims would get suspicious if he wore them when he made initial contact with them. It figures that he must be very good at touching the minimum amount of surfaces possible, and cleaning up afterwards. He's only made a couple of mistakes; getting scratched by the cat, and leaving semen on the garage floor after raping Danielle."

Catherine tentatively raised her hand, and the DCI nodded for her to speak.

"He probably handed the first contaminated bottle to James, and let James help himself after that. He also would have handled the only unadulterated bottle, which he drank. He then cleaned both those bottles afterwards."

Everybody looked round. Catherine blushed at the sudden attention, but carried on.

"Did the lab test for DNA on the bottle without the poison?"

The DI answered her. "Yes, it was clean. The mouth of the bottle had been wiped as well. But very good, that scenario is certainly plausible."

Tom Kelly coughed, and continued with his review of the physical evidence. Looking for information about the nail guns used by the suspect, he'd paid a visit to a large builders' merchant and showed the sales staff a blown-up picture of the nails used in the Dundee cat case, and one of the actual nails recovered from the fibreboard raft. He glanced occasionally at his notebook as he spoke.

"Let's start with the heavier nail, from the James Prentice murder. It's a four inch nail fired by a pneumatic air framing nailer, and would have needed an air compressor, or more likely a tank of compressed air, to power it. Even when the trigger is squeezed, the gun only fires a nail when the nozzle is pressed against something solid. The depth the nail is driven into the wood is adjustable. This type of nail gun is mainly used in the building trade for putting up frames for houses, or other large wooden construction projects. Our nail was fairly generic and could be used in a number of different guns. The nailer would have done the job very quickly and efficiently, but both the gun and an air tank would have had to be carried to the scene and back. It would help to explain the large number of footprints on the route between the fence and the building." He looked up. "Any questions?"

There were none.

"The nails used on the cat were different. They were much smaller, and were fired in with a finishing nailer. These are often cordless, and nails are propelled by a small explosive gas charge, although they can also be air driven. They are generally used for skirting boards and door facings in the building trade, and they're also widely utilised in mass furniture manufacturing.

"The sales guys were very helpful and gave us a catalogue showing all the nail guns that they sell and They marked one or two of the most popular ones in each category, just to give us an idea of what we're looking for. None of the building contractors we've contacted knew of any stolen nail guns, but this guy could have bought these new. A foreman at Balfour Beattie suggested looking at dispersal sales; a large number of building firms go into liquidation every year and it's an easy way to buy second hand building gear, with relative anonymity. There are five or six companies who organise these sales in central Scotland. We've contacted all of them, and they are providing us with records for the last three years. Incidentally, the nails that were used on Danielle Simpson were standard six inch nails, and clean of any forensic traces. We think he used the same hammer to nail her up as he did to kill her with. The block that the killer used to hoist the body up before crucifying her was also clean of fingerprints or DNA, but there were some blue polypropylene rope fibres wrapped round the shaft of the pulley."

He looked round at the DI, as if to say that's all he had.

When Tom Kelly was handed the job of auditing the evidence, it left the job of office manager to the second sergeant. Neil Thompson was in charge of the incident room, and its day-to-day running, including communications. David Anderson turned to him and asked him to talk about all the sightings of the suspect.

"We've got a few eyewitnesses, and a little bit of CCTV footage. The woman in the Moorcroft off-licence in Renfrew remembers refusing to let James Prentice purchase some White Lightning cider, but she served a man about ten minutes later who purchased a couple of bottles of the same brand. When she looked out of the door, she was sure she saw James and this man walking away together in the direction of the Babcock Factory.

"The description she gave was of a man about five feet ten, medium or slim build, with a completely bald or close shaven head, possibly in his thirties, wearing some kind of sportswear – tracksuit bottoms or possibly sweats, a dark baseball cap, and trainers.

"A motorist going to Glasgow Airport from his home in Renfrew to start his early morning shift saw a man crossing the Inchinnan Swing Bridge at about four a.m., and said there was a dark car, possibly something like a Mercedes or a BMW, parked about a hundred yards short of the bridge. The man he saw seemed to almost change his mind halfway over, but then continued walking. He didn't get a good look at him, but said he was of medium build and average height.

"DC Douglas and Mr. Henderson traced the fish tank used in one of the first cat killings to a large pet store in

Abbotsinch Retail Park. The shop lady who made the sale gave a very good description of a man very similar in appearance to the one described by the woman in the off-licence. She also came in and did an E-fit picture for us, which is now up on the board, and which ..." he turned to the DI, "... may be released to the press to help locate this man."

David Anderson nodded and explained that they were waiting another twenty-four hours to avoid alerting the suspect while some other lines of enquiry were being completed, before his sergeant continued with his report.

"Further eyewitnesses came forward after the discovery of Danielle Simpson's body. Three women saw her leave the District Bar, where she was a barmaid, at the end of her shift. She was in the company of a man with a very similar description to those we've had already, although they said he might have been taller, maybe even six feet tall. Again, he wore a baseball cap.

"As some of you know, from CCTV footage on Paisley Road along from the District Bar, Danielle can be seen getting into a dark BMW, probably a five series, according to our resident car geek, with a man who could easily fit the previous descriptions given by all the other eyewitnesses. Unfortunately the camera was more than three hundred yards away and the pair of them, and the car, were facing away from it. Enhancing the video failed to make the number plate readable.

"DC Douglas managed to find another possible eyewitness, after looking for unusual patterns of antifreeze purchases. A man answering the description of our suspect bought two packs on three occasions over a five month period at a filling station in Barrhead, and two of these purchases were during the summer. He drove a dark grey BMW. Regrettably they only keep their CCTV tapes for two months, but they will contact us if the person returns to buy any more. The owner, who had served the customer on two occasions, thought that he would recognise the man."

This had come in just before the briefing started, and Catherine hadn't had a chance to tell Eddie.

The DI interjected again. "Let's get the E-fit picture circulated around all the filling stations and auto part shops in the area. If he's going to buy any more, I want to know about it." He turned again to Neil Thompson. "Anything else on the other vehicle?"

"No. It's a truck, probably a Transit with a tipper body, that's what was used to collect the aquarium from the pet store. Again, no numbers, but the saleswoman described it as blue and silver, with yellow and black markings, which could be half the trucks in Glasgow."

"Anyone else have anything?" The DI waited for a few seconds. He must have had second thoughts about his conversation with Catherine the night before, because he brought up the subject himself. It was either that, or he hoped Eddie would make an arse of himself.

"Eddie, our veterinary advisor, thinks he might have something."

Eddie, suddenly thrust centre stage, turned to address the whole room. He spoke hesitantly at first.

"As I explained a while ago to Detective Inspector Anderson, there's a link between childhood cruelty to animals and people continuing this abuse as an adult. There's also evidence that these people are more likely to be violent towards humans as well. By interviewing animal welfare personnel from a variety of organisations, we hoped to identify individuals who might fit into this category, but this has proved to be more difficult than expected, as these groups don't keep records as far back as we want to go."

A muffled derisive laugh came from the back of the room, and a few others looked sceptical. Eddie recognised the cynic as the disparaging detective who had sneered at him in the very first interview he'd had with the DI, but he ignored him and persisted in presenting his evidence to the squad.

"However, when I talked to the local Cat Protection coordinator, who has been involved in cat rescue services for over thirty years, she remembered a case from twenty years ago when a boy of six or seven impaled a litter of kittens on the spikes of an iron fence. The interesting thing about this is that she reckons it happened in the Ferguslie Park estate, and she named two possible streets where she thought the family might have lived."

"How are we supposed to find someone without a name, for a crime that was never on record, from twenty years ago? I suppose we'll be getting a medium in next." It was Eddie's pal, the sarcastic detective, who spoke out, but in fairness, he was probably voicing the thoughts of the majority of the assembled squad.

"Well, Detective Constable Douglas, on hearing this and having watched the speech expert's film made from PC Hamilton's testimony a number of times, realised that both 'Ferguslie Park' and 'Woodvale Drive' were recognisable on the video as places named by Craig Ferguson before he died." He turned pointedly to his heckler behind him. "Has everyone seen the film?"

An embarrassed silence fell on the room. The DCI had a deeply concerned look on his face, and was furiously making notes. David Anderson replied stonily that he'd had a quick look at it, but felt that the words were undecipherable and that he had failed to understand any of them until DC Douglas had hazarded a guess as to their significance. He had the grace to request that Catherine should play the video to the squad on the large screen in the incident room, which was connected to one of the computers on the workbench. A DC closed the blinds after Catherine had plugged the USB drive into the PC, and opened the file to play it.

There was a stunned silence while the short film ran, and for a few seconds afterwards, then the room erupted as everyone tried to speak at the same time.

The DI shouted for calm and suggested that Eddie or Catherine should speak first. Catherine stood up, walked over to the whiteboard, took the pen from the WPC, and wrote "Ferguslie Park" and "Woodvale Drive" on the board.

"Anything else?"

"Blue Wicked." This was one of the DCs. It was added to the board.

"Antifreeze." The DCI, this time.

"Estate." One they hadn't spotted, but obvious once it had been pointed out.

Catherine waited a few seconds, but people seemed reluctant to stick their necks out and guess. "Any more?"

When no one volunteered any further suggestions, she took out a piece of paper and copied the words on to the board. As she did, there were murmurs of recognition and comprehension from the group.

Once she had finished, the board read:

Ferguslie Park

Woodvale Drive

Blue Wicked

Antifreeze

Dark BMW

Other end

Ma Ma's hoose (my mother's house)

"We think that James was trying to tell the attending officer that the suspect lived in or near to Woodvale Drive, at the opposite end of the estate from where James stayed with his mother, and that he drove a dark coloured BMW. He also tried to tell him further details about his killer, like the Blue Wicked adulterated with antifreeze, confirmed by what we already know."

The DI, who'd belatedly realised that he should have come back into the station the previous evening and checked the film, covered himself by trying to take a little of the credit.

"When DC Douglas told me about this last night I was initially sceptical, but I was keen to bring this up today, as it could be the break we need to catch him. I want the whole squad out in Ferguslie Park today, and every last house visited. Take copies of the E-fit to show to the residents. Sergeants Thompson and Kelly will organise you into pairs. Any questions?"

The DCI, like many in the room, hadn't expected that the killer would have had a background in one of the more deprived housing schemes in Scotland. He said, "I will be surprised if the killer comes from somewhere like Ferguslie Park. We're talking about someone who's well organised, methodical and with enough knowledge to leave minimal forensic traces at very violent murder scenes. This type of serial murderer is usually white collar, educated. But, it's all we've got, so let's find out, one way or the other."

Catherine spoke just as everyone started to get up. "Can I ask everyone if you can take a quick look at the film again before you leave? There are still a few phrases on it that we haven't yet identified, and they could be significant. The file is available on the network. If you think you've got an idea about any of Craig's words, write them on the board, however silly you think your suggestions are."

While Tom Kelly and Neil Thompson were pairing up the officers and assigning each pair to a specific street for house-to-house enquiries, the DCI was having a quiet word with David Anderson. Eddie overheard him tell David Anderson, in a cold and clipped tone, that they needed to have a word in his office as soon as the house-to-house enquiry was organised. The senior officer then left, and everybody gradually filed out of the room after him. As the DC who had laughed at Eddie passed by Catherine, he leaned over and spoke quietly to her.

"Lucky, DC Douglas. Fucking lucky bitch."

Eddie didn't hear what he said, but he saw the change on Catherine's face, and he started to move towards them, until Catherine caught his eye and mouthed "no".

David Anderson came over to Eddie once everyone had left, and thanked him once again for his input. He then spoke to Catherine.

"You haven't done yourself any harm here, Catherine. We'll make sure this is all noted, and I'm sure you'll get an excellent assessment next time around."

"Thank you, sir, but Eddie had a hell of a lot of input into this, too."

"Yes, I appreciate Eddie's help, but he'll not be looking for a sergeant's post in the next few years, will he?" With that, he left, leaving Eddie and Catherine alone.

"Well done, I think you impressed everyone, especially the DCI."

"I suppose, but David Anderson can be so patronising. All that was missing was the pat on the head."

"Better than a pat on the arse," Eddie said, grinning.

"Very funny, Mr. Henderson. Did you notice that I've not been assigned to the house-to-house operation?"

"Do you think that's deliberate? Maybe they think you're too smart to be wasted on mundane stuff."

"Now you're being patronising," she said, but she was smiling as she spoke.

"What did DC Plonker say to you? I saw the expression on your face."

"Nothing I can't handle, Eddie, but thanks for trying to come to my rescue. I'm just glad I managed to stop you, or the cat would definitely have been out of the bag, and the arseholes in the squad would have had a field day."

-o-

They arrested Jacko later that morning. By then the squad, numbering twenty-eight, had covered the bulk of the bottom end of Ferguslie Park. Catherine, it turned out, was part of the coordinating unit at the station, gathering information as it came in from the groups on the ground. Very soon they had a name for the suspect, supplied by a number of the estate's residents when they'd seen the E-fit. Andrew Jackson, often known as Jacko, had been born in Ferguslie Park and still lived there. A number of older people in one particular block of flats remembered the incident of the impaled kittens and eventually, although the family had moved to another street in the estate, an address had been suggested, and confirmed by reference to the voter's register. Jacko's mother put up more of fight than he did when they arrested him, but his father never moved from his chair, making some comment along the lines that the boy always was a no-good waster.

When Catherine saw the suspect being brought in, she was surprised how nondescript he looked, and if she hadn't known of the terrible crimes he'd carried out, she might even have felt sorry for him. He was examined by the duty police casualty surgeon, who passed him fit to be detained and interviewed.

During the search of the house, in Jacko's bedroom, one of Sergeant Kelly's four DCs found two new and three used, but clean, orange boiler suits which must, they reckoned, have been washed at least once, and probably by Jacko's mother, which begged two questions. Did she know something about his crimes and turn a blind eye? And why the hell did he keep the boiler suits?

They also unearthed a second pair of Air Max 90s, in addition to the ones Jacko was wearing when he was arrested, which were bagged and removed for forensic examination. In a drawer at the side of the bed, there was a folding Stanley knife, a pack of paper face masks, a box of latex medical gloves, half a dozen packets of black rubber gloves of the type use for heavy duty cleaning, and a few pairs of leather rigger's gloves. He'd been clever enough to use the durable rubber or leather gloves for the more physical tasks, to avoid the risk of the surgical gloves bursting and leaving his fingerprints at the murder scenes.

The team searching the house failed to find keys for the BMW or the truck, and there was no sign of the nail guns, compressor, or any of the blue rope.

Interviews with Jacko's neighbours and other residents of the estate did give CID considerable background on him. Innocuous, almost to the point of anonymity, Jacko was seen as a loner, a bit of a mummy's boy. He had few, if any, childhood friends that they knew of. Apart from the kitten incident, which some of them remembered, there was nothing remarkable about him.

An older teacher, still working at the primary school he'd attended, described him as an average achiever, despite being brighter than most. When the class collected frogspawn and nurtured it in a tank in the class, he would stare at it for long periods just to watch the tadpoles eating each other until the surviving ones got bigger, developed legs and became young frogs. When the rest of the class was out at play one day, he stayed behind, and when the teacher finished her mid-morning cup of tea in the staff room, she found her pupil watching the tank intently as a dismembered frog was being eaten by the three other remaining inhabitants of the tank. He was clever enough to tell her that the creature had been attacked by its companions but she saw something in his eyes and knew that he had been responsible for the frog's mutilation. When she tried to prise the truth from him, he coolly and calmly argued his innocence, until she found herself almost believing him.

In secondary school, he often frustrated teachers who felt he had the ability to achieve reasonable academic success, but they all eventually gave up on him when he refused to respond to their encouragement.

When he left school, he was more often than not unemployed, but held a job from time to time that required him to wear a hi-vis jacket. There were a couple of reports that he spent a bit of his time over in Renfrew; nobody knew if it was a girl that was the reason, but most, especially women, doubted it, saying that he was a bit creepy. One neighbour said she'd seen him being dropped off at the end of the street in a lorry, by a fellow worker. She never got a good look at the driver, but he'd worn a hat and sunglasses on both occasions.

Catherine was present for two sessions of Andrew Jackson's interviews at Paisley police station and, despite her training, she found it chilling. He refused the offer of legal representation and seemed to revel in being able to talk about the crimes, giving the officers questioning him as much detail as they asked for; so much, in fact, that they came to the conclusion very quickly that Jackson was unquestionably the perpetrator of all the murders, and the cat killings as well.

When they asked him the reason why he'd started his killing spree, he'd told them that he hated jakeys and junkies. When they delved further, he admitted to always having enjoyed killing things, from a very early age, starting with beetles, butterflies and worms. He discovered torture before he was even at school, when an older child showed him how to use a piece of rounded glass from a broken bottle to focus the sun's rays to burn holes in paper. The young Andrew had turned this technique into a method for vaporising the internal organs of insects, causing them to struggle violently and sizzle, before popping in a puff of smoke.

The incident with the kittens had probably been the tipping point, as it provided him with two motives for his later crimes. The mother cat had the litter in a corner of the bin store at the back of the houses where Jacko's family lived. When the kittens were only a couple of weeks old, some of their eyes as yet unopened, Jacko had taken them one at a time and impaled them on a series of fence spikes behind the bin store while the mother cat was in her owner's house being fed. At first nobody knew who'd done it, but it came to light, when the owner asked around, that "Giro" George, a local junkie, had seen the boy kill the kittens, and he was asked to be present when they confronted the boy.

Jacko's father was drunk, as he often was, when the neighbour and his wife came to the door with "Giro" George and accused the boy of the kittens' deaths. The junkie's account was believed, which surprised the young Jacko, as his eyes looked empty and he could hardly string two coherent words together, but the boy's previous history of abusing small creatures lent credence to the story.

Jacko, no stranger to a beating from his drunken father, was whipped within an inch of needing to be hospitalised. As it was he didn't attend school for a week, and when he did, he still had the yellow and black remnants of bruises that he dutifully told the teacher were due do a tumble down a flight of stairs. Again.

During the beating, within earshot of the cat's owners and George the junkie, Jacko's howls and the thuds of his father's blows mingled with the sound paternal advice that was being delivered; that if the boy ever chose to repeat his actions again, Mr. Jackson senior would not be so lenient with him.

Embittered by his beating and the fact that a drug-using scumbag had been believed over his own protestations of innocence, Jacko withdrew further into himself, and was clever enough to never be caught again, until his arrest for the four murders. He harboured a hatred of cats, junkies and alcoholics that would ultimately lead him to commit the series of crimes that shocked the whole of Scotland.

During the interviews, he admitted to a series of additional animal cruelty incidents, some of which Eddie found on the list he had compiled back at the start of the investigation. The CID officers needed only to prompt him occasionally with a question designed to steer his boastful ramble in the direction they wanted.

He candidly admitted that in his early teens he started to

achieve sexual arousal during these episodes.

His use of antifreeze started when, in his late teens, he found a bottle in the outside cupboard used by his parents to store all the assorted household paraphernalia that was deemed unsuitable for inside the house. He never questioned why it was there, as his father had never owned a car, to his knowledge, but it ended the search for an easy and almost untraceable way to kill cats, and he embarked on the spree that Eddie's spreadsheet file had alluded to.

He told the detectives that after a while killing them at a distance didn't deliver the satisfaction that he remembered as a child, or the sexual arousal he enjoyed as a teenager, so he started devising ways to further his pleasure during the killings. The aquarium was inspired by his desire to watch one of his antifreeze victims die at close hand, and it opened up a whole new world of possibilities when he realised that antifreeze was a freely available method of immobilising cats enough to be able to do all sorts of other things to them.

He gave less away about his stay in Dundee, saying only that he had a casual job on a building site for a few months and had dossed down in a Portakabin on the job. He described the cat killings he had carried out while he was there in much greater detail, and it was at this point that the police were completely convinced that they had the right man for the Dundee killings as well.

His confession allowed the police to fill in many of the gaps in their knowledge, and confirm most of the facts they'd already identified.

He'd graduated to killing what he called "non-people", the alcoholic or drug using jakeys that he so despised, when he realised how easy it would be, and what an escalation of arousal and satisfaction he could expect. He had to disguise the taste of the antifreeze a little for his human victims by mixing it with some of the real stuff, if only for the first few drinks, but he liked the inevitability of the method: even if the subjects of his torture survived it, they were doomed by the damage already done to their bodies by the chemical he'd used to control them.

This proved to be critical for him in the Craig Ferguson murder. Jacko described how, just as he was nearing the point when he hoped he could somehow get the bar to come out of Craig's mouth, he heard a banging and shouting at the front door of the block and realised that he had to leave. He gave the bar a few more blows, until he could see the bulge at the base of Craig's neck, then cleaned up the scene as quickly and as thoroughly as he could, including any areas he had touched the day before. Fortunately for him, he hadn't taken the BMW to the flats when he'd returned to torture Craig.

He confirmed Catherine Douglas's theory about the bottles found in the James Prentice murder; he'd only wiped the first bottle he'd given to Craig, which he'd handled, and the bottle he'd drank from himself. In all the murders, he doctored all the drinks in his bedroom, and wiped them all afterwards, before returning them to their cardboard boxes for transport.

He was very proud of his record of leaving little or no forensics at the crime scenes, but was disappointed at the DNA the police had retrieved from the drop of semen he'd left on the garage floor. He also explained why he'd killed Danielle with a hammer. It was during one of the interview sessions when Catherine was present, and she told Eddie later that it was one of the most chilling things she had ever heard.

"Andrew, why did you kill Danielle with a hammer? Did she taunt you for having a small dick, or did you not manage to keep it up?"

The DI's question riled him and, for once, he lost his composure.

"No fucken way man, ah did her good an' proper, man. She wis squealin' like a fucken piglet. That wis the problem. The gag slipped an' she wis makin' a fucken racket, an' ah thought ah heard a car cummin', so ah had tae shut her up. Ah didnae want her tae be able tae tell onyone aboot me, so ah gied her a couple o' taps on the heid tae make sure. But naw, she knew she'd been shagged, nae worries there, man."

"What about your semen, Andrew? That was a big mistake, yes?"

"Aye, it wis, but it wis the only wan. Ah was aye careful, an' ah always wore a condom when ah had ma wee wank when ah killed them aw, but ah must hae spilled some when ah took it aff, after ah did that wee junkie hoor."

"Did you shag the boys as well, Andrew? Are you a bit of a shirt lifter too?"

Angry again, Jacko vehemently denied that he was in any way a homosexual.

They asked him about the car, and the truck.

"When ah saw yehs oan the telly efter ah killed the wee hoor, sayin' ye were lookin' fir a dark BMW, ah just left it up at Darnley wi' the keys in it. Some wee spanner'll be ridin' aboot in it thinkin' he's the king o' the toon. Ah wiped it aw first, but that disnae matter noo. Ah borrowed the truck aff a site ah wis workin' on."

He told them that after he discovered who Danielle's uncle was, which had given him a bit of a fright, he'd disposed of all the stuff that could connect him with the murders; the car, the nail guns and the compressed air canister, which he said he got refilled at one of the tool hire places, so he never had a compressor.

In between interviews Catherine phoned Eddie and told him of the progress they were making. He would have liked to ask him a few questions about the cat killings, but Catherine said there was no chance he'd be allowed to be in on one of the interview sessions.

He suggested to her that they should ask Jackson if he'd repeated all the cat killing methods on humans, in case there were any undiscovered bodies, and when she mentioned it to the DI, he said that she could do it during the final session with Sergeant Kelly, whom she briefed before they started.

The sergeant let Catherine do the questioning initially, working off a printed schedule detailing all the remaining lines of enquiry that the DI and the DCI wanted covered, mainly to do with cross-checking stuff they already knew. When she finished the series of questions that she'd been told to ask, Tom Kelly took over.

"You told us there were no other victims. Why did you stop? Did you lose your bottle after Danielle, because you made an arse of it?"

"Whit the fuck at ye talkin' aboot? She's deid, isn't she?"

"Aye, but not the way you planned it, Jacko." It was the first time any of his questioners had used the name most people knew him by, and was intended to catch him off guard.

"Fuck youse. For aw ye knaw, there could be mair bodies lyin' somewhere."

"No, we caught you before you could finish the game you started with the cats, didn't we. Anyway, you seemed happy to boast about all the rest. Why wouldn't you do that if there were others?"

Jacko was beginning to become irritated.

"Listen, cunts, ah'm sayin' fuck all else."

"You failed Jacko. We got to you before you could complete all the killings you intended. Didn't we?"

Jacko didn't respond, and after a few minutes, the sergeant suspended the interview. After Jacko had been taken away, he turned to Catherine.

"I think he would have told us. What had he got to lose?"

-o-

Six hours after his arrest, Andrew Jackson was charged with the murders of Danielle Simpson, James Prentice and Craig Ferguson, and remanded in custody. At his remand appearance the next day, the judge ordered a full psychological examination which, two weeks later, showed no reasons to suspect that he wasn't fit to face trial.

CHAPTER 12 Doubts

"What's bothering you, Eddie? You've been very quiet this morning. Got a hangover?" she teased.

The previous night's impromptu party had kicked off with a "few" drinks to celebrate having arrested and charged Andrew Jackson with one of the murders, and the fact that he was giving a full account of his crimes. Being a Friday, at four o'clock the DI told everyone to knock off early and added that anyone who fancied a celebratory pint or two, and a curry, should make their way to The Kelbourne, or meet in the Pride of India restaurant at seven. There was a buzz of conversation all evening about Andrew Jackson's confession, and the new information they'd learned from it. Eddie and Catherine had got back to his flat just after eleven, both pleasantly drunk, but capable of some sexual fireworks which only just reached the bedroom. Now they were lounging about and making a leisurely breakfast.

"No, I'm at that stage when my head knows I've had a good drink last night, but you wouldn't actually call it a hangover. That's not it."

"What is it, then? Is it because the case is over? Sometimes our guys get withdrawal symptoms after a big investigation ends. And you have the added trauma of going back to being just a vet." She smiled.

Eddie looked at her, saw that she was taking the piss, and smiled sarcastically back.

"I'm quite happy being a vet, although I'd be lying if I said I didn't get a buzz from being involved with this investigation." He scratched his head. "There's something niggling me, and I don't know what it is."

"I know what you mean. You haven't been part of his interviews but you've seen the transcripts, and I've told you what the ones I was involved with were like. Are you completely happy that Jackson is telling the truth?"

Eddie looked at her, curiously. "So you're having doubts as well, then?"

"I don't know. I was probably OK with it, until Neil Thompson said something last night in the restaurant. He told me that 'he didn't trust the wee bastard', which is a funny thing to say about a serial murderer, but the DI interrupted before he could say anything else. What do you have problems with?"

He shook his head. "I can't put my finger on it."

She sighed. "No, I guess I can't either. I want to be convinced that everything's done and dusted, but there's just something that's not right."

"Are you going in today?"

"I'll maybe head in for an hour this afternoon to finish up the paperwork and clear the cupboard they called my office. It's my responsibility to sort out all the documentation generated by our part of the investigation."

"There won't be any charges brought for the cat killings, will there?"

She smiled. "No. Not with four murder charges against him."

"Remember when that was all we were investigating?"

Catherine put her arms around Eddie as he fried some bacon. "I'm glad we did, otherwise we would never have met." She kissed the back of his neck teasingly, and Eddie dropped the rasher he was turning, burning himself with the splashes of hot oil.

"Shit!" he said, "you're dangerous! Sit down and behave yourself." He waved her in the general direction of the sitting room and feigned annoyance.

Catherine pretended to be in the huff, but sat on the couch with her legs stretched out, letting her dressing gown fall open just a touch to distract him further.

He brought over the bacon butties and coffee and sat next to her on the couch, still not quite believing that she had picked him to be with.

They didn't bring up the subject of the enquiry for a while, because what started as a little teasing during breakfast ended up back in the bedroom, where they stayed until lunchtime.

-o-

She returned from the station about four, after a couple of hours that saw her box up all the papers pertaining to Jackson's animal welfare crimes and complete all the outstanding tasks that were expected of her.

Eddie was at the kitchen door again, playing with his Post-it notes. He'd removed them all and piled them up on the kitchen table, and then divided the glass down the middle with a marker pen. He'd written a title at the top on each side, "Solid" on the left, and "Shaky" on the right, and was in the process of putting the notes back in their newly designated places.

"I see you like to use technical terms," she said, laughing.

He'd already stuck a whole sheaf of notes on the left hand side, overlapping each other, under the "Solid" heading, and there were one or two on the right. There were also a number of Post-its straddling the line in the centre.

"Hiya." He glanced at her, his mind on the task in hand. "It sums it up though, that's all it is; a few doubts."

"Why do you think this will help now?" she asked. "It didn't help last time."

"You say that, but how do you know it didn't? Perhaps it helped us to organise the whole thing in our minds, gave structure to our ideas."

"Very profound, Dr Henderson, but I'll have to take your word for it."

"Well, I thought that I'd sort out which areas I have doubts about, and the ones there's no problems with. For instance, if Jackson's DNA is a match with both the samples we have, then it will go into the "Solid" section, but until the results come back, we'll leave it sitting in the middle; on the fence, so to speak."

"OK. Let me give you a hand. It'll be quicker with two. And the DNA result should be in today, by the way. They were rushing it through."

"That's quick. It will be a relief to have it confirmed, but I'm sure there's no doubt about it. What else is happening?"

"They're going to do identity parades with the women from the bar, the pet shop and the off-licence, and there are still a few open lines of enquiry running. The DI, Sergeant Thompson and about six DCs are still working on the investigation until it's all wrapped up."

"Right." He showed her a pile of new notes. "I've added a few more. I think that's brought everything up to date."

They continued sorting through the notes, most of them ending up on the growing stack down the left hand side of the glass. Occasionally, Catherine would show Eddie a note and ask him if he had any issues with it, and vice versa.

By the time the pile of notes on the table had dwindled to nothing, one side of the door was bristling with notes, as if the door had grown a paper beard, while the other side was far less crowded. There were probably more in the vertical line of notes hiding the dividing line down the middle than there were on the "Shaky" side.

Eddie removed the large collection of notes they were happy with, and put them in a clear plastic folder that he produced from his desk in the living room. He then piled all the notes from the centre line on the table.

"These have mostly minor issues, or we're just waiting for results. There's no point in spending a lot of time on them just now. We should start with the ones we definitely aren't comfortable with."

Eddie spread out all the remaining notes over the whole glass pane.

"Now, let's see what we've got."

There were eleven of them. Catherine and Eddie took turns to read them out to each other.

"Women in District Bar – Jackson's height."

"CCTV outside pub."

"Aquarium stand."

"Access to buildings."

"Jackson's confession."

"Craig Ferguson's last words."

"Danielle, support while nailed to door?"

"Car not found."

"Truck not found."

"Getting James into river."

Eddie had his say first. "The first two are about the same thing: the height discrepancy. The issues with assembling the aquarium, nailing Danielle to the garage door and getting James Prentice into the water are of practicality. Could one man have done them on his own?"

"I don't know. It would have been very difficult. And did Jackson have easy access to the premises used for the murders? None of them showed signs of forced entry, so he must have had keys for them."

"Or he scouted around for unlocked buildings."

"I suppose, but what about the fact that no trace of the car or the truck have been found? That's a bit unusual, isn't it?"

Eddie had to agree. "Yes," he said, "and it's not the only thing that's a bit strange. What about his interviews? Does his confession not sound a bit rehearsed? You were there, what did you think?"

"No, on the whole, I just think he enjoyed telling us about it and he knew too much for it not to be mostly true. But I think there's a couple of areas where he wasn't quite as forthcoming. I'm still suspicious that there might have been more murders, but I can't understand why he wouldn't want to tell us about them, unless he was protecting someone else."

"We still have to try and decipher the rest of Craig Ferguson's words. There's a few that we haven't got yet."

They took a moment to reflect, then Eddie voiced the growing feeling they both had.

"We've got to consider the real possibility that there are two of them, haven't we?"

-o-

Three events took place the next day, which were each in their own way critical in the case against Jacko.

First, his DNA matched the samples recovered from both the garage floor in the Danielle Simpson murder and the cat's claws that Eddie had provided.

Secondly, all the women but one who had taken part in the Identity Parades picked out Jacko. The lone dissenter was one of the customers from the bar where Danielle worked, who just wasn't sure enough to say for certain. The filling station owner had no such doubts, which pleased the DI, in no small measure.

Finally, a subcontractor who did regular maintenance work for a property management company admitted occasionally employing workers on a cash-in-hand basis, one of whom was Andrew Jackson. The builder only came forward when he heard that one of Jackson's fellow workers had recognised him and had already contacted the police.

The property management company was the one retained by the legal practice whose client list included the former owner of the house where Danielle Simpson had been murdered. The assumption was that Jackson had used his employment to find a suitable site for his plans for Danielle, and had borrowed and copied keys that allowed him easy access to the secluded garage.

Employment records from other building contractors and property maintenance firms in Glasgow and Dundee also started to flood in, and the DI looked around for the nearest targets to sift through them. The wide boys in the squad were good at looking busy elsewhere when things went a bit slack, so it was Catherine and two of the youngest DCs who were assigned the task of wading through each new package, searching for signs that Jackson had worked for the company at any stage. They concentrated initially on the companies that had maintained or provided security for the properties used by Jackson as locations to torture and kill his victims, but when nothing obvious appeared, they had to widen the search to include all of the employers on the list.

Catherine spoke with Eddie about the slow tedium of trawling through sheet after sheet, contacting each employee to check that Andrew Jackson had not used a false name. Eddie suggested putting all of the employees' names onto a spreadsheet, along with their contact details, the dates and locations of their contracts, and their employer's identity. It was then easy to sort it by name to see if there were any patterns which could indicate that Jackson, or anyone else, had had access to all the buildings that murders had been committed in.

He set it up for her, and when she showed Neil Thompson the next day how it would save time in the long run and perhaps turn up some extra information, he told her to go for it. She made three copies of the spreadsheet, as Eddie had advised, and demonstrated to the two younger detectives what she wanted them to do.

With three working on it, the lists grew rapidly over the next couple of days, even with more data arriving on a regular basis. At the end of each day, she would copy the two younger men's lists and add them to her own, then take the file home to let Eddie play around with it. She justified his involvement by telling herself that Eddie had never been taken off the case, and was still officially being retained as a consultant on the investigation.

-o-

Eddie was home before her, so when Catherine arrived at Eddie's flat she opened the door to the smell of a freshly cooked omelette and toast, and was welcomed by Eddie with a kiss and a glass of wine, and instructions to sit down at the table and dig in.

When they'd finished eating, she picked her bag up from the floor by the door, where she'd thrown it when she got home, and fished around in it for her USB stick.

"Put that in your laptop," she said, handing it to him. "I've put some video on it for us to take a look at."

He took it from her, plugged it into his computer and sat down on the couch.

"I didn't know you were so open-minded. I'll watch it, but it's not really my thing, unless you've done one of yourself, just for me." He grinned, until a cushion caught him firmly across the back of his head.

"Idiot!" she said, still wielding the weapon she'd used to punish him with. "It's work. The CCTV footage from outside the pub, and a few new bits. We think we've got more clips of Jackson on film, buying the insulated fibreboard."

Eddie immediately became serious, and she smiled inside at the change in him when something technical stirred his interest.

"Right," she said, sitting down beside him, "watch the two new pieces of film we have, and then look at the footage from outside the pub again. The owner of this yard recognised Jackson from the picture we released, but it took him a while to dig out the right tapes."

Eddie watched intently as a grainy black and white picture of a builders' yard appeared on the screen. A small transit type truck with an aluminium tipper body pulled into view, and the driver jumped out.

Eddie pointed. "That's Jacko."

The man entered the sales office and came out a few minutes later clutching a piece of paper, probably an invoice. He then disappeared out of shot, but returned a short while later and loaded a number of large, thick boards on to the back of the van, then got in and reversed to turn the truck round. Eddie got a glimpse of a face behind the windscreen as the man drove out of the yard.

"Why did he buy so many sheets? One of these is probably the board the poor bastard was nailed to." Eddie felt strange watching the start of a process that he knew ended in a life cruelly snuffed out in the most horrific way.

"I know. Watch the next bit." Her training made her just a little better at dissociating herself from the victims. For a CID officer, it was the only way to survive in the job.

The second clip was almost identical and Eddie thought that Catherine had screwed up and put the same clip on the film twice, but when Jacko got out this time, he was wearing sunglasses and a baseball cap, and when he came back out of the office, he was carrying a couple of large plastic bags, which he flung in the back of the truck. As before, Eddie got a brief glimpse of his face as he drove off.

"What do you think?" Catherine asked, pausing the film.

"Well, I suppose it's too grainy to get the registration number, but it would be nice to know what he bought the second time he was in, although I could hazard a guess."

"You're right about the number plate, but have a look at this."

She reached into her bag and pulled out a photocopied invoice, which she handed to Eddie.

"False name," he observed, "and no surprises. Two types of nail cartridges, polypropylene rope, ten orange boiler suits, a hammer, various plastic funnels, standard four-inch nails. It's all here. And look at the date: 2009. Why the hell did this guy keep the security tapes?"

She laughed. "Get this. The owner was investigated by the Inland Revenue about ten years ago, and they spent about four weeks pulling his company apart, trying to prove he ran two cashbooks. Pissed him off and nearly brought his business to a standstill, all over what he called a malicious tip-off. The Revenue never got him, but ever since then he keeps a video record of everyone who visits the yard, and he can tie each one up with an invoice if the taxman ever comes calling again."

"Smart. And it's lucky for us he did, but it only corroborates what we already know."

"Watch them again."

He looked at her inquiringly, but replayed the clips.

When the clips had finished, he nodded.

"Are you thinking the second man isn't Jacko? The quality's not good enough to recognise faces, but I'll agree there's something different about him."

"I couldn't take it to the DI, but to me, they're different men. The second one seems taller, or thinner, and they walk differently. Look."

She played the clips again. Although Eddie had his doubts

about Jacko working alone, he wasn't convinced that there was enough on these clips to persuade the DI to look seriously at it, especially as Catherine's boss seemed determined to declare the case closed.

"Now watch the CCTV clip from outside the bar again," she said.

As Eddie watched it, Catherine spoke. "That's the taller version of Jacko, isn't it?"

"It would seem that way, but what if it was just Jacko and he was trying to change his appearance, by wearing higher shoes or something? That would also affect his walk, wouldn't it?"

"I never thought of that, but why would he want to do that?"

"Well, he was planning mass murder. I would assume that he would want to hide what he was doing."

"There's more. Look at Angela Robb's film again. It's on the USB drive too."

They watched it, and Eddie still couldn't make the missing words make any sense.

"I think he's trying to say 'someone else' and possibly 'two of them'. I know it's not very clear; I've watched it fifty times, and although it's not actually Craig's words, it was voiced by someone who witnessed them. It's amazing that we've got as much from it as we did."

"They're not as clear-cut as the others, but it's certainly the best match so far. See what David Anderson thinks." Even as he said it, he could imagine the DI's predictable dismissal, but if it was as she thought, it was too important to sit on it.

They discussed the pros and cons of taking it to the DI. She was reluctant, as she felt they had too little to convince him with, but in the end Eddie managed to persuade her to talk to Sergeant Thompson. He switched off his laptop and walked over to the shelves where he kept his CD and DVD collection.

"Now, let's forget about work for a while. I've got a pile of films here that I've been meaning to watch for a while. Pick one, and I'll pour us another glass of wine."

"I didn't know you were so open-minded. I'll watch one of them with you if that's what turns you on, but it's not really my thing." She grinned, dodging the cushion tossed her way as he headed for the kitchen.

-o-

"Thanks for listening, Sergeant. You probably think I'm overreacting, but should we take it to the DI?"

"I've got a couple of concerns about Jackson myself. Even so, I'd normally say no if one of my DCs came to me with something as flimsy as this, but you've had good instincts so far, no doubt aided by your very good veterinary friend, so I'm inclined to take it a bit more seriously."

She hoped that he didn't notice her blushing, and she lost a bit of her composure at the thought that their relationship was being talked about, but she didn't try and deny it.

"Who knows?"

"There's some talk that you two might be an item, but no one knows for definite. I only knew for sure the other day."

"How did you find out we were together? We've been very careful to keep it to ourselves; I didn't want it to complicate things while Eddie was involved with this investigation."

"Don't forget I'm a detective." He grinned. "I saw Eddie almost come to your assistance at the briefing, when that prick made some underhand remark to you, and I also saw the look you gave Eddie to tell him you could handle it yourself. Only couples do that, in my experience." He smiled kindly at her. "Listen, you deserve somebody decent after the way that arsehole sergeant cheated on you, and Eddie seems like a nice bloke. I'll not say a word to anyone, so if you want to keep it to yourselves for a while, that's fine. But people will gossip, and however you try and hide it, it'll be next to impossible not to give it away."

She was about to reply, but he hadn't quite finished.

"Oh, and by the way," he added, "I think he's a very lucky young man."

This time she knew he'd notice her blushes, but she didn't mind. She realised that he was just looking out for her.

"Thanks Sarge; he is a nice guy, but I'd rather keep it to myself until this is all wrapped up."

"And that brings us back to what we should do now. Why don't we just keep an eye on it? I'll get you put back on the squad, as we're still working on a few areas of the investigation that need tidied up. You can concentrate on the ones where we have issues; those that you and I think would benefit from another look. I can give you some help but the rest of the squad will be busy enough making sure all the information we have already stands up to examination, so you'll be mostly working on your own. We'll go to the DI if and when there's something a bit more substantial."

"That would be great Sarge; I'd be happier doing something, even if it eventually comes to nothing." She hesitated. "Listen, I've been running a lot of this stuff past

Eddie; have you got any problems with that?"

"Well, officially he's just been retained as an animal welfare consultant but, seeing as that side of the investigation has had a major influence on the outcome, and Jackson's capture in particular, I think he has a right to be involved in some capacity. Just be careful. Remember he's not police."

-o-

"We ran a fantastic enquiry, and I must thank my team for their methodical approach and hard work."

Eddie watched the press conference with interest, and a little bit of cynicism. David Anderson spoke first, and tried his best to steal most of the credit for the arrest and charging of Andrew Jackson for the four murders.

"Andrew Jackson is an evil man who preyed on some of the most vulnerable members of society, those with serious addiction issues. The Strathclyde police force takes the welfare of every sector of our society seriously. The streets of Glasgow, Renfrew and Paisley are now much safer with this man in custody."

The DCI, while giving him his moment of glory, wasn't going to let him get away with all the credit. When it was his turn to say a few words, he made sure that everyone knew that the success of the investigation was not just down to the cleverness and efficiency of the police.

"We shouldn't forget that this murder inquiry started as an animal welfare investigation. Without the persistence and abilities of the SSPCA inspectors and the veterinary consultant on this case, we might still be a long way away from where we are today. Having said that, I would like to echo Detective Inspector Anderson's praise for all my officers who took part in this investigation, and who did a tremendous job. I'd also like to thank the Scottish public for their assistance in finding this cold and callous killer."

Eddie, basically a shy person, was glad that he hadn't been named. It avoided having to answer questions from curious clients and staff at the practice.

-o-

When Catherine got in from work, she updated Eddie on the case, told him about her meeting with Neil Thompson, and explained what she'd been doing since.

"We got the results back on Jackson's Air Max 90s. They found mud in the treads that matched the ground near to the loading dock at Babcock's. Seems that the soil there is quite unique, full of contamination from years of factory debris. Sergeant Thompson is going to allow me to follow up on the areas of the investigation we have doubts about. I've been completing the file of contractor's employees, and I've also scanned any information relevant to our concerns on to my USB pen. It's just about full."

"I'll have a good look at your list later. I've had a few ideas that might help. And I've borrowed an aquarium from the pet superstore identical to the one used by Jackson when he killed the cat. I wanted to see if one man could assemble it by himself."

"And could you?"

"I haven't tried it yet; I thought I'd wait until you were about. I also wondered if it might be possible to validate whether the man on the CCTV footage from the pub could be someone else other than Jacko."

"How do you plan to do that?"

"Can we get access to the camera that took those pictures?"

"I suppose so. Why?"

"Well, you are about the same height as Danielle, and I am three inches taller than Jackson. If we park a car in the same spot, you and I can do a quick reconstruction. We should be able to tell if the man in the film is my height or Jacko's. We could also do that with the builders' yard."

"OK, I'll go with that. Anything else?"

"Can we get access to the Babcock factory, and the store?"

"Yes, it shouldn't be a problem. I can see where you're going on this one. The two people question?"

"Yes, we can pick up a bit of fibreboard at the builders' yard. He says we can borrow one and try out the CCTV camera."

"Oh, you phoned him, then."

"Aye, I thought it would be worth a go. What about the Danielle Simpson crime scene?"

"Can I ask what you want to look at there?"

"Whether or not one person could lift up a body, and nail it to the door."

"And you've already got some rope here."

Eddie looked slightly embarrassed. "No, but we can pick up at the builders' yard too."

"I suppose they have that in stock, too." She was laughing now.

"OK, OK, take the piss. I just thought it was worth doing. What about Saturday?"

"Eddie, you're so romantic. There's me thinking you

might take me away for a nice weekend break, as we're both off."

"We could still do that. I've got Monday off as well." He could see the benefits of a weekend away with Catherine, but he was also desperate to find out if there was any substance to their suspicions that somebody else was involved in the killings with Jackson.

-o-

In the end, their Saturday investigations ran into Sunday, but they did get away for a night after that, catching one of the best autumn days to explore the hills and forests around Pitlochry, staying in a beautiful little hotel just outside the town.

Even there, their conversation occasionally came back to their growing belief that they were looking for a second killer.

Early on Saturday, when they'd turned up at the CCTV control centre at Blochairn, in Glasgow's east end, the supervisor was waiting for them. They explained what they wanted to do, and he said he would make sure the camera was trained on the right spot, and that he would have a copy of the tape ready for them by the time they returned.

The owner of the builders' yard was equally helpful. He watched while Eddie retraced the footsteps of Jackson and his alleged accomplice, and gave them the tape to take away with them. He also donated a short length of rope and a board similar to the one James Prentice floated to his death on.

By the time they reached the factory it was just before three o'clock, but the security guard said he was in no hurry and that they could take as much time as they needed. He hung around to watch, curious and most likely bored, and this proved very useful. Eddie set up his video camera on a tripod to catch the experiment on film.

Eddie drilled some holes in the board with his small cordless drill and fashioned some handholds and footholds from short sections of rope that he threaded through them. He placed the board on the floor inside the store, and Catherine got on to it and held on as best as she could, using the holds Eddie had made. Eddie then attempted to lift the board out through the door. As he slid it along the floor, it made obvious marks on the concrete. When he reached the doorway, he had to tilt the board to get it through and he struggled to make it. As he pulled and twisted, Catherine's bodyweight moved to the side, and she did well to hold on. As the board scraped through, it shed pieces of insulation, and marked the doorway, and got stuck halfway through. By the time Eddie released it and got it out into the yard, he was pouring with sweat. Catherine got off the board and they inspected it. There was a fair bit of damage to the board, and a couple of large gouges out of it.

Making use of the idle security guard, they repeated the procedure with the two of them carrying the board, Catherine clinging on to the hand and footholds as before. Although they still had to tilt it to get it through the doorway, it was much easier and it caused virtually no additional damage to the board.

Eddie photographed the board and checked that the video camera had recorded their efforts. By now the light was fading, and hunger and tiredness persuaded them to call it a day. After collecting the tapes from CCTV control, which were ready as promised, a carry-out curry, a glass of wine and an early night left them refreshed enough for an early start the following morning.

After breakfast, Eddie and Catherine let themselves into the practice where he had stored the aquarium kit. Leaving the actual aquarium aside, he started to assemble the stand as per the instructions. He soon got into difficulties. The stand was designed, once it was assembled, to derive its strength and rigidity from the weight of the tank. As such, it was very unsteady until the tank was placed on it. Eddie made four or five attempts to place the tank on the stand, using his knees to try and stop it from shifting, before he gave up, exhausted. Without someone to help steady the stand, it was impossible.

After a short rest, and still on film, they tried again, with Catherine holding the stand this time, and Eddie managed it in a few minutes, with little effort.

Sitting down for a quick lunch gave them a chance to have a breather, before heading out to Giffnock and the garage Danielle had died in. Letting themselves in with the keys they'd collected the day before at the lawyer's office, they set up their recording gear, attached a pulley similar to the one currently residing in the evidence store to the garage roof, and rigged a length of polypropylene rope through it.

Catherine then put on three or four layers of old clothing to protect her body from the rope sling that Eddie was going to try to support her weight with.

Again he struggled to manage on his own, not only to lift Catherine, but to hold her suspended while he tried to position her as Danielle had been on the garage door. There was a way of securing the end of the rope to the garage lock mechanism that allowed him to free his hands, but even then it would have been difficult, if not impossible, to hold someone's limbs in place and use a hammer to drive home the nails at the same time. If Danielle had been even partly conscious and had resisted in any way, a second person would have been essential.

Eddie transferred all the footage they'd taken with the camera, plus the new CCTV clips, on to his laptop, while they showered and chucked a few items in a bag. Later, curled up on a couch in front of a roaring fire on a romantic Perthshire autumn evening, they watched the film clips on Eddie's laptop.

Although later in bed they couldn't keep their hands away from each other, as was often the case in the newness of a relationship, they were both more subdued in their passion; a reflection of their shared concern that there was still a multiple killer out there, perhaps with further murders on his mind.

-o-

Catherine and Eddie sat in the room with Sergeant Thompson as he watched all the video they'd pulled together to try and convince him that Andrew Jackson had not worked alone.

"I can see where you guys are coming from, and I think we should put some more effort in to follow this up, but I'm not convinced we have enough here to persuade the DI that there were two killers. My concern is that if we go to him with it now, when it's a bit subjective, it could be counterproductive. I could see him telling us to stop dicking around, wrap up the investigation and move on. My advice is to continue our enquiries discreetly, and I'll drag it out for as long as it takes to get something a bit more substantial."

Catherine had warned Eddie that this would be the probable outcome, even though they both believed that the individual from the original clips was close in height to Eddie in the reconstruction videos, and so very likely taller that Andrew Jackson, and that their recordings of the aquarium assembly and of their reconstructions at the crime scenes showed that it was unlikely that Jackson had acted on his own.

"There's a couple of other things, sir," Catherine said. "Neither the car nor the van has turned up yet, and neither have the nail guns or a compressor or air tank."

"There could be any number of explanations for that. Anything else?"

"Yes. None of the crime scenes showed any signs of forced entry, and Jackson only had access to one of them through his employment. We think his accomplice is also in the building or security business and could get hold of keys for these locations."

"Then that's an area we can concentrate on. Plus, let's keep looking for the vehicles. It's a pity we haven't got access to Jackson, to see if he has any explanations for all these discrepancies."

"I know sir, but we'll work on these other areas."

"If another victim turns up, we'll be able to question him. In the meantime, I'm not trying to be negative; I think you have something here, and I'm impressed with what you've done already. We just need a bit of patience and restraint here, and it will come. Keep me in touch with what you are doing at all times."

-o-

The flow of information from building contractors and security firms had slowed to a trickle, but they had amassed a vast amount of employment details with possible connections with the murder locations. Most of it was now on the spreadsheet and Catherine and Eddie spent a few hours every night sorting through it, trying to find any pattern that could point to Jackson's killing partner.

A few days after their meeting with Sergeant Thompson, a few significant bits of information fell on to Catherine's desk.

The letters that Catherine had sent out to GP surgeries belatedly bore fruit, when a doctor's receptionist working at a health centre in Paisley phoned to say that a man had been treated for infected cat scratches on his hands and arms on the third of June. She gave Catherine the name of a patient, who lived in Renfrew. When Catherine phoned him, he knew nothing about his supposed injuries. After questioning him further, she realised that Jackson had used the man's name and address to get medical attention, but he must have guessed, or known, that he was registered with the practice, that he was roughly the same age as Jackson, and that he wasn't a frequent attender of the practice who would be easily recognised by the doctor or his staff.

When she phoned the surgery back, the woman confirmed that the man hadn't been seen by a doctor during the previous four years, but when he came in to be treated for the infected scratches, she thought he had been accompanied by a friend, a taller man about the same age and build.

Catherine then spoke to the doctor who told her that the man had refused to attend the hospital as advised, so she'd given him a course of antibiotics and insisted that he needed to go to casualty if it got any worse. She never saw the man again.

Another piece of the puzzle fell into place when one of the dispersal auctioneers contacted CID with details of the purchase of an LDV Maxus 3.5 tonne LWB single cab tipper, a compressor and an air driven nail gun at an auction of building equipment from a well-known contractor who'd gone into liquidation in February of 2009. The purchaser had paid in cash, and the name and address registered with the auctioneers turned out to be false. They were able to supply a registration number for the vehicle and the make and model number of the nail gun, but so much time had passed, nobody could remember anything about the buyer. They promised to send over a copy of the bill of sale. Jackson must have purchased an air tank elsewhere, but he'd lied about the truck and the compressor.

Catherine checked with the vehicle licencing authority in Swansea, but the truck hadn't been road taxed since the date of purchase. Catherine presumed that it was seldom used and was kept in an off-road location the remainder of the time. She put the registration number of the truck on to the PNC vehicle list, on the off chance it would turn up at a routine check.

When she told Eddie that evening he was optimistic that all this information would eventually yield results, but in the meantime he reasoned that Jackson's accomplice must be on their list of building and security employees, and that they should be able to narrow it down.

First of all, Eddie selected all the companies that had done work at any of the locations where either cats or people had been killed, or had provided security for those places. He then highlighted all the employees who had worked with at least one of the companies at any one location. Finally, he cross referenced these locations to see how many employees had connections with every single location. Eddie was surprised to find there were fifteen employees in this category, but he reasoned that this was common within the construction, security and maintenance industries, where there were large number of workers who moved around regularly.

Of these fifteen, only five had worked in Dundee during the time the three documented cat cases had taken place. All but one of them had current addresses on the south side of Glasgow.

Eddie printed out a list of the names and gave it to Catherine, and she said she'd have a word with the sergeant in the morning with a view to checking those five out, and contacting Dundee CID to do a little bit of investigating at their end.

Satisfied that they were making progress, they shared a bottle of wine and watched a subtitled French film on Channel Four, before falling into bed an hour or two later than they'd intended.

-o-

Eddie headed to work the following morning knowing that he had a busy day ahead. The routine surgery at the practice was spread pretty evenly between all the members of the small animal team, but each vet, although not having a specialised field of expertise, tended to have a recognised area where they had a bit more ability than some of the others. It could be quite random. Gavin, for instance, did most of the orthopaedic stuff, but also did mammary strips, while Eddie seemed to have a knack for cruciate ligament repair, so this was the one orthopaedic operation that Gavin didn't regularly do.

Today, Eddie had two bitches to neuter and one cruciate ligament to fix, in a young Labrador called Henry. He had already checked the X-rays that had been taken the week before, so he wasted no time in anaesthetising Henry and putting the new synthetic ligament in, still leaving him the two spays after lunch.

After he'd finished the op he checked his phone. A text from Catherine had come in about 11.30, telling him that three of the men on the list had been checked and eliminated on the grounds of age, appearance and in one case, ethnicity. Eddie tried phoning her, but got no answer, so he replied to her text, telling her to be careful.

When he'd finished his second op of the day, he checked his phone and saw that he'd missed a call from her. He logged into his voicemail and heard her slightly garbled message. She had visited the address listed for the fourth man on her list, Spencer somebody, and had been suspicious, so was following him. She also said that she'd sent a message to Sergeant Thompson.

Eddie tried to call her, but her phone was switched off, which surprised him, as she had often told him that her golden rule was to always have her phone on as a line of communication while she was working. He sent a text to tell her to contact him again as soon as she could, and returned to the theatre to anaesthetise his last patient.

As he operated on the dog, he was working on cruise control, his mind more and more on Catherine; *where is she; why isn't she answering her phone?* He couldn't bring himself to hurry the surgery: he knew that could be a recipe for disaster, but it seemed to be dragging on forever, as he agonised about Catherine's wellbeing.

Eventually, he placed the last of the skin sutures, wrote up the dog's meds, left instructions for her aftercare and made for the door. The nurse shouted after him as he ran through reception, but he didn't hear her.

He dived into his car and gunned it out into the street, narrowly avoiding hitting one of the other vets on the way out. As he sped up the road, he took a quick look at his phone: no more calls or messages. He drove on, glancing in his rear-view mirror, not wanting to be pulled over for speeding when he really needed to find out where Catherine was.

He arrived at the police station within a few minutes, ran past the desk sergeant, flashing the visitor's badge he still had, and went up the stairs two or three at a time. He looked in at the squad room, which was deserted, and hurried on up the corridor. Neither of the two sergeants was in their shared room, and he went on up the stairs at the end of the corridor. He knew there was no point in talking to one of the DCs, and while Sergeant Thompson would have been the most likely officer to listen to him, and act, he wasn't available, so he headed for the top floor, where he knew the DI and the DCI had their offices.

He scanned the doors and about halfway along, he saw DI Anderson's name. Praying that he was in, he rapped on the glass, turned the handle and walked straight in.

David Anderson looked up sharply from his paperwork.

"Eddie, what can I do for you?"

Out of breath, and frantic with worry, Eddie struggled to speak.

"It's Catherine. She's in trouble. I think."

"Eddie, sit down, you're in a hell of a state." He rose from his chair and made Eddie take the seat in front of the desk. "Now, start again. Where is DC Douglas?"

Eddie didn't know where to start, as he realised the DI didn't know about either their suspicions that there was a second murderer or their investigation, and he was even more sure he didn't know about their relationship. He decided to leave that bit out, and concentrate on the investigation.

"I was trying to get in contact with Sergeant Thompson, who knows all the details. We have all been following up on some loose ends from the investigation, and we've come to the conclusion that Jackson was not working alone."

The DI looked furious.

"And just when was I to be told about this?"

"I don't know; that was Sergeant Thompson's call. Where is he?"

"At a family bereavement; why?"

"Because Catherine tried to contact him earlier today."

Eddie went on to explain everything, from the CCTV evidence, to their experiments to back up their second suspect theory, and their search through the employee records. He then told him about the messages and phone calls that Catherine had made, and how her phone had been registering as switched off for the last few hours.

"She never does that," he said, "she always has her phone switched on."

The DI looked at him strangely.

"Catherine and I are in a relationship. She tells me stuff."

"And what do you want me to do?"

Eddie couldn't believe his ears. This was one of the DI's squad, possibly in trouble, and he was asking him?

"I don't know, but what if she's found a suspect, and he's realised she's tagged him, there's no saying what he might do."

"Eddie, you're probably reading far too much into this. For a start, we don't have any firm evidence that there is a second suspect, and it would seem unlikely that DC Douglas would have found him on her own if he did exist. It's even less likely that she would be harmed by him. I can understand why you might be worried and emotional, but you mustn't let personal feelings cloud your judgement."

Eddie asked him if he could call Sergeant Thompson, as

Catherine might have left a more detailed message on his voicemail.

"I'll see what I can do. The best thing you can do is go home. DC Douglas will hopefully contact you there. I will be in touch once I have talked to the rest of my officers."

He got up to show Eddie out, and put a patronising arm around his shoulder. "On you go Eddie, let us deal with this."

-o-

Furious but beaten, Eddie left for home; he had only driven a short distance when he realised that the DI was going to take no effective action and his chest tightened painfully. He hoped that he was wrong, and that Catherine was waiting for him at the flat with a non-functioning phone.

When he reached home, he shouted her name as he opened the door, but there was nothing.

For five minutes, he just sat with his head in his hands, then he seemed to galvanise himself. He fired up his laptop and opened the spreadsheet containing the names of the men that Catherine had planned to investigate. Eddie ran the searches again, and printed out the results. He looked down the list to the fourth name, and looked at the address.

It was in Renfrew, and the man's name was Spencer Naylor.

CHAPTER 13 Catherine

Catherine Douglas had been bright at school, and pretty enough in her own way. She was regarded as a bit aloof, so she didn't have a string of young male admirers running after her in her teenage years, but had a small circle of good friends of her own sex that she retained into adulthood. She was always very good at sport, and was a better than average achiever academically. Under pressure from her peers, teachers and parents, she applied and got into university to do a degree in languages, but although she did well in her studies, she was restless and unfulfilled.

She lost her virginity at fresher's week to an opportunistic third year student, mainly because she felt ridiculous arriving at university still a virgin, and had a couple of other "flings" in her first year before acquiring a steady older boyfriend for the rest of her time at university. By then, she had blossomed into a lovely young woman and developed a nice way of rebuffing the frequent attention of the male students in her year who, if she was honest, she found irritating and shallow.

In her fourth year, she attended an undergraduate careers conference, intended to match students up with companies and organisations looking for graduates to work for them. Strathclyde Police had a small stand at the show, tucked away in a corner and poorly attended. Catherine found it by accident while looking for the toilet, and spent the rest of the afternoon talking to a female Detective Inspector about a career in the police force.

Unlike ninety per cent of her classmates, Catherine didn't return to university for an honours year. Instead, she left with an ordinary degree and joined the police, much against the wishes and advice of her parents, friends and boyfriend, a postgraduate PhD student whose next career stage was to move abroad to one of the universities in the USA; he had expected Catherine to up sticks and join him.

When she told him that her intention was to stay in Scotland *and* become a policewoman, he tried to lay down an ultimatum; that it would be difficult to continue their relationship at a distance, and she should really take this into consideration.

She duly did and, to his surprise, decided that it would be best if they both went their separate ways. She and a few friends went backpacking in Europe for six weeks, where she found it easier than she expected to forget him.

During her induction into the police at the Scottish police training college at Tulliallan, she excelled, and was given the prize for the top cadet at her passing out parade. While she was there, she met and started going out with a newly appointed sergeant from Paisley, who was there doing a course at the same time.

Her probationary year flew in, and her first uniform posting was on the north side of the river, in Maryhill. She also became engaged to her sergeant, and moved in with him. They were seen as the ideal couple; good-looking, affable, and with good career prospects; they would have made an ideal pair for a police recruitment poster.

He seemed to always find excuses why they shouldn't get married, and as neither of them wanted kids, it wasn't a pressing issue. He was one of the most popular officers on the force, and although they were together a lot, they had their own independent lives as well. He was good to her, and she knew that she'd be happy with him for the rest of her life.

When she went back to Tulliallan to do her sergeant's

course and exams they were in contact nearly every day, and she went home at weekends to see him. The course was supposed to finish on a Friday, but there was a weekend function for visiting police dignitaries and the college wanted a day to prepare for it. The tutors did an extra couple of evening sessions early in the week, and let the students away late on the Thursday afternoon.

Catherine thought she'd surprise her fiancé, so she hadn't told him she was coming home early. She let herself in, keeping as quiet as possible and, seeing his coat hanging up, assumed he would be in the sitting room watching TV. She crept through, but there was no one there. It was then she heard a noise in the bedroom and, horrified, she recognised the sounds of a couple having sex. She could see a girl's naked back through the partly opened door and his body under her, with various items of police uniform strewn over the floor and on the chair next to the bed.

She backed out quietly, leaving a note saying what she'd seen, and that she would make arrangements to have her stuff picked up over the weekend.

Within a week, he had moved in with his new companion, and the flat was put on the market. She stayed with her mum and dad for a couple of months until she bought a smaller flat in one of the nicer parts of Paisley, where she had lived alone until she met Eddie a few years later.

Her confidence had taken a knock, and she hadn't applied for any acting sergeants' posts, a common prelude to gaining a permanent position.

As she went into work the morning after she and Eddie had whittled the number of possible suspects down to a shortlist of five, she mulled over the possibility of getting her career back on track and applying for the first vacancy for a sergeant's position that came up.

When she arrived at the station she went straight to find Sergeant Thompson, but one of the DCs told her that he was away at a funeral and might not be in at all that day. She left a copy of the list on his desk, having first written on it a brief summary of how they'd got this far, and a note saying that she was going to start following up the suspects. She had a look in the squad room, to see if there was a spare DC around to help her, but the only officers present were all busy.

By the time she'd seen the first three men on the list, she was beginning to wonder if they were thinking along the right lines. All three were easily eliminated from suspicion, as with no stretch of imagination could they have looked anything like the man she'd seen on the CCTV clips. She sent Eddie and Sergeant Thompson texts telling them this, then headed over to Renfrew to check out number four. On the way she stopped at a café and had some soup, a roll, and a cup of tea.

She had worked the area as a uniformed probationer, so she knew roughly where the street was, in the Newmains area of the town, a seventies social housing development. She parked the car in the nearest available space, about a hundred yards away. Checking the address again, she walked towards the house.

The woman who answered the door was about sixty, Catherine guessed, or perhaps a badly aged fifty. She presumed it was Spencer Naylor's mother. Catherine showed her ID card.

"Mrs. Naylor? I'm Detective Constable Douglas, from Paisley CID. I was hoping to talk to Spencer."

"He's no' in at the moment."

"Do you know where he is?"

"Naw. Ah don't."

"When will he be home, Mrs. Naylor?"

"Ah couldn't tell ye, miss, he didnae say."

"Will he be home today?"

"Probably no'. He's workin' away."

"I thought you said you didn't know where he was."

For the first time, the woman looked flustered.

"Ah don't knaw where he is, ah just knaw he's workin' away somewhere."

"Right. I'll make a note of that. Do you have a contact number for him?"

"Naw, he sometimes phones when he's away, but he disnae huv a mobile."

"That's interesting, Mrs. Naylor. We can check that up."

Catherine stood for a few seconds, saying nothing. It was the woman on the doorstep who looked away first.

"If he does contact you, or he comes home, can you get him to contact me? My number's on here." She handed over her the card, then walked away. The woman watched her for a few seconds and then slammed the door.

Catherine walked past her car and round the corner. She saw an open doorway into one of the blocks of three storey flats, and slipped inside. Taking a chance, she took the first flight of stairs. As she had hoped, there was a window facing back the way she had just come, but it was just too low. She climbed up to the first floor landing, then up another flight. This window was much higher, and she could just see the Naylor house.

Something about Mrs. Naylor had annoyed her. She hadn't

even asked why Catherine wanted to speak to her son and she had glanced to the side a couple of times when the young detective had mentioned him.

She tried phoning Eddie and Sergeant Thompson, but reception on her phone was down to one bar so she sent a text to the sergeant, in the hope that he was back in work, telling him where she was and why.

She looked out again, then pulled back from the window as she saw a man come out from the passageway between the Naylor house and the neighbouring one.

"Fucking right!" she muttered under her breath, uncharacteristically. He looked just like the person in the CCTV footage. He was walking briskly, nervously looking up and down the street as he came towards her. She shrank further into the stairway, away from the window, as the man that she knew must be Spencer Naylor passed by the building she was hiding in. She got a good look at him; close up, he didn't look as much like Andrew Jackson as he had from a distance or on video, but she could understand why some people confused the two men.

She watched as he disappeared down the road, and raced down the stairs to follow him. A woman coming out of her flat on the first floor looked at her strangely, but Catherine ignored her and rushed to the front door. She stuck her head out first, but he'd already turned the corner, heading towards the main road.

Walking as fast as she could, occasionally breaking into a trot, she made it to the corner just in time to see him turn right on to the main road. She suddenly realised that she could see part of the massive Babcock factory complex in the distance, the scene of James Prentice's murder. Her excitement grew as more and more about the pairing of Jackson and Naylor began to make sense.

As she walked she tried phoning Eddie again, but only succeeded in reaching his voicemail. She left a message as she hurried towards the main road, just giving brief details of the man she was attempting to follow. She was so intent on speaking into the phone that she almost reached the corner without taking care that Naylor wasn't looking back at her.

He wasn't, but he was making for a row of shops that looked as if they would once have had flats above them. The upper floors had been demolished, leaving a terrace of single storey retail units with flat roofs, so typical of Glasgow and its surrounding urban areas. There was a mini-mart, a launderette, a hairdresser, and one boarded-up empty shop in the centre of the forlorn row.

Catherine had to dodge behind a parked van as Naylor looked back before diving into the narrow alleyway between the shops and the adjoining row of houses. She tried to phone again, and cursed as she saw the low battery warning flashing on the phone. She thought she'd got a text off to the sergeant telling him where she was, but she couldn't be sure. She tried to text Eddie but the phone died completely on her.

She hesitated for a moment, weighing up the risk of letting this chance slip against the personal danger she might be putting herself in if she pursued it any further without backup. She looked around for a public phone, but there was none in sight. Reasoning to herself that the suspect didn't know she was following him, she decided to see if she could find out where he had gone, then, no matter what, she would retrace her steps to her car, connect up the mobile to its charger and phone the station.

She made her way down the alley, trying to remain inconspicuous, and entered the service yard behind the shops. A collection of large commercial wheeled bins, some stacks of bound cardboard, and a large enclosed skip cluttered the space. She could see that each shop had access to the yard, mostly through doors protected by steel roller shutters. All of them at her end were closed, but she could see a partly opened one beyond the skip.

She cautiously crept along the side of the skip, losing sight of the door as she did, but as she got near the corner, the doorway again came into view. She didn't take her eyes off it in case somebody came out, which allowed Spencey, standing hidden on the other side of the skip, to sneak up behind Catherine and grab her. He put his hand around her nose and mouth to muffle any sounds she might make, and encircled her midriff with the other arm, lifting her off her feet and propelling her rapidly towards the open door, then inside the shop. On his way through he kicked the internal wooden door shut, and it locked behind them.

The room they were in was dark and her legs gave way as he slammed his knees into the back of her. She fell forwards, still firmly in his grip. Even though she landed on something cushioned – *probably a mattress*, she thought – his full weight landed on top of her and the breath was knocked out of her. While she was still heavily winded, he pulled her arms behind her back and bound her wrists tightly with sticky gaffer tape. He then put a folded cloth across her mouth and wrapped another length of tape around her head to keep it in place.

Despite weeks of self-defence training at various police training courses she had done little to resist but, albeit belatedly, the mechanism that prompted her to fight finally kicked in and she lashed out hard with her legs and caught her attacker firmly on the kneecap. He grunted, swore, and stood up, aiming a hard kick to her right side, which connected with a sickening thud. A searing pain passed through one side of her chest, and she briefly wondered if she was having a heart attack, but reasoned that it was more likely that he had broken one or more of her ribs.

While she was immobilised again, this time by pain, he used the opportunity to bind her legs, again using gaffer tape. She was absolutely powerless, and he made sure he had complete control of her by doubling up all her bindings with rope. She knew without being able to see that it was the blue polypropylene rope that they had found at all the other crime scenes, and that she had gone, by making one major error of judgement, from hunter to victim.

She forced herself not to cry as she thought first of her parents and then of Eddie. She tried not to think of what might be coming; her only slight hope was that Naylor wanted to use her to try and barter for Jackson's freedom.

She numbly observed in the gloom that her attacker, looming over her, was wearing surgical gloves.

"I expect yer wunderin' why yer here, ya dozy bitch."

That hurt nearly as much as her side, hands and feet. She made no sound, until he grabbed the handful of hair that was tied back and yanked her to her knees.

"When ah ask ye sumfin', ye fucken answer, right?"

This time she nodded, and made an affirmative grunt.

"That's better, filth; just remember who's in charge, here."

He walked over to the wall and turned on the lights, a series of overhead fluorescents. She blinked uncomfortably as her eyes became accustomed again to brightness. She looked round and realised that she was in an abandoned butcher's shop; the rails and hooks that had held sides of beef, lamb and pork still present. A now silent refrigerated counter ran half the length of the room, its quiet hum probably dormant for years. A large white insulated door with oversized handles told her where the cold store was, and she wondered which of these fixtures her captor had in mind for her torture, which she already knew, to her terror, was inevitable.

Where the doorway and display window had once been she could see a wall of insulation board that she recognised as similar to the stuff used in the James Prentice murder. She knew now why they'd purchased the extra boards, and presumed it was not for heat insulation; it would be just as effective at keeping any sound she might make within the building.

"Nice, eh?"

She looked around, and nodded, deciding that not antagonising him was her first priority.

"The shops aw close at five. After that, nae cunt will be able tae hear us. Until then, Ah'm gonnae keep that gag oan ye. Don't bother tryin tae get oot o' thae ropes, ah'll no' be fawr away."

He pulled over a metal chair with a PVC and foam seat, and hauled her onto it, tying another rope around her waist and the seat to hold her in place. He then picked up her shoulder bag and rifled through it, finding her purse, and opened out the section her cards were stored in.

"Catherine, eh? Too nice a name fir a piglet, ah'd say."

He approached her and started going through her pockets one by one. She cringed as his hand brushed against her breast while he removed her CID identity card from the inside pocket of her jacket, and when he picked her phone and her set of keys out of her skirt pockets, he made sure he'd felt right to the bottom reaches.

Looking at his face while he searched her, however, she didn't get any sense that there was anything sexual in his actions. Nevertheless, she was worried that he might find out about Eddie and her. He now had the keys which would provide him with access to Eddie's flat, and perhaps a motive for going there. She'd only had a set for a few weeks and now she was wishing he'd never given them to her.

He put the bunch of keys to one side, as if to say that he'd deal with them later. He saw that her phone was switched off, and when he tried to switch it on, it would only display the red 'low battery' symbol on the screen.

She saw him shaking his head and heard him tutting, and she realised that there were good and bad sides to her dead phone. It meant that even if anyone was looking for her they wouldn't be able to find her by locating her phone. On the other hand, this Naylor guy wouldn't be able to know who she'd called or sent texts to in the last few hours, unless he had a charger for it. She was glad now that she didn't have one of the most up to date smartphones, because she knew he didn't have the same phone as her when he dropped it on the floor and ground it to pieces with his heel.

She tried to think of the best way to play it. Telling him that she'd phoned for backup might make him panic and run, but she was pretty sure he would kill her first. No, the best way to act was to convince him that there'd been no calls for help, that no one knew where she was and that no one was coming to save her.

She was surprised and strangely proud that despite her fear she was still able to think clearly, but she knew that if he got round to harming her that could easily change.

"Ah'm Spencey, by the way," he said, as if they'd met in a bar, or at some work-related function.

There were obviously a few things he wanted to say without her being able to interrupt, because he kept her gag on to start with, but she got the impression as he talked that at some point during the proceedings he would want her to be able to respond. She reckoned she would have at least a few hours before he took the gag off, and he might want her unharmed for a little while afterwards to get information from her about Jackson. She silently prayed, although she wasn't religious, that Eddie or Sergeant Thompson would realise that she was missing and work out where she'd gone.

"Ye must hae thought ah wis a right silly bastard, thinkin' ah didnae knaw ye wid wait fir me tae appear efter ye'd talked tae ma mither. Ah don't knaw if ye were waitin' fir me tae come hame, or ye'd guessed ah wis in the hoose, but ah saw ye haulin' yer daft wee arse intae thon flats and ah thought therr wis a gid chance yehs wid follow me, an' here yehs urr."

She knew she'd been stupid, but the last thing she needed was for him to point it out. With hindsight, she should have gone and called for backup first. She could even have asked in one of the shops for the use of their phone.

"That's the trouble with you polis, ye think people like us cannae be as clever as youse. Just because we talk like this, an' cos o' where we come fae, doesnae make us thick. Yer probably thinkin' that yeh've got Jacko, an' yeh've found me, but once ah've dealt wi' you, ah'm out o' here, and no cunt'll ever find me."

He walked away, not waiting for her response. For a short while she neither heard nor saw anything of him. She was desperate for a drink of water, and she knew that sooner or later emptying her bladder would become an issue, but even if she could have asked for a drink or a toilet visit, she was determined not to. She doubted whether Naylor was capable of feeling sympathy for her, so that wasn't a route worth going down. Instead, she felt she needed to show him she was stronger than she really felt.

It could have been fifteen minutes or an hour; Catherine was having great difficulty keeping track of time. Occasionally she heard sounds behind her, but she couldn't identify them. At one point she thought he heard him talking on the phone, then laughing, but she couldn't be sure. Then he was in front of her and to her horror, he was holding a large butcher's knife and a bottle of blue fluid.

"Thirsty, cunt?"

He reached round to the side of her face and ripped off the gaffer tape holding the gag in place, then put the knife against her throat. "One squeak frae you and ah cut wan o' yer ears aff, or maybees a finger."

She kept quiet. Her two hours' grace had shrunk to nearer one. He lifted up her blouse with his left hand and sliced down through the buttons to expose her chest, with only her bra covering her nakedness. She flinched as he inserted the tip of the knife under the short strap between the cups, and flicked the knife outwards, splitting her bra in two and exposing her breasts, her chest now heaving in terror.

He placed the tip of the knife against her left nipple and told her that she needed to have a drink with him. He placed the bottle to his lips and took a quick sip. She tried to see if the level of fluid in the bottle had changed, but she couldn't quite say for sure.

He put the bottle to her lips and gently increased the pressure of the knife on her flesh. "Take a drink, cunt."

Tears running down her face now, she took a mouthful and pretended to swallow, then gagged, spilling some of the sweet liquid from her mouth, and feeling it run down her chin and drip onto her chest.

She felt the sudden pressure, the sharp pain and the warm flow of blood as the knife sliced into her. It wasn't much more than a nick, but the effect was to make her gasp, and almost choke on the liquid that was still in her mouth, swallowing some of it. Pressing home his almost complete control of her, he put the bottle to her lips again, and told her again to drink.

This time, she tried to swallow, just a little, and retain the rest of the fluid in her mouth. He seemed to be fooled, as he smiled at her and nodded approvingly. She repeated this a few times, wondering how much of the stuff was fatal, and whether it was even worth trying to delay the inevitable. When he wasn't watching, she let it trickle slowly from her mouth and down onto her lap, to join the pool of blood gathering from the steady dripping of her sliced nipple.

After a while he seemed to be satisfied, and he put the bottle down on the counter, checking that the level had gone down. Again she took the opportunity to dribble the contents of her mouth down her chin, and, once more, he appeared not to notice. The taste wasn't unpleasant, just sweet and sickly. She didn't know if it was her imagination, but she was starting to feel light-headed, and if she hadn't been in such a horrific situation she might have given in to its dulling effect. For a moment she wondered if Naylor was taking the piss and it was just alcohol he was giving her, but then she remembered Eddie telling her that the initial effects of ethylene glycol were very similar to those you would get from any other alcoholic drink, and the taste wasn't too unlike that of any of the alcopops that had become so popular.

"How's Jacko?"

The question shocked her. Was all this just for an update about his evil friend? She dredged up the courage to fight him from depths she didn't know she had.

"Fine. He confessed to everything. He knew we had him."

"Good lad. That wis oor agreement if wan o' us got caught. He didnae say nothin' aboot me, though?"

She took a gamble. "He did. How do you think I got to you? There was nothing else that could have led me to you."

"Baws tae that, whore. The place wid be swarmin' wi' pigs if he'd told ye. How did ye find me?"

"I'm telling you; he didn't give us your name, but he told us roughly where you lived, and who you worked for." She remembered the name of one of the companies he'd worked for, and told him. For the first time during their short conversation, he looked slightly uncomfortable. She knew she had to keep him wanting more information from her, to make keeping her alive more useful to him than having her dead.

"Ah don't believe ye, Jacko widnae dae that." He looked thoughtful. "How did yehs catch him, then?"

"He was careless. He raped Danielle Simpson and left us a semen sample on the floor, so once we had him in custody, we had the evidence to convict him."

"Silly wee cunt. Ah wundered at the time why he fucking chibbed the hoor. He told me she'd got the gag off and started shouting. Ah wis only away fir ten minutes tae get some scran, an' when ah came back, her heid wis melted. Ah told him just tae finish the joab."

She didn't know what was worse; the casual banality of the two killers taking a break from Danielle's torture for a Scotch pie buttie, or the dismissive way he talked about snuffing out her life. She told him that Jacko had described the rape to her, and how Danielle had threatened him that she would tell his mate, and he'd panicked and hit her with the hammer when he heard Spencey coming back. She willed him to believe her lie. It helped that it was probably close to the way it had happened.

"Silly wee bastard. Wan mistake. An' he told me the video didn't work. He must hae switched the fucken tape." He started laughing.

She'd hoped that he would react more to the news of his partner's deceit.

"That's not how we found him."

"How then?" he asked, annoyed at her, and perhaps Jacko, too.

"That was the amazing part. Somebody phoned in with a name and possible address, after they remembered Jacko impaling a litter of kittens on a fence as a boy. It was just a matter of time until we found him after that."

She was becoming stronger, encouraged by the fact that he hadn't tried to make her drink again.

"Anyway. He told us that he had someone else helping him, but that he was the main man."

"Yer lyin', ya snidey wee minge. Jacko would never hae said thon. He knew that ah wis the wan that was in charge."

He got up and slapped her face, hard. She tried not to, but she started sobbing quietly. "Why should I lie? I'm going to die anyway, now that I've drank that stuff."

"True," he said, "ah suppose yer right. While we're on the subject of the truth, who did ye tell before ye came here? Ma guess is naebody."

Catherine's sobbing became louder. They were real tears that she'd managed to hold back until he'd started forcing her to drink antifreeze, but she also realised that he might believe that her breaking down meant that she had lost all hope, confirmation that she hadn't told anyone. She knew that her survival depended on how much of the antifreeze she could avoid drinking, and how soon somebody managed to find her.

She tried to get herself together for one last effort to make "Spencey" postpone any plans that he had for her by engaging him in some sort of dialogue.

"Why didn't you and Andrew Jackson complete the series?" she asked him, just as he picked up the bottle again.

He laughed.

"Whit makes ye think that?"

"Well, all the cats you killed, and the way you killed them. You haven't managed to use all those methods on people yet, and you're never going to do it now; you'll have enough trouble just avoiding getting caught. I left details of who I was going to investigate, and they'll get around to finding you eventually, especially if you kill me."

"Ah bet ye asked Jacko the same question. Whit did he say?"

"We asked him if there were any more victims. He initially said there weren't, but when we wound him up a bit, he hinted at there being others. He'd admitted to all the rest, so why wouldn't he tell us details if there were any more? It's not as if it would make any difference to his sentence, as he'll never get out anyway."

"Fucken discipline, hen, fucken discipline. Good on ye, wee man. Ye see, he wid only give ye whit ye already hud. He was a clever wee bastard. You do know that once all the fuss has died doon, in a couple o' years, ah'll go an' visit the wee cunt."

"You'll get caught before that. You'll never see Jacko again."

He laughed again. "Ah wid have a bet on wi' ye, but yeh'll no be aroon fir me tae cash it, so there's nae point."

"So ye did kill others, then?"

"Always the fucking polis, eh? Well, ah'll tell ye; whit way o' killin' did ye think we missed?"

"We never found any bricked up victims, or anyone that was strung up."

Spencey went over to the counter and picked up a plastic bag, took out a brown envelope and tipped the contents on to the glass surface. He picked up one of the small digital video tapes from the pile and walked somewhere behind her, returning with a video camera. He ejected a tape from it, holding it up to let her see. "This is you, for my collection."

So he was taping all this. Her head slumped, although she didn't know why his filming her made it any worse. He put the other tape in and flipped the small screen round to an angle where she could see it.

At first, because of the size of the screen and the bright fluorescent lights, she couldn't make out anything, but Spencey went over and switched the lights off directly above where she was sitting. She could then see that she was looking into some kind of narrow pit, and two young men were staring up at her, agony etched on their drawn faces. They were holding each other up, although it would have been doubtful if there was room for them to sit down even if they wanted to.

"That was efter three days, an' they were boufin', man. Therr ain sick an' piss an' shite; If ah'd been them, ah think ah'd huv had the baws tae kill wan an' other. As it wis, they lasted another two days. The top's aw covered over noo, so the smell doesnae bother nae cunt."

Catherine felt sick. She didn't know if it was what she had just seen, the fact that he was taping what he was doing to her, or the toxic effects of the ethylene glycol beginning to make her ill.

"So that's yer walled up cunts." He put the tape back in the camera.

He walked behind her again and she presumed he was putting the camera back on a tripod again.

He spoke from behind her. "Every one is on tape; ah'll be takin' them wi' me, just fir auld times' sake. Ah doan' huv the wan wi' Jacko giein' that young crucified burd a seein' to, but apert fae that, there's only wan missin'."

He walked round in front of her. He was holding a length of blue polypropylene rope, with a noose knotted at one end. "Whit wis that ye were whinin' aboot a minute ago? We hadnae completed oor 'series', wis it?"

Catherine could only watch, numbed and horror-stricken, as he looped the long end of the rope over one of the butcher's hooks hanging from the rail on the ceiling. He then went behind her, tilted her chair backwards, and dragged it across the floor until she was directly under the hook.

She screamed, and shouted for help. She tearfully implored him to let her live, knowing that it was of little use.

From behind, he yanked her head back by her hair and placed the noose over it, tightening it onto her neck. Perversely, she thought of their experiment at Danielle Simpson's crime scene, when Eddie had tried to hoist her up; how uncomfortable it had been, despite the padding.

This would be ten times worse.

Spencey walked round in front of her and took hold of the free end of rope dangling from the hook.

Smiling at her, he started to take up the slack until she could feel the rope cutting into her neck, the knot snagging one of her ears, causing it to fold painfully, and the rough abrasive rope pinching the skin at the back, just at her hairline.

He took the end of the rope and wrapped it round a metal toggle sticking out from the white tiled wall. Walking over to his latest victim, her neck craned to try and relieve as much pressure as possible, he stuck his face right up close to hers.

"If it hadnae been you, ah wid huv had tae find a wee jakey burd, so yeh've saved some cunt's life, the day. Ye can think o' that when yer danglin' therr."

He took the knife again, for the last time, and cut the bonds tying her to the chair. He grabbed hold of the rope again and pulled, this time with all his weight on it.

"Ye'd better climb, bitch."

Suspended a foot off the ground, and choking, she desperately swung her legs, trying to feel for the chair. It took her three attempts, and she just about lost consciousness; the lack of oxygen, the pain, and the constriction around her neck making her eyes bulge and her vision blur. Eventually she managed to half-stand up on the chair, easing the pressure. She gasped desperately, filling her lungs with cool, delicious air, but Spencey took up the slack again, grinning at her.

"Ah've left ye maybees just enough slack tae breathe a wee bit, as long as ye stay balanced, an' ye don't pass oot. Ah'm just gonnae get ma shit taegether, but ah'll be hereabouts for another wee while, an' ah'll take the video wi' me before ah go."

A few minutes went by, and she thought she heard some music from the back of the shop, and a door slam, but she may well just have imagined it.

Dangling there, trying to keep her balance, she knew that her strength, both mental and physical, was limited, and that at some point soon, one way or the other, her full weight was going to hang from that rope and finally extinguish her life.

CHAPTER 14 Brian

Eddie sat staring at the fourth name on the list for no longer than five minutes, trying to take deep, slow breaths and control his rising panic. The one thing he had was this Spencer Naylor's address, but he didn't relish the prospect of going there on his own. Apart from Neil Thompson, there was nobody in the police who he could turn to, and unfortunately the sergeant was out of reach just when he needed him.

He hesitated, because there was no rational basis for the action he was about to take other than the fact that the guy was a true friend; in desperation, he opted to phone Brian and ask for his help. He was certain his pal would drop whatever he was doing to help, but even he was surprised when Brian arrived within twelve minutes of his call.

"Ye owe me a taxi ferr," he said, on stepping into Eddie's flat.

In the car, on the way to the Naylor address, Eddie told Brian just as much of the story as he needed to know for him to grasp the seriousness of the situation. When they were almost there, Eddie had sudden doubts about what they were doing, then he saw Catherine's car sitting in the same street, not more than a hundred yards from the house.

It was Brian that urged caution. "If ye march in therr, gung ho, ye'll just alert them that ye knaw sumfin'. Let me go and ask for him – maybe they'll think ah'm just an ordinary gadge, a friend o' his."

Although Eddie saw the benefit of this, he watched with more than a little apprehension as his friend approached the house. The door was answered by a woman, who listened for a while, said a few words, then closed the door as Brian turned to retrace his footsteps.

When he got into the car, Eddie grilled him impatiently about what had been said.

"Nothing much, Eddie, but the auld bag's hidin' sumfin, ah can just tell. She said she didnae knaw wherr he wis, but that he's away wi' his work an' she hasnae seen him for two or three days."

"I'm going to phone the police. They've got to respond to an emergency call."

"Whoa, Eddie. Think aboot it carefully before ye do sumfin' stupit. First; whit are ye goan tae tell them? That yer burd, a polis wummin, hus been kidnapped? They might no' even come oot. Second; if they do, they'll send a perr o' uniforms who'll barge in mob handed. Ah don't think she's there. The auld bag's no nervous enough. Ah think she's coverin' for him, but no necessarily pert o' it."

Eddie knew he was right. His only option was to go back to the DI, or try and get hold of the Detective Chief Inspector, and plead with them to do something. He said this to Brian.

"Eddie, if that's whit ye want tae dae, ferr enough, but therr's another option. Ye said that this nut job killed Muller Simpson's daughter, right?"

"Muller Simpson?"

"Arthur Simpson. Everyone knows him as Muller. He's heavy duty."

"Oh, Arthur Simpson. Aye, but it was his niece, Danielle."

"Get in contact wi' him. He'll help ye."

"How the fuck do I get in contact with him? And why the fuck would I?"

"Listen, the word's out that he's lookin' tae tan this guy Jacko once he gets in tae jail, proper. But he disnae knaw aboot this other bam. If he did, he'd want a word wi' him, wouldn't he?"

"OK, so you think it's a good idea to get a Glasgow gangland boss involved in helping what is currently a police investigation? Are you fucking mad? We'd get put away ourselves! How's it going to help Catherine?"

Brian turned to Eddie and gripped his arm.

"Listen, mate. You've been ma friend since we wir in prams, an' ah sometimes wunder why ye bother. Ah know this girl means everything tae ye, and a widnae say this if ah didnae think it wis true, but if ye call the polis she's deid: This cunt's maw will phone him, an' he's off, an' ye never see Catherine again."

Eddie crumbled. His lip quivered and his eyes filled. Brian felt compelled to look away, but he didn't.

"Okay." Very quietly, Eddie gave in. "How?"

"Give me two minutes."

He got out the car, mobile in hand and walked up and down the street, head nodding as he talked. Eddie, sitting in the car, numb, couldn't hear what Brian was saying, but the conversation didn't last long. He got back into the car.

"We've to wait here. He's coming."

They sat, saying nothing, Eddie with his head in his hands. Brian put his arm round Eddie's shoulder.

"We look like a couple o' poofs here."

Eddie laughed, involuntarily. He turned to Brian. "Thanks."

-o-

A silver Mercedes glided past and stopped outside Spencer Naylor's house. A squat, menacing man got out and approached the front door. He had a three-quarter leather jacket and the walk of a boxer. The same woman opened the door, spoke to the man and let him in, closing the door behind them.

The two other men in the Mercedes got out, looked across at Brian and Eddie, and nodded, before walking up the path, opening the door and going in.

"Let's go." Brian told Eddie.

They got out, walked down the street and followed the two men into the house. Eddie briefly wondered to himself how the fuck it had come to this.

Nobody could remember who had given Arthur Simpson the handle "Muller", or why. Perhaps, Eddie thought, he had a passion for those little rice pudding pots as a teenager, or it could have been that his scoring ability in backyard football games and squat appearance reminded his friends of Gerd Müller, the world class German footballer. Or maybe it was because "muller" often refers to destroying something, a nod to his more violent side. Whatever the reason, the name stuck, and he entered his twenties, and the start of his career as a professional thug, as "Muller" Simpson.

Eddie had never been as close to anyone who exuded malevolence the way Arthur Simpson did. The man had sat Spencer Naylor's mother down in a high backed chair in the centre of the combined living and dining room. A cowed older man, about the same age as Spencer's mother, sat in an easy chair; the TV was still on, and Eddie was amazed to see him still watching it. A younger man stood at the kitchen door, which led into the only other downstairs room.

The gangland boss nodded to Eddie and Brian, but spoke to the woman.

"Now, we would like a word with your Spencer, and you're going to tell us where he is. That's the deal."

Eddie could see that the mother was a tough old bag, and she resisted bravely.

"Ah honestly don't knaw where he is. Ah've already told yehs aw."

Arthur Simpson was shaking his head. "I don't think you're quite grasping the situation here. Not telling me where I can find Spencer is not an option that is available to you, or your family. Now, I'll ask you one more time. Where is he?"

Eddie was aghast at the implied threat and felt sick at the thought of what this thug would do to her. He silently willed her to talk, but even as he watched he saw her steel herself.

"Ah cannae tell yehs whit a don't knaw, ah'm sorry."

Arthur Simpson barely moved. He just shook his head sadly and nodded to the tall, thin one of his two companions. Eddie didn't really see the man move until it was all over. Before he had time to comprehend what was happening, Arthur's assistant had grabbed the younger member of the family and pulled him, screaming, into the kitchen.

"Shut the fuck up, or ah'll break your fucking arm," was his advice to young man.

Arthur's heavy set employee moved over to where he was standing, and moved behind Mrs Naylor, putting his hands gently but firmly on her scrawny shoulders. His boss pulled a pair of latex medical gloves from his pocket, and casually put them on, then sauntered through to the kitchen where the young man, presumably Spencer's younger brother, sobbed quietly. He opened one of the kitchen drawers and, just in view of the mother, pulled out a large carving knife. He felt the edge of it, and replaced it, lifting out a second one, a smaller knife that may well have cut the vegetables for the pot of soup sitting on the cooker. The edge seemed to meet the gangster's approval this time, as he made a show of testing the blade by slicing into a ripe banana picked from the coloured glass fruit bowl. He squeezed the banana, and the flesh erupted through the cut skin.

Eddie had a good view of both the kitchen and the living room. At a nod from the gangster, the tall, thin thug lifted the brother and shoved him face down on the table, the boy now whimpering pathetically. Eddie saw the gangster, now out of the woman's sight, open the freezer door and, after looking inside, pull out a bag of ice cubes. He turned and, incredibly, winked at Eddie.

His henchman then ripped Spencer's brother's tracksuit bottoms downwards, exposing a largish white pair of arse cheeks, enclosed in a pair of off-white Y-fronts. These were also yanked down and Arthur "Muller" Simpson moved round behind him. His helper leant over, holding the quivering young man's hair with one hand, leaning heavily with his forearm and elbow on the small of his back, and hooked one of his legs around the victim's knee to stop him kicking.

Arthur Simpson reached under and caught hold of the young man's testicles and pulled. The youth let out a scream, which was quickly muffled by the tall, thin man's free hand reaching round and grabbing a handful of his face, fingers closing around his nose and mouth, and squeezing hard.

"If none of you tell me where Spencer is, in about ten seconds one of your sons is going to lose a testicle. Thirty seconds after that, he's going to lose the second one."

Eddie looked around the room. Brian stood impassively. The father cowered in his seat, still sneaking glances at his TV programme blaring away in the corner, good cover for any other sounds that might originate from within the house. The large thug, looking relaxed, hovered behind the mother, ready to restrain her if it became necessary.

The mother was harder than Eddie would have believed. Maybe Spencer was her favourite, but she didn't budge or say a word. The boy obviously didn't know where his brother was, and the father, if he did know, was more frightened of his wife than of the men who now terrorised his family.

Arthur Simpson cupped the son's balls in his hand and firmly "sliced" a testicle with one of the ice cubes. A half-strangled scream came from the boy; Eddie was convinced that the tall, thin thug was manipulating his captive's mouth and nose as if he was playing some kind of obscure musical instrument, producing just the right note of terror and pain for effect.

Weeks later as an experiment a curious Eddie, in his bathroom, took an ice cube and ran it across his own testicle. Even though he knew what was causing it, the cold sharpness of the ice on his scrotum and the wetness of the melted water felt uncannily like how he imagined having an incision made into his testicle might feel. He'd seen Arthur Simpson give an extra squeeze of the testicle at just the right time, and a pinch with a fingernail, which could have only heightened the sensation of being castrated.

"That's one away. They say you can father as many children and shag as many women with one testicle as you can with two, so now's the time to speak up if you ever want grandchildren."

He paused.

"Your son, Spencer, and his little cunt of a friend crucified and raped my wee fucked-up niece, then caved in her pretty little head with a hammer."

He paused again, Eddie knowing that he was genuinely choked with emotion.

"Your other son is dead, there's no question about that. I'm going to kill him. And not in a nice way. You have a chance to save one of your sons. Don't be a hard bitch; do the right thing."

He cupped the testicle again, his hand wet with melted ice, as if soaked with blood. The thug let another scream escape from Spencer's brother's mouth.

His mother finally saw the stark reality of the choice she had to make. She visibly slumped, but did not cry or bleat.

"He uses the auld butcher shop in Paisley Road, at Moorpark, as a store. Ah think he took her there. Ah didnae knaw whit he done. Honest."

Arthur nodded at the man holding the boy down, who let him go. He collapsed, clutching his groin to stop the blood flow then, incredulous at finding himself intact, put his hands up to his face and wept uncontrollably.

His mother rushed through, expecting the worst and, seeing the boy unharmed, screamed and rushed at Arthur, trying to punch, kick, gouge and bite the man who had tricked her into giving up her other son. Arthur Simpson smiled and held her arms, while the blows from her feet hardly seemed to affect him. The heftier of the two thugs grabbed her and squeezed until she stopped struggling.

The gangland boss spoke to all three of them. "My good friend here is going to stay and make sure none of you does anything silly like trying to warn Spencer about us. He has my permission to do *whatever* it takes to make sure that doesn't happen."

He had a quiet word in the ear of the sidekick who was remaining with the family, then turned to leave. Going down the path, he took Eddie aside. "Eddie, we'll do our best to get your policewoman out of there, but I'm just telling you this, friendly, like. It's not my top priority, so you do not, and I'll repeat it just so you can't say I didn't explain it to you afterwards, *you do not* contact the police until I say so. Right? Capisce?"

"That's fair. I just want to get her out in one piece, and I'll not do anything to stop you doing what you need to do. But once I'm in there, and I see she's still alive, I'm phoning an ambulance."

"You've got balls, I'll say that for you. OK, we have a deal. I owe you that for finding this bastard for me."

He put his arm round Eddie's shoulder, as if he were a concerned friend. They were just coming to the gang boss's car when Eddie realised he desperately needed to stop on the way to the abandoned butcher's shop,

"Mr Simpson, I need to buy some alcohol on the way."

His new "friend" reached inside the glove compartment of the car and pulled out an unopened bottle of vodka, which he handed over with a puzzled look. "Here, but now's not the time for it, Eddie."

Eddie shook his head. "No, not that," he said, taking the bottle from Simpson. "If she's still alive, she'll be really sick. The bastard will have given her antifreeze and this is the only antidote. It's critical for her survival."

Arthur Simpson nodded, understanding. "Let's go."

-o-

They drove past the front of the row of shops, in convoy, and then turned into the service road leading to the back yard. Eddie parked his car beside the Merc. The two men got out of it and made for the back of the shop they'd been told Spencer would be in. Eddie followed anxiously, held back by Brian, keen to keep him out of harm's way.

The steel shutter door was up, but the inner wooden door was locked. The thin thug went back to the car and returned with a sledgehammer. Arthur Simpson motioned for Eddie and Brian to stand back and then counted down from three with his fingers. The sledgehammer shattered the lock with the third blow, and the two men were inside within seconds, Brian and Eddie close behind.

The two gangsters grabbed Spencer, who had succeeded in removing the insulation board covering the front door of the shop, but had failed, in his panic, to open it.

The sight that greeted Eddie haunted him for the rest of his life. An almost unrecognisable, half-naked Catherine was hanging by the neck from a rope strung up to a hook on the steel butcher's rail that ran the length of the shop. She was limp, her feet perched precariously on a chair, one side of her chest caked with blood, her skirt soaked with what could have been a mixture of urine, saliva and blood. Eddie roared for help and grabbed her, trying to lift her and take the strain off the noose strangling her, knowing that she was already dead.

Brian saw the knife lying on the worktop, grabbed it and stood on the chair to slice the rope. Catherine's body fell, toppling the chair with Brian on it, and the two of them landed on top of Eddie, the knife clattering off into the room.

Eddie furiously pulled at the noose, but it had worked its way deep into her neck and it was difficult to loosen. He screamed at Brian to get the knife, and when he did, he worked the tip of it under the rope where the knot had formed, leaving a small gap, and sliced it open.

He put his ear to her mouth, and thought he could hear a slight rasp. He checked her wrist for a pulse. He couldn't feel one, but when he felt the base of her neck below the damaged area, he was sure he could feel a faint beat. He put his ear to her chest, telling Brian to get his stethoscope from the car.

The two gangsters had both of Spencer's arms twisted up his back and were marching him towards the back door. They stopped in front of Eddie and Arthur Simpson looked down at Catherine, his eyes full of genuine pity, but with a grim look of barely suppressed rage behind them.

"You can phone now. We're out of here. Anything you want to say to this cunt?"

Eddie shook his head, took one last look at the man who had done this to his Catherine, and went back to trying to revive her.

Brian arrived with Eddie's stethoscope just as Spencer was being hustled out the back door and into the Mercedes.

Eddie, the comfortingly familiar earpieces in his ears as he listened to Catherine's faint heartbeat, didn't hear either the car speed away or Brian calling 999 and telling them to "Send a fucken ambulance as quick as possible 'cos there's a polis wummin dyin' here."

The response was overwhelming. The first police car arrived within three minutes, followed by half the Paisley constabulary. The ambulance took seven minutes, by which time Catherine had opened her eyes for a few seconds. Brian had, when Eddie asked him, fetched the bottle of vodka, and as soon as she was able to lick her swollen lips, Eddie was dipping his finger in the bottle and touching it to her mouth.

The paramedics were horrified when they arrived to find Eddie drip feeding neat vodka to a patient with severe neck and throat injuries, but Eddie's quiet but authoritative determination, the reasons he gave them for doing it, and Brian showing them the bottle of blue liquid, convinced them to let Eddie continue administering the "medication" while they fitted a neck brace and loaded her on to a stretcher. Even in the ambulance, Eddie continued to feed her with the best eighty-seven per cent proof Russian vodka that money could buy, all the time talking to her, telling her why he was making her drink the stuff, that he loved her and wasn't going to let her die now that he'd found her.

A number of things came together to save her life, although even after a week the medical profession still couldn't say what kind of life that might be.

She'd managed to spit out about half of what Spencer had given her to drink, and she'd kept him talking long enough to avoid him force-feeding her the whole bottle. They knew from the remaining fluid, which was a mixture of a little vodka and a lot of antifreeze, and the size of the bottle, how much ethylene glycol she'd ingested, and it was significantly – perhaps fatally – toxic. The fact that it contained some alcohol, and Eddie had managed to get a decent amount of vodka into her quickly, helped, as did the alcohol drip they put her on when she was admitted to the Royal Alexandria Hospital in Paisley. She was also immediately put on kidney dialysis, and her neck assessed to see how much damage had been done.

There was some nerve damage to the spine caused by the prolonged stretching of her vertebral column, which the doctors hummed and hawed about, saying that she might not recover. Eddie wasn't worried as much about that, as she had some sensation and movement and he was quietly confident that she would eventually make a full neurological recovery.

Her second lucky break was that the rope noose, like the one that was used in one of the cat cases, had been knotted in such a way as to avoid a relatively quick death by strangulation. Catherine had also somehow managed to turn her body so that the knot slid round to the front, giving her windpipe just a little bit of room to function, although in the process, she caused a horrific amount of soft tissue injuries, and may have put more pressure on the spinal nerves. Eddie reckoned she was unconscious when he got to her and if she hadn't turned the noose she would almost certainly have died.

Finally, if Eddie and Brian hadn't got to her as quickly as they did, she wouldn't have survived the hanging or the poisoning. If the ethylene glycol had been in her system for another few hours, her kidneys would have been irreparably damaged. As it was, she had an estimated forty per cent of kidney function remaining, which the doctors hoped might improve with time.

CHAPTER 15 Spencey

At the hospital, while Catherine was being treated in the high dependency unit both before and after surgery, Eddie was by her side as often as he could be. Her determination to fight for her life, demonstrated during her captivity and torture, was as strong during her medical treatment, but the dark terror she sometimes awoke with and the waves of depression that washed over her, unannounced, made having to be with people, even Eddie, difficult.

Neil Thompson was one of the first to visit, and was almost inconsolable in his guilt and grief. Both Eddie and Catherine assured him that he'd called it right by delaying taking their suspicions to the DI, a belief borne out by David Anderson's reaction to Eddie's desperate plea while Catherine was in Spencer Naylor's grasp.

Sergeant Thompson was also full of remorse over his lack of response to Catherine's texts and the missed call: he hadn't had his phone with him at the funeral, and hadn't checked it until it was all over. He'd only rushed into work when he'd seen the late news on TV.

He spoke with Eddie after they'd left Catherine sleeping, exhausted by his visit.

"Would it help if you were to take a look at everything we've found since you got her out of there?"

Eddie looked surprised. "Does David Anderson know anything about this? I would have thought he would have been keeping me as far away as possible from the fallout."

Eddie had narrowly escaped a charge of assaulting a police officer having taken a swing at the DI in the hospital corridor outside Catherine's room, after the pompous policeman had made a crass comment about how everything had turned out OK in the end while visiting Catherine's bedside. He didn't do much damage, but David Anderson bleated loudly about having Eddie arrested for an unprovoked assault. Eddie suspected that the reason that nothing ever came of it was due to the alleged intervention of the DCI, advising his colleague that it wouldn't be politically expedient for him to take the matter any further, and that a DI post in another division might be a good idea for a fresh start, if he was lucky.

"I don't give a shit. You and Catherine have earned the right to know everything."

Eddie had travelled in the ambulance with Catherine on its short journey to the hospital, so he hadn't had time to take in any details of the scene of her horrific ordeal, so he welcomed the chance to inspect the butcher's shop in more detail, and catch up on how the investigation was progressing.

The sergeant looked embarrassed, as he broached a sensitive subject with Eddie.

"Catherine's not fit to be involved at the moment, but we have to ask her some questions, along with you and Brian. I'm sorry, but it's necessary. We'll leave Catherine's interview until later, when she's stronger, but we need to talk to you as soon as we can."

Eddie knew that he could never reveal the full details of how they'd found Catherine and Spencer Naylor. Brian, with a life of experience in trying to remain unnoticed by the police, was hardly mentioned in reports by the first officers on the scene. Eddie explained his friend's involvement away as peripheral but supportive.

During his interview with the sergeant he didn't mention

Arthur Simpson or his affiliates. Spencey's family said nothing, having been heavily warned by the gangland boss and additionally cautioned by the minder left to supervise the parents and traumatised sibling that any hint of them going to the police would be met at a later date with appropriate retribution. Their neighbours, made aware of "Muller" Simpson's reputation, were reticent about coming forward with any information when they were questioned.

Eddie, in the end, told a version of the truth that only Brian knew was limited in its accuracy. In his account, he said that he had questioned the family, who had let slip the location where Spencey might be holding Catherine. When Neil Thompson presented this scenario to the family and asked them if it was true, they'd agreed.

Eddie told him that he and Brian had rushed there to find Catherine abandoned, close to death, the building otherwise unoccupied. Eddie surmised that Spencey had fled, forewarned perhaps by a phone call from one of the family members.

The sergeant also made a point of conducting Brian's short interview, and led Brian through a series of questions that made it easy for him to corroborate Eddie's statement. Brian had already conferred with Eddie, and both knew exactly what to say, but there was no doubt a more robust line of questioning might have thrown up one or two inconsistencies.

Although the police put a massive manhunt in place for Spencer Naylor, no sign of him was ever found, although the BMW that he and Jacko had used, registered in Spencey's name, eventually turned up in Liverpool.

The LDV truck had been located in a small yard in front of the railway arches near central station in Glasgow. A week after it had appeared on the PNC stolen vehicle list, a uniformed officer remembered seeing a truck of that description sitting in the same place for two or three days, and had radioed it in.

When they examined the truck, they found two sets of prints; Andrew Jackson's, and another matching a set taken from Spencer Naylor's house.

Neil Thompson also took Eddie back to the disused butcher's shop, which had been a gold mine of evidence. Amazingly there were no significant fingerprints other than Eddie's, Catherine's and Brian's, but some DNA from nasal hair matched hair and skin cells taken from Spencey's bedroom.

Two nail guns turned up, along with empty and full antifreeze containers, a couple of boiler suits and the ubiquitous rope used in most of the killings, but the most significant find was the empty video camera and a pile of tapes, which documented all but one of the murders, and many of the cat killings.

A second search of the Jackson house turned up the missing tape; a record of Danielle Simpson's murder. He'd hidden it from everyone, including Spencey, behind a loose piece of the skirting board in his bedroom, and it showed the full horror of what she'd gone through before she'd goaded him into ending her torture swiftly, and more mercifully than he'd intended.

There was no footage of Catherine's torture and Eddie couldn't bring himself to watch any of the others. It would have felt voyeuristic to him, but he did listen while Neil Thompson described in detail how the tapes confirmed what they already knew, filled in the many remaining gaps in their knowledge, and refuted some of Jackson's lies, told mostly when covering up for his friend.

They didn't explain how or why Jacko and Spencey had

become partners in their gory enterprise or what the true nature of their relationship was, but they did help locate the two missing victims, both young men with severe addiction problems who, the best of friends before their incarceration, ended their lives in each other's dying embrace.

Jackson, when faced with the irrefutable evidence that he had committed these additional murders, had admitted them and told the police where they could find the bodies.

From the bricked off corner of an infrequently used warehouse, the Dundee police removed the bodies of Michael Ford and Stuart Lees and, after they'd been processed as the law demanded, the Fiscal released them to their families.

"Leesy" and "Fordy" had been the killers' second and third victims. Returning to Dundee, they'd lured the unsuspecting duo out to the warehouse on the pretext of easy sex, drink and drugs. They must have been disappointed when only one of the three was on offer, and even more so when they woke up, dying, incarcerated in an eighteen inch square cell together.

-o-

About a fortnight after Catherine left hospital, Eddie had a visit from a new client with a young dog that quite patently did not belong to him. Eddie had last seen the man at Spencer's house, on the day Catherine had come so close to death. He was the one who'd remained behind to guard against a mother's last attempt to save her evil son's life.

There was nothing wrong with the dog, but the man indicated that the animal was probably going to be unwell the following day, and that it would require Eddie to do a call-out to his house to give the pup whatever treatment might be necessary.

When the client rang the next day to ask for a home visit and Eddie was specifically requested, the practice staff took this as a normal occurrence, and duly dispatched Eddie to handle the call.

When he arrived at the house he was shown into the front room and sheepishly informed that the dog, called Tyson, had improved dramatically since they'd phoned. Eddie examined it to make sure, and the dog was removed to the adjoining room, leaving Eddie alone for a minute.

He waited patiently, playing out a charade that wouldn't have looked out of place in a De Niro or Pacino film.

Eventually, Arthur Simpson appeared at the open door, entered, and shook Eddie's hand. Motioning Eddie to sit, he did the same, and pulled out a padded envelope. From it he extracted three photographs, a piece of paper, and a digital video tape.

"Have a look," he ordered Eddie.

Eddie blanched when he saw the first picture, which he studied with revulsion. The second and third were fully worse, and together they showed the various stages of the punishment meted out to Spencer Naylor and the agonisingly slow termination of his life. Eddie looked at the time stamps on the three photographs which, if genuine, meant that Spencey had lasted for six days.

"You can only look at these here, today, and then they will be destroyed. However, there's a website with a collection of photographic stills from "slasher" horror movies which has, spread amongst its bona fide pictures, unidentifiable close-ups of parts of these photographs, and other similar ones. If you should ever need to show your policewoman friend what happened to her abductor, they'll be available. She'll just have to take your word for it that it's him, unless they ever demolish those new Clydeside residential developments and dig up the foundations."

He reached out and took the photographs from Eddie, and gave him the sheet of paper. Eddie could see an internet address on it. He folded the note and pocketed it.

He then handed Eddie the video tape. Eddie immediately knew what it contained.

"What do I do with this?"

"Do what you like, I thought it might be of use to you as evidence."

Eddie pocketed it. Arthur Simpson hadn't finished.

"I've left Andrew Jackson alive for now, but every so often I'll arrange for something extremely unpleasant to happen to him, so that he spends the rest of his prison life in fear, just waiting for the next time. He'll never get out alive, and he'll never know what happened to his pal, but it will eat away at him wondering why he's never been in touch."

The gangland killer's face held a look of grim satisfaction.

"Any questions?" he added.

Eddie, still shocked, could only think of one.

"Did he say why he got involved with Jackson in the killings? I mean, we think we know Jackson's motives, but not Naylor's."

"Funny you should say that; it was one of the things I wanted to know, and he was quite forthcoming about everything, when we asked."

Arthur smiled thinly at that.

"He told us that he and Jacko had killed some kittens when

they were just young boys, and that Jacko had shouldered all the blame for it without grassing on him, and had taken all the punishment, as well. Spencey never forgot this, and although he moved to a different estate a few years later, they always kept in touch. When Jackson started killing cats, Spencey went along with it just for the fun of it, but soon realised that he got a huge hard-on from planning the killings that Jacko would then put into effect. It was Spencey's idea to see if they could do the same with people. He reckoned nobody would bother too much about junkies and alkies."

He smiled again, and Eddie shivered.

"There wasn't much he didn't tell us, in the end."

He looked up at Eddie, not expecting any understanding or approval.

"Listen. You helped me find my poor wee niece's killer and allowed me to deal with it in my own way. For that, I'll be forever in your debt. OK, without me, you may well have lost your little copper girlfriend, but that's by-the-by. You also, very sensibly, kept my name out of the investigation, for which I'm grateful, if a little surprised. If there's anything I can ever do for you, I'll consider it. I suspect that you won't ever ask, because, deep down, and a little self-righteously, you probably feel disgust and revulsion at what I've done. But think of this. At any point, did you do anything at all to try and stop it, when you knew what was inevitably going to happen?"

Eddie bowed his head and gently shook it. By the time he'd raised it again, the gang leader had gone.

-o-

Later, tears running down his face, he made himself watch the film of Catherine's ordeal, as much to justify to himself the actions he'd taken to find her and his overlooking of the abduction and subsequent killing of Spencer Naylor. The footage ran up to a few seconds before Arthur Simpson had burst in; the rest had been deleted. After he'd watched it Eddie wondered if he should find a way to get the tape to the squad still working on the case, but it would mean others seeing Catherine naked, vulnerable and humiliated, and he knew she wouldn't want that.

-o-

Eddie wheeled Catherine through the Rothiemurchus Forest; although she could walk, she still used the wheelchair sometimes, because she tired easily. Every day she was getting stronger, and was now talking of a phased return to work. The nightmares were becoming less frequent, and she was learning how to subdue the occasional panic attacks that had once threatened to ruin her life.

She'd even laughed when, before they'd left Paisley for a week's break in the heart of the Cairngorms, Eddie had invited Brian over to his flat to thank him for his part in saving her life.

Eddie had got annoyed when Brian had tried to wind him up about his new career as a detective, and retorted, "If you call me 'Ace Ventura' one more time, I'll fucking cry."

He could see a vast difference in her from the shocked and tearful victim that Neil Thompson had interviewed as soon as she was strong enough to tell them the full story. She had been barely conscious when her rescuers had burst in, so knew nothing of Arthur Simpson's part in saving her life. Eddie decided to keep it that way, although it hurt him to keep secrets from her.

He'd never mentioned Spencer Naylor's fate to her, or the

ongoing mental torture of Andrew Jackson, and part of him doubted that he ever would. It would be unfair to burden her with knowledge of a crime that she would naturally feel compelled to report, and if he let her know that Spencey had been executed, he'd also have to tell her of his and Brian's part in getting Arthur Simpson involved, their intimidation of her attacker's family, and the ultimately horrific torture that took place before Spencer Naylor died.

For a while, it looked as if their relationship might founder. She couldn't bear him looking at her with pity and, apart from the medical staff, she hated to have anyone touch her, even Eddie. She knew her mood swings made her difficult to be with at times, and she felt that he would be better off with someone who didn't have her emotional or physical scars.

But underneath it all, she remembered, as she'd lain dying, the look in Eddie's eyes when he told her, in her badly damaged state, that he loved her.

EPILOGUE

Detective Inspector Neil Thompson sat at his desk. His sergeant entered the room and dropped an old newspaper on his desk with a thud. It was a copy of the Dundee Courier, dated Wednesday, seventh December, 2010.

"I don't know how this was missed, sir. We might have to visit Jackson in prison."

He looked up at the newly promoted Sergeant Catherine Douglas. He could barely see the scars now; the doctors had worked miracles, in his mind, and she was almost back to being the person and the police officer that she had been before the attack two years earlier. They'd never found so much as a trace of Spencer Naylor and he wondered how painful that was for her, knowing that he was still out there somewhere, even though his team had never officially stopped looking for him. He knew she was still with Eddie, that they were happy, and he was glad.

He turned his attention to the page in front of him.

A nineteen-year-old woman committed suicide yesterday by throwing herself off a railway bridge on to spiked railings. She was a known drug user, and was under the influence of a cocktail of heroin, cocaine and antifreeze at the time of her death.

End.

ACKNOWLEDGEMENTS

I would like to thank Peggy Ann Arthurs for being the first person to read the book, for being so supportive of my writing, and for all her helpful suggestions about promoting my books. Big thanks also to Greig for helping with my CID research, to Tel G. for checking all the lawer speak, to Cara for the veterinary research and to Ronnie Milton for background on the Renfrew area.

The comments and feedback that I got from my other proof readers were very much appreciated. They were Michael, Elaine, Mark Johnstone, Theresa Murphy, Hamish, Mary, Julie and Katrina.

Thanks also go to Julie Lewthwaite, who edited the book for me, and to Keith Nixon for recommending Julie and his words of advice.

Thanks to Cat for the cover, again, although her comments about my valiant attempts at artwork bordered on the rude.

And once again, thanks to my wife, children and all my extended family and friends for their general support and encouragement.

-o-

If you enjoyed this book, and wish to recommend it to a friend, they can obtain the opening chapters free of charge at: **www.bluewicked.co.uk**. The website also contains additional material connected with the book.

GLOSSARY

Medical and Veterinary terms

[Abdomen] The body cavity that contains the liver, kidneys, stomach, intestines, spleen, pancreas and bladder, etc.

[Abdominal] Relating to or of the abdomen

[Addison's disease] The adrenal gland produces insufficient hormones to control levels of glucose, sodium and potassium

[Addisonian crisis] Sudden collapse when Addison's disease becomes critical

[Adrenal glands] A pair of small gland near the kidneys which produce the hormones aldosterone and cortisol

[Aldosterone] A hormone that controls the electrolytes, sodium and potassium, in the blood

[ALT] A chemical in the blood that is used to measure liver function

[Anal gland] A scent gland near an animal's anus used to mark territory. Sometimes becomes blocked or over-full

[Anti-emetics] Drugs used to control vomiting

[Assays] Measurement of levels of chemicals, usually in the blood

[AST] A chemical in the blood that is used to measure liver function

[Ataxia] Imbalance, lack of fine control of movement

[Barium study] Still or multiple frame X-rays taken after barium has been given to show gastrointestinal function

[Bile acids] A chemical in the blood that can is used to measure liver function

[Biochemistry] A study of how biology works at a chemical level

[Blood glucose] The basic fuel carried round the body by the blood; controlled by insulin, cortisol and other hormones

[Carpal] The wrist area

[CPL] Cat Protection League, a UK-wide cat welfare society, now called Cat Protection

[Contusion] Bruising

[Cortisol] A hormone that controls blood glucose and many other chemical levels in response to stress

[Cranium] The part of the skull that contains the brain

[Creatinine] A chemical in the blood that is used to measure kidney function, and also muscle damage

[Cruciate ligament] There are two of these ligaments in each knee; rupture of one causes severe lameness

[Deposits] Small amounts of a substance laid down within an organ, or in a tube such as an artery or the intestine

[Depression fracture] Usually the skull, when broken bone is forced into the brain by an external impact

[Dialysis] External cleansing the blood of waste products when the kidneys fail to perform this function

[Diaphragm] The muscular sheet that separates the abdomen and the thorax, allowing breathing to take place

[Differential diagnoses] A list of possible causes for a group of symptoms

[Distally] Further away from the torso, usually on a limb

[DNA] The chemical chain within a cell nucleus that is the blueprint for an individual, and is unique to them

[E. Coli] One of many bacteria that can cause serious blood poisoning, an infection called septicaemia

[ECG] Electrocardiograph, a measurement of the electrical activity of the heart

[Electrolytes] Ions within the blood that keep us alive, including sodium, potassium, chloride and calcium

[Entire] A male animal that has not been castrated

[Ethylene glycol] A chemical, similar to ordinary alcohol, which is used as antifreeze, and is highly toxic

[Exotics] Animals kept as pets, excluding dogs and cats, such as chinchillas, lizards, snakes and monkeys

[Fibrosis] An organ's normal tissue is replaced by scar tissue due to disease or trauma

[Fix] Preservation of a tissue by a chemical, usually prior to microscopic examination

[Foramen magnum] The opening at the back of the cranium, into the spinal canal

[Formol saline] A solution used to preserve pathological specimens

[Frontal area] The forward part of the cranium \ brain

[Gastric foreign body] A swallowed object in the stomach, usually plastic, metal or similar

[Gross examination] Inspection of something pathological with the naked eye

[Haematology] The examination of blood cells

[Heart base] The part of the heart where all the vessels leave and enter

[Histological] Examination of a stained thin section of tissue using a microscope

[Histopathology] Microscopic examination of diseased tissue

[Hypoglycaemia] Low blood sugar, usually as the result of too much insulin

[Insuloma] Insulin producing tumour of the pancreas

[Intracranial] Inside the cavity formed by the bones of the skull

[IV drip] Fluid therapy given intravenously

[Mediastinum] The central part of the chest between the lungs that contains the heart, trachea and oesophagus

[Mesenteric] Contained within the thin sheet that connects the intestines to the body

[Metacarpal] The bones immediately distal to the wrist

[Metatarsal] The bones immediately distal to the ankle

[Microchip] A small electronic device injected into an animal as a unique identifier

[MRI scan] Magnetic Resonance Imaging: a way of visualising the internal structures of the body

[Neuter] An operation to remove a male or female animal's ability to produce offspring

[Non-pyrexic] Does not have a high temperature, or fever

[Oesophagus] The tube that passes food from the pharynx to the stomach

[Oxalate crystals] A type of crystal that grows within the kidney after antifreeze is ingested

[Parvovirus] A serious viral infection that causes severe diarrhoea and vomiting

[Pathology] The study of disease; the effect a disease has on the body

[Petit mal] A mild form of epileptic fit

[Pharynx] The part of the throat behind the tongue, before the oesophagus

[Phlebitis] Inflammation of the veins

[Physiology] A study of how biology works at a functional level

[Proximal] Closer to the torso, usually on a limb

[Pulmonary] To do with the lungs

[Rectal lavage] Where fluid is pumped into the rectum, then flushed out

[Renal failure] If kidney function falls below a certain level, filtering of the blood becomes compromised

[Spermatic] Connected with sperm production, or with the sperm themselves

[SSPCA] Scottish Society for the Prevention of Cruelty to Animals

[Syncope] Short period of missed heartbeats leading to a brief collapse

[Talus, calcaneus and the navicular bone] Some of the bones that make up the ankle

[Tarsal] Referring to the ankle

[Thoracic] Within the chest

[Thoracic opening] The small gap in the chest wall at the neck that the trachea and oesophagus pass through

[Thorax] The chest

[Toxicity] How poisonous a substance is

[Toxicology] Testing to determine the levels of a poisonous substance

[Trachea] The windpipe, carrying air to the lungs

[Transverse] Refers to something aligned across the body or limb

[Tubules of the kidney] Microscopic tubes that concentrate urine and filter impurities

[Unfixed] Tissue sent to the lab without being preserved, usually to test for bacteria or toxic substances

[Urea] A safe way for the body to excrete the by-products of protein metabolism; rises in levels of urea in the blood may indicate kidney failure

[Viral myocarditis] A virus infection of the heart muscle which can cause heart failure

Police terms and acronyms

[Actions] Police officers' records of their daily findings

[Black light] Ultraviolet light that shows up various bodily secretions

[CCTV] Close Circuit TeleVision

[CID] Criminal Investigation Department

[DC] Detective Constable

[DCI] Detective Chief Inspector

[DI] Detective Inspector

[DS] Detective Sergeant

[E-fit] An electronically assembled estimation of a criminal's appearance from eye witness reports

[ID parade] Identity parade

[PC] Police Constable, the lowest ranked uniformed police officer

[PF] Procurator Fiscal, the prosecuting arm of Scottish law

[PNC] Police National Computer; a database of criminals, wanted vehicles, missing persons, etc.

[Probationary year] The twelve months after police college when a new police officer works under supervision

[Productions Officer] The officer overseeing the material evidence relating to the investigation.

[Remanded in custody] A prisoner is sent from a court to be kept in prison

[SOC team] Scene of crime team, who complete the forensic examination of a crime scene

Glasgow Slang

[Aboot] About

[Ae] Of

[Aff] Off

[Ah] I

[Ah'll] I'll

[Ain] Own

[An'] And

[An' aw] As well

[Anither] Another

[Arse-bandit] Gay man

[Askin'] Asking

[Auld] Old

[Aw] All

[Aye] Yes, Always

[Awready] Already

[Baith] Both

[Bam] Nutter, stupid

[Barras] Glasgow's famous East End market

[Bas] Short for bastard

[Bein'] Being

[Boattle] Bottle

[Boufin'] Smelly or disgusting

[Broo money] Social Security payments

[Buckie] Buckfast a fortified wine, favoured by young Scots drinkers

[Burd] Woman \ girlfriend

[Burst ma baws] Annoy me

[Calm the beans] Calm down

[Cannae] Cannot

[Comin'] Coming

['Cos] Because

[Coupon] Face

[Dae] Do

[Deid] Dead

[Dilutin' juice] Concentrated fruit squash

[Do-ins] Beatings

[Doon] Down

[Doss] Sleep \ find a bed

[Drinkin'] Drinking

[Dyin'] Dying

[Efter] After

[Fae] From

[Fanny] Woman \ sex

[Faur] Far

[Filth] Police, derogatory term

[Fir] For

[Fit] Foot, twelve inches

[Frae] From

[Fucken] Fucking

[Fuckwit] Derogatory term for someone stupid

[Fur] For

[Furst] First

[Fuzz] Police, derogatory term

[Gaff] Home \ house \ place to stay

[Gaggin'] Desperate \ needing

[Gear] Drugs

[Gettin'] Getting

[Gie] Give

[Gimme] Give me

[Goat] Got

[Goin'] Going

[Gonnae] Going to

[Greet] Cry

[Grun] Ground

[Guid] Good

[Hadnae\hudnae] Hadn't

[Hame] Home

[Haud] Hold

[Haun] Hand

[Headin'] Heading

[Heid] Head

[Hoose] House

[Hud] Had

[Hunner] Hundred

[Huv] Have

[Huvn't] Haven't

[Huvvin'] Having

[Intae] Into

[Isnae] Is not

[Ithers] Others

[Jacksie] Backside

[Jakey] Alcoholic \ street person

[Jestin'] Kidding

[Jist] Just

[Kiddin'] Kidding

[Knaw] Know

[Knawn] Known

[Lappin'] Consuming \ soaking

[Lend a few quid] Borrow some money

[Ma] My

[Ma] Mother

[Mair] More

[Maistly] Mostly

[Man] Often added to the end of the sentence, addressing the listener

[Masel'] Myself

[Maw] Mother

[Maybees] Maybe \ Perhaps

[Melted] Battered \ hit firmly

[Mind] Remember

[Minge] Vagina \ derogatory term for woman

[Missus] Wife

[Mister] term for a child addressing a man

[Mither] Mother

[Mooth] Mouth

[Nae] No

[Nae probs] No problems \ OK

[Naebody] Nobody

[Needin'] Needing

[No] not

[Noo] Now

[Nuthin'] Nothing

[O'] Of

[Oan] On

[Offy] Off-licence \ liquor store

[Onywan] Anyone

[Onyway] Anyway

[Oot] Out

[Park yer arse] Sit down

[Perr] Pair

[Pig] Police, derogatory term

[Plook] Spot, Pimple

[Polis] Police

[Poontang] Girls \ sex

[Rippin' the pish] Taking the mickey

[Roon] Round

[Rozzer] Police, derogatory term

[Score] Get drugs

[Scran] Food

[Seen] Saw

[Shirt-lifter] Gay man

[Shitehole] Disgusting building \ room

[Sleekit] Untrustworthy, slimy

[Smack] Heroin

[Snidey] Sneaky

[Somewan] Someone

[Spanner] Daftie

[Special brew] Very strong lager, favoured by alcoholics

[Stayin] Staying

[Stevo] Nickname. Many names are shortened and have 'o' added on

[Stupit] Stupid

[Sumfin' / somethin'] Something

[Swallae] Drink

[Tae] To

[Tanned] Drank \ beat up \ break into

[Tap] Ask to borrow something

[Taxi ferr] Taxi Fare

[The berries] Brilliant

[The dug's baws] Equally brilliant

[Therr] There

[They'rr] They're

[Thon] That \ Those

[Topped] Killed

[Trustin'] trusting

[Til] Until

[Voddy] Vodka

[Watter] Water

[Wan] One

[Weans] Children

[Wee] Small

[Wernie] Weren't

[Wherr] Where

[Whit] What

[Wi'] With

[Willnae] Will not

[Wir] were

[Wis] Was

[Wrang] Wrong

[Wummin] Woman \ women

[Wunderin'] Wondering

[Wunnered] Wondered

[Wur] Were

[Ya] You

[Ye] You (singular)

[Yehs] You (plural)

[Yer] Your

[Yersel'] Yourself

Made in the USA
Columbia, SC
20 August 2018